Amy's Diary

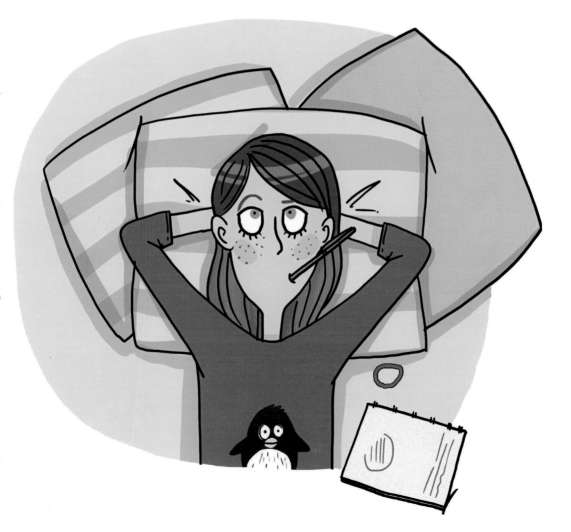

MORE GRAPHIC NOVELS AVAILABLE FROM charmz

STITCHED
MARIAH McCOURT
AARON ALEXOVICH
The First Day of the Rest of her Life

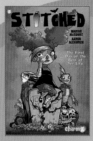

STITCHED #1
"THE FIRST DAY OF THE REST OF HER LIFE"

STITCHED
MARIAH McCOURT • AARON ALEXOVICH
Love in the Time of Assumption

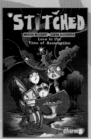

STITCHED #2
"LOVE IN THE TIME OF ASSUMPTION"

GFFs
GHOST FRIENDS FOREVER

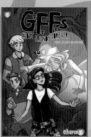

G.F.F.s #1
"MY HEART LIES IN THE 90s"

GFFs
GHOST FRIENDS FOREVER
WITCHES GET THINGS DONE

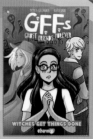

G.F.F.s #2
"WITCHES GET THINGS DONE"

Chloe
The New Girl

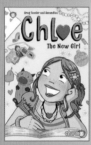

CHLOE #1
"THE NEW GIRL"

Chloe
The Queen of High School

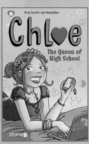

CHLOE #2 "THE QUEEN OF HIGH SCHOOL"

Chloe
Frenemies

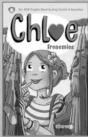

CHLOE #3
"FRENEMIES"

Chloe
Rainy Day

CHLOE #4
"RAINY DAY"

PATRICIA LYFOUNG
The Scarlet Rose

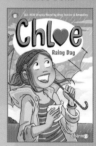

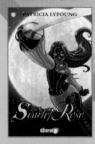

SCARLET ROSE #1
"I KNEW I'D MEET YOU"

PATRICIA LYFOUNG
The Scarlet Rose
I'll Go Where You Go

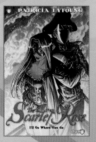

SCARLET ROSE #2
"I'LL GO WHERE YOU GO"

PATRICIA LYFOUNG
The Scarlet Rose
I Think I Love You

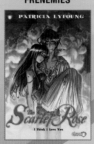

SCARLET ROSE #3
"I THINK I LOVE YOU"

PATRICIA LYFOUNG
The Scarlet Rose

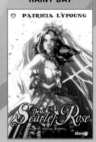

SCARLET ROSE #4
"YOU WILL ALWAYS BE MINE"

Amy's Diary
Space Alien... Almost?

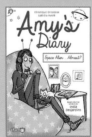

AMY'S DIARY #1
"SPACE ALIEN... ALMOST?"

Sweeties
CHERRY SKYE

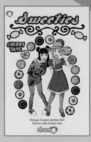

SWEETIES #1
"CHERRY SKYE"

Monica
WHO CAN AFFORD THE PRICE OF FRIENDSHIP TODAY?!

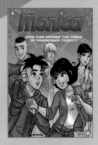

MONICA ADVENTURES #1

Ana
COSMIC RACE
THE RACE BEGINS

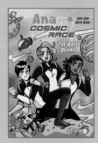

ANA AND THE COSMIC RACE #1
"THE RACE BEGINS"

SEE MORE AT PAPERCUTZ.COM

Amy's Diary

Space Alien... Almost?

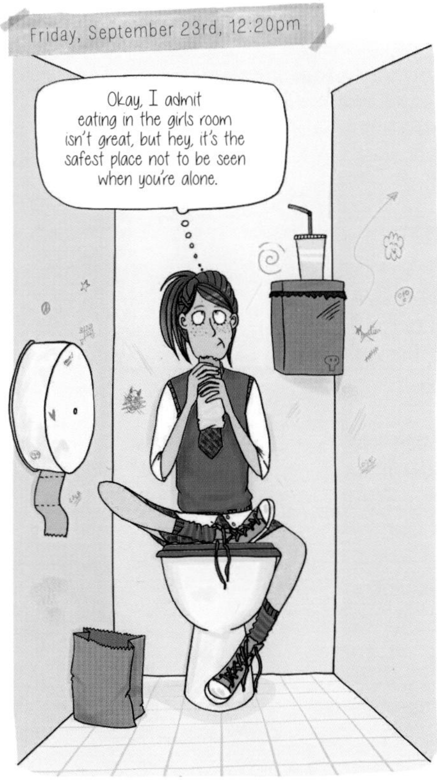
Friday, September 23rd, 12:20pm
Okay, I admit eating in the girls room isn't great, but hey, it's the safest place not to be seen when you're alone.

Base on the novels by INDIA DESJARDINS

Adaptation — VÉRONIQUE GRISSEAUX

Illustration — LAËTITIA AYNIÉ

charmz

NEW YORK

To Véronique and Laëtitia, a crackerjack team able to capture Amy's universe so well.
Elsa Lafon, who always manages to "stir things up" for me.
Florence Maine, Michel Lafon's entire team, as well as the Jungle team for this lovely project.
—*India*

Thanks to Véronique, India & Aurélie (Amy), Jungle…a high-octane team forever and ever.
—*Laëtitia*

What a pleasure it was to work on this volume!
Thanks to Laëtitia, Florence, Mélanie, Héloïse, and Estelle.
And thanks to India for having trusting me with AMY!
—*Véronique*

"SPACE ALIEN… ALMOST?"
Le Journal d'Aurélie Laflamme [AMY'S DIARY] volume 1 *"Extraterrestre…ou Presque"* © 2015 Jungle/Michel Lafon.
All Rights Reserved. www.editions-jungle.com. Used under license.

English translation and all other material © 2019 Papercutz. All rights reserved.

AMY'S DIARY #1
"Space Alien… Almost?"

Based on the novel by INDIA DESJARDINS
VÉRONIQUE GRISSEAUX—Comics Adaptation
LAËTITIA AYNIÉ—Art, Color, Design
JOE JOHNSON—Translation
BRYAN SENKA—Lettering
LÉA ZIMMERMAN—Production
GRANT FREDERICK—Editorial Intern
JEFF WHITMAN—Editor
JIM SALICRUP—Editor-in-Chief

Charmz is an imprint of Papercutz.
Papercutz.com

Hardcover ISBN: 978-1-5458-0215-1
Paperback ISBN: 978-1-5458-0214-4

Printed in India
February 2019

Charmz books may be purchased for business or promotional use. For information on bulk purchas-
es please contact Macmillan Corporate and Premium Sales Department at
(800) 221-795 x5442.

Distributed by Macmillan.
Frist Charmz printing.

SEPTEMBER

The End of the World

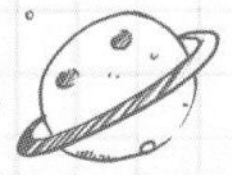

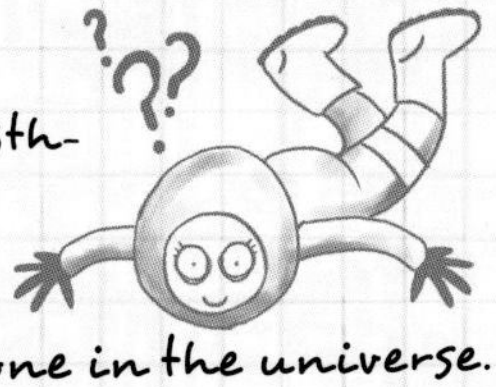

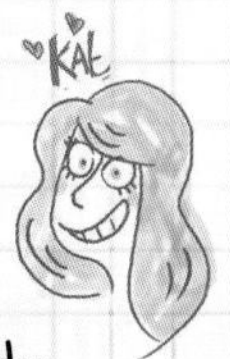

Kat

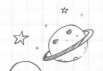

-Tuesday, September 13th-

7:05pm:
Sometimes I feel alone in the universe. I don't get along with anybody, except for my best friend, Kat, but ever since we got into an argument over something stupid, we're not talking anymore. There's my mom, of course, (she's downstairs in the kitchen making some spaghetti sauce and it smells soooooo good), but I can't really tell her everything and she gets on my nerves sometimes. Like right now.

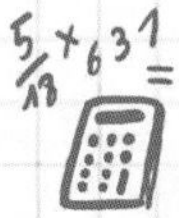

5/13 x 631 =

7:10pm: My mom's calling me to tell me dinner's ready.

7:12pm: Okay, I'll go downstairs and eat...But first, I've got to point out that I'm being punished, because I made a little, let's say, "behavior mistake" at school. Honestly, I don't deserve my punishment. I just played a little joke on the math teacher (who, let me point out, has been a real pain since the beginning of the year). She shouted in class: "You must follow the process or you'll miss the train for your diploma!" And I answered: "We'll catch a boat..." and then found myself in the principal's office:

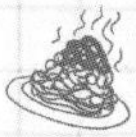

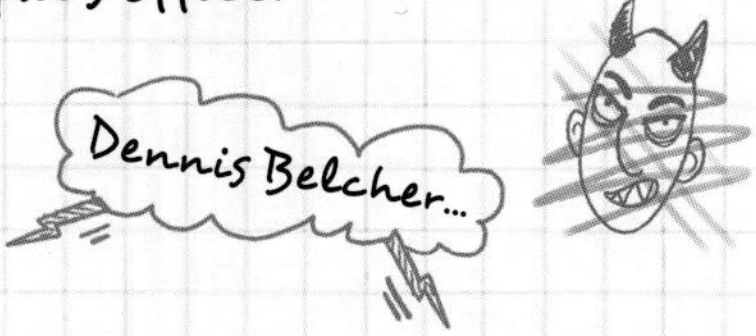

Dennis Belcher...

7:16pm: Okay, I've got to go have dinner.

8:35pm: Great...My mom's decided my punishment would be not getting to watch "One Tree Hill." That sucks! What's more, she told me the principal wanted to see her tomorrow to talk about my grades. Tssk! I was just starting to hate him when she said: "He's cute."

Cute handsome? Or cute nice? Argh!

Does she have a crush on him or something?!

10:00pm: My mom came into to my room and saw me crying. She told me she didn't know "One Tree Hill" was that important to me and let me watch it on my computer. But I wasn't crying about that. I was crying because I was thinking about my dad, who's not here anymore...

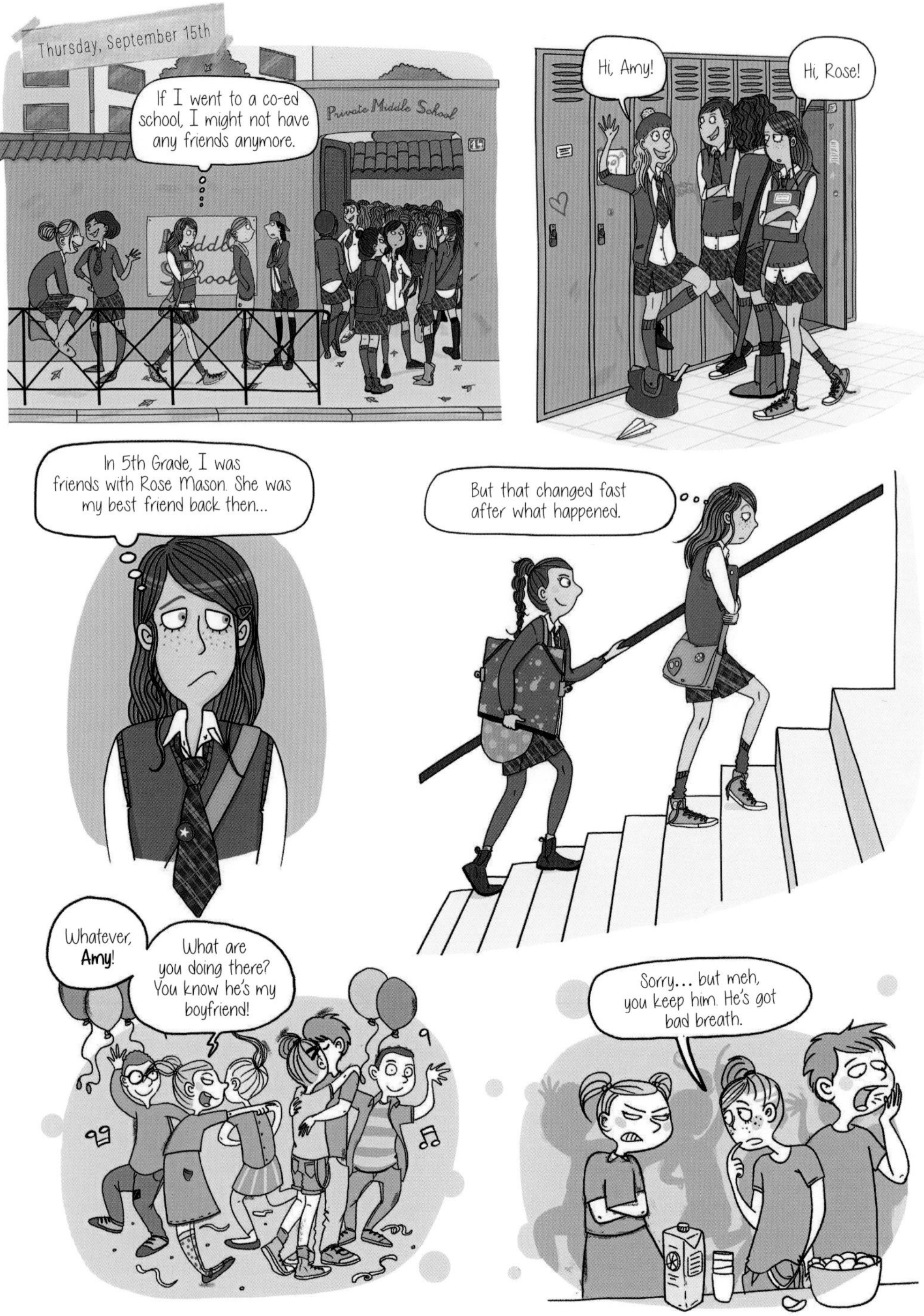

Thursday, September 15th
If I went to a co-ed school, I might not have any friends anymore.
Private Middle School
Hi, Amy!
Hi, Rose!
In 5th Grade, I was friends with Rose Mason. She was my best friend back then...
But that changed fast after what happened.
Whatever, **Amy**!
What are you doing there? You know he's my boyfriend!
Sorry... but meh, you keep him. He's got bad breath.

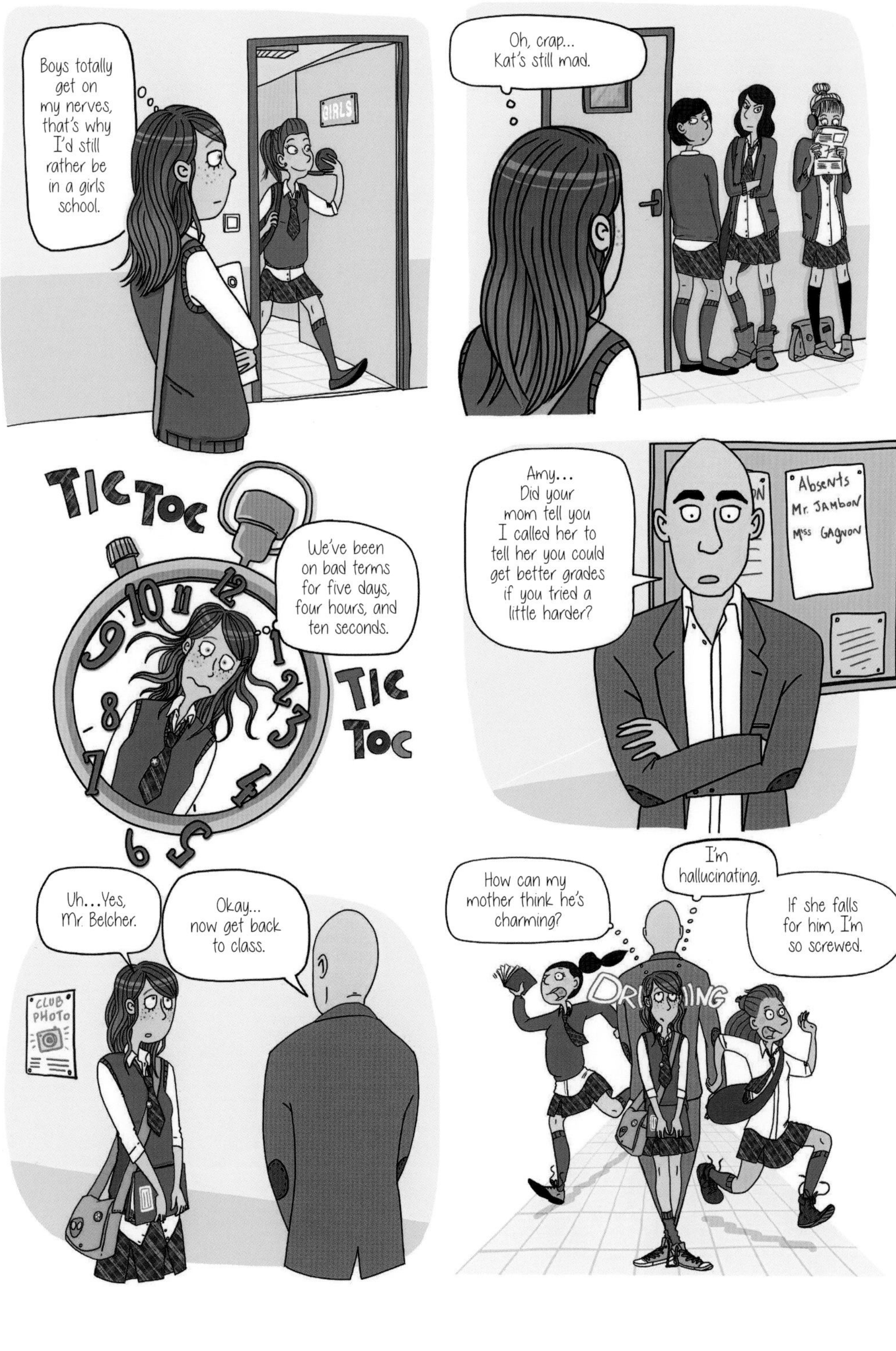
Boys totally get on my nerves, that's why I'd still rather be in a girls school.
GIRLS
Oh, crap... Kat's still mad.
TIC TOC
We've been on bad terms for five days, four hours, and ten seconds.
TIC TOC
Amy... Did your mom tell you I called her to tell her you could get better grades if you tried a little harder?
Absents
Mr. JAMBON
Miss GAGNON
Uh...Yes, Mr. Belcher.
Okay... now get back to class.
CLUB PHOTO
How can my mother think he's charming?
I'm hallucinating.
If she falls for him, I'm so screwed.

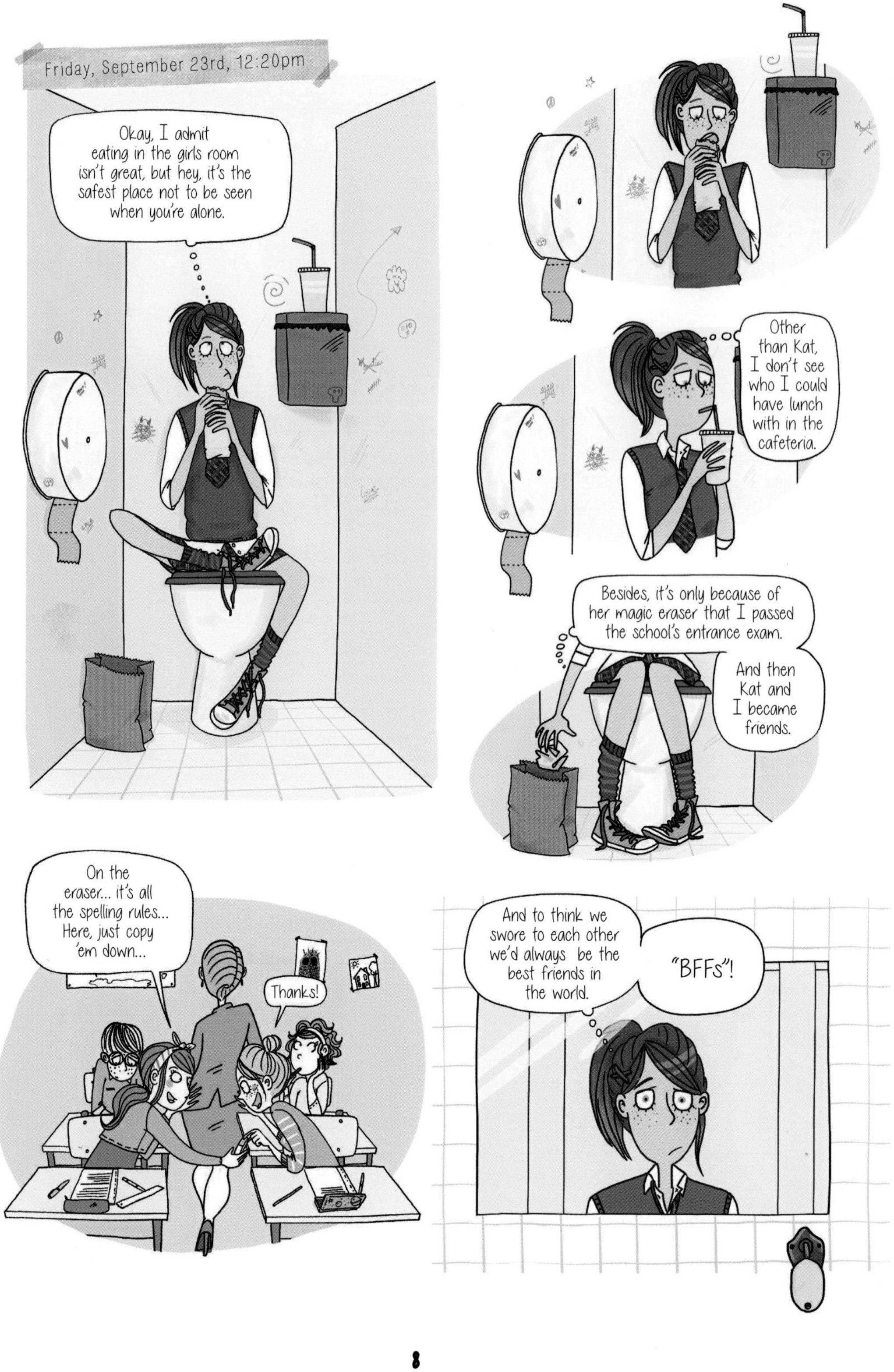
Friday, September 23rd, 12:20pm
Okay, I admit eating in the girls room isn't great, but hey, it's the safest place not to be seen when you're alone.
Other than Kat, I don't see who I could have lunch with in the cafeteria.
Besides, it's only because of her magic eraser that I passed the school's entrance exam.
And then Kat and I became friends.
On the eraser... it's all the spelling rules... Here, just copy 'em down...
Thanks!
And to think we swore to each other we'd always be the best friends in the world.
"BFFs"!

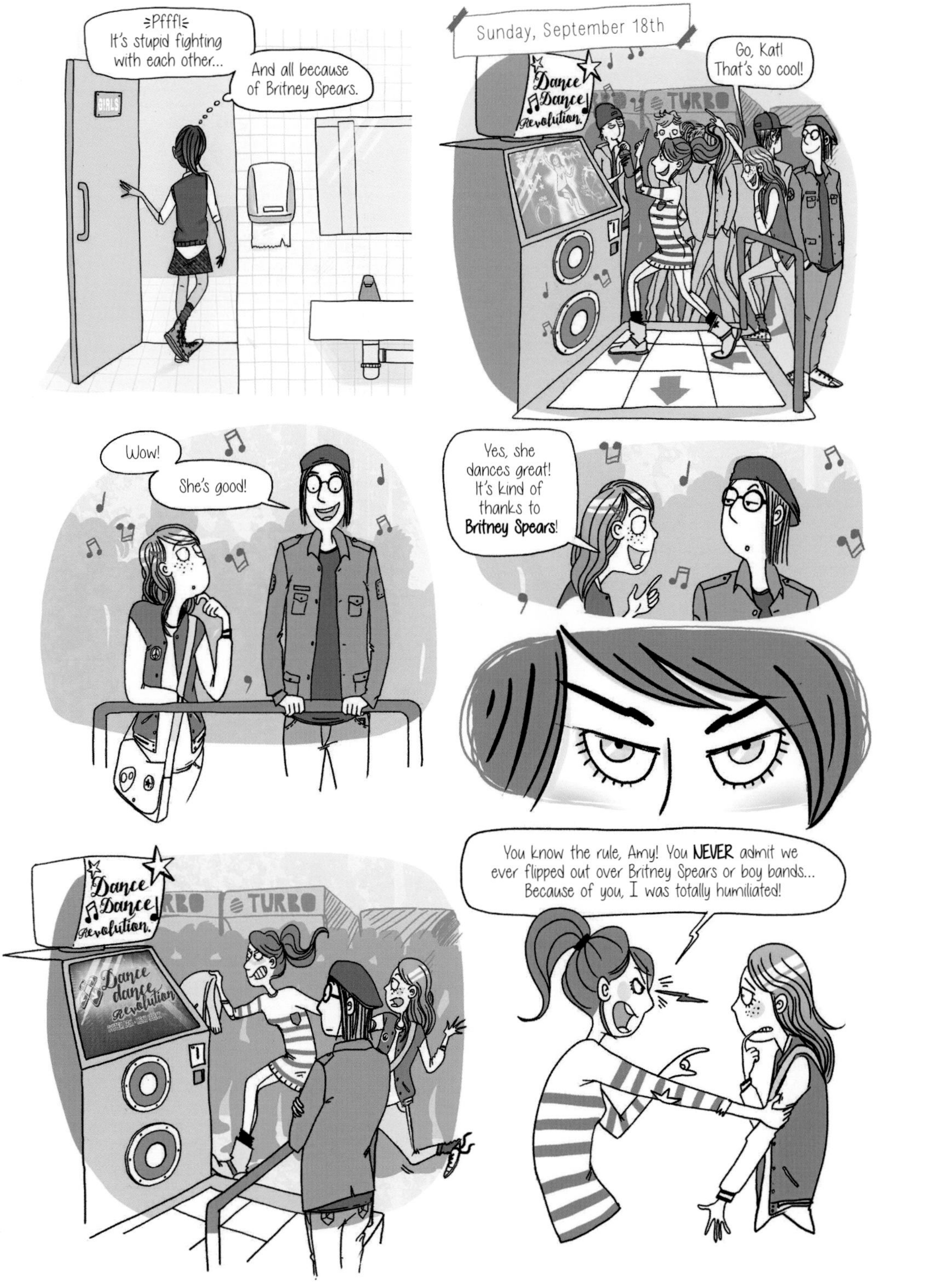

=Pfff!=
It's stupid fighting with each other...
And all because of Britney Spears.
GIRLS
Sunday, September 18th
Dance Dance Revolution
TURBO
Go, Kat! That's so cool!
Wow!
She's good!
Yes, she dances great! It's kind of thanks to **Britney Spears**!
Dance Dance Revolution
TURBO
Dance dance Revolution
You know the rule, Amy! You **NEVER** admit we ever flipped out over Britney Spears or boy bands... Because of you, I was totally humiliated!

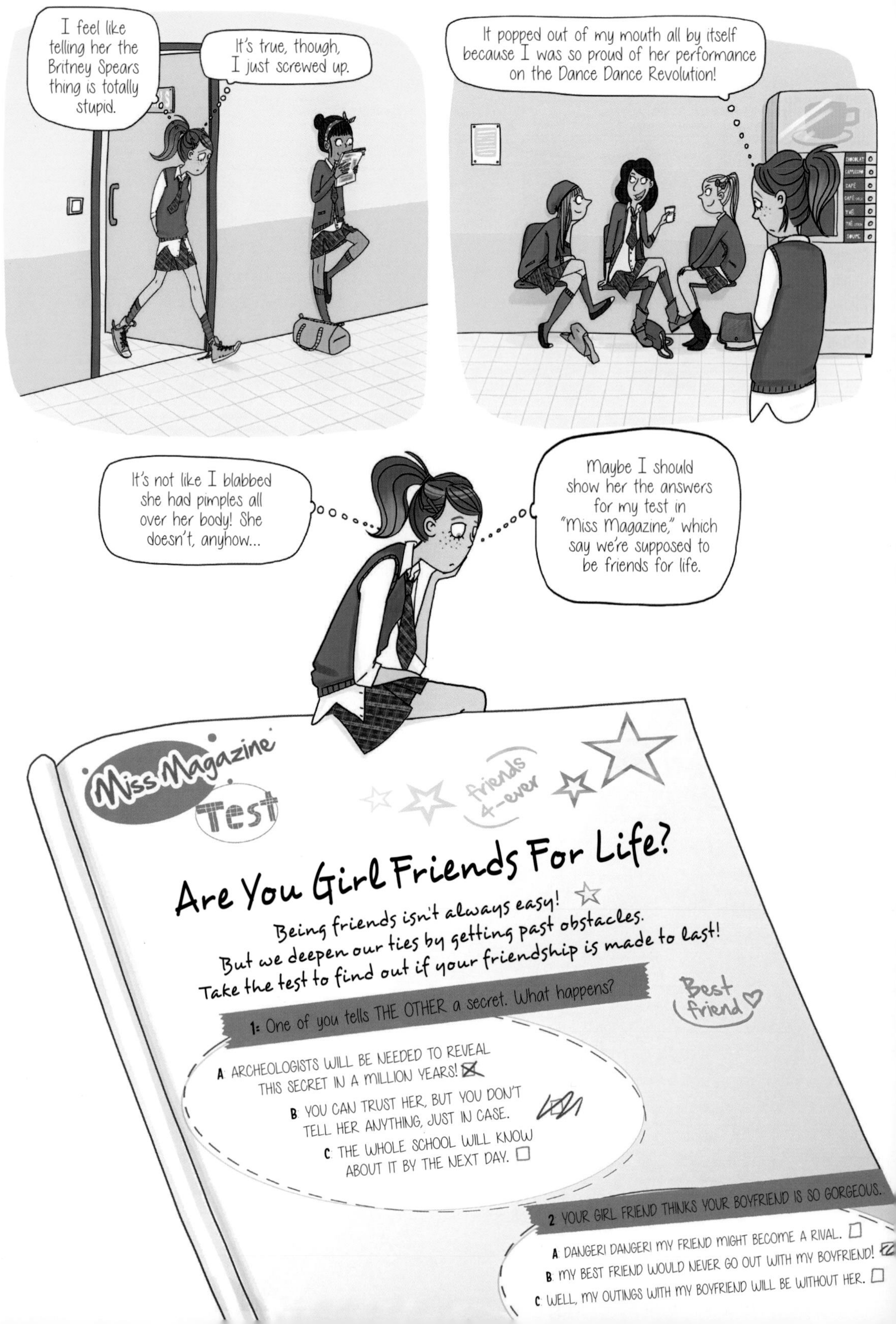
I feel like telling her the Britney Spears thing is totally stupid.
It's true, though, I just screwed up.
It popped out of my mouth all by itself because I was so proud of her performance on the Dance Dance Revolution!
It's not like I blabbed she had pimples all over her body! She doesn't, anyhow...
Maybe I should show her the answers for my test in "Miss Magazine," which say we're supposed to be friends for life.
Miss Magazine
Test
friends 4-ever
Are You Girl Friends For Life?
Being friends isn't always easy!
But we deepen our ties by getting past obstacles.
Take the test to find out if your friendship is made to last!
Best friend
1: One of you tells THE OTHER a secret. What happens?
A: ARCHEOLOGISTS WILL BE NEEDED TO REVEAL THIS SECRET IN A MILLION YEARS!
B: YOU CAN TRUST HER, BUT YOU DON'T TELL HER ANYTHING, JUST IN CASE.
C: THE WHOLE SCHOOL WILL KNOW ABOUT IT BY THE NEXT DAY.
2: YOUR GIRL FRIEND THINKS YOUR BOYFRIEND IS SO GORGEOUS.
A: DANGER! DANGER! MY FRIEND MIGHT BECOME A RIVAL.
B: MY BEST FRIEND WOULD NEVER GO OUT WITH MY BOYFRIEND!
C: WELL, MY OUTINGS WITH MY BOYFRIEND WILL BE WITHOUT HER.

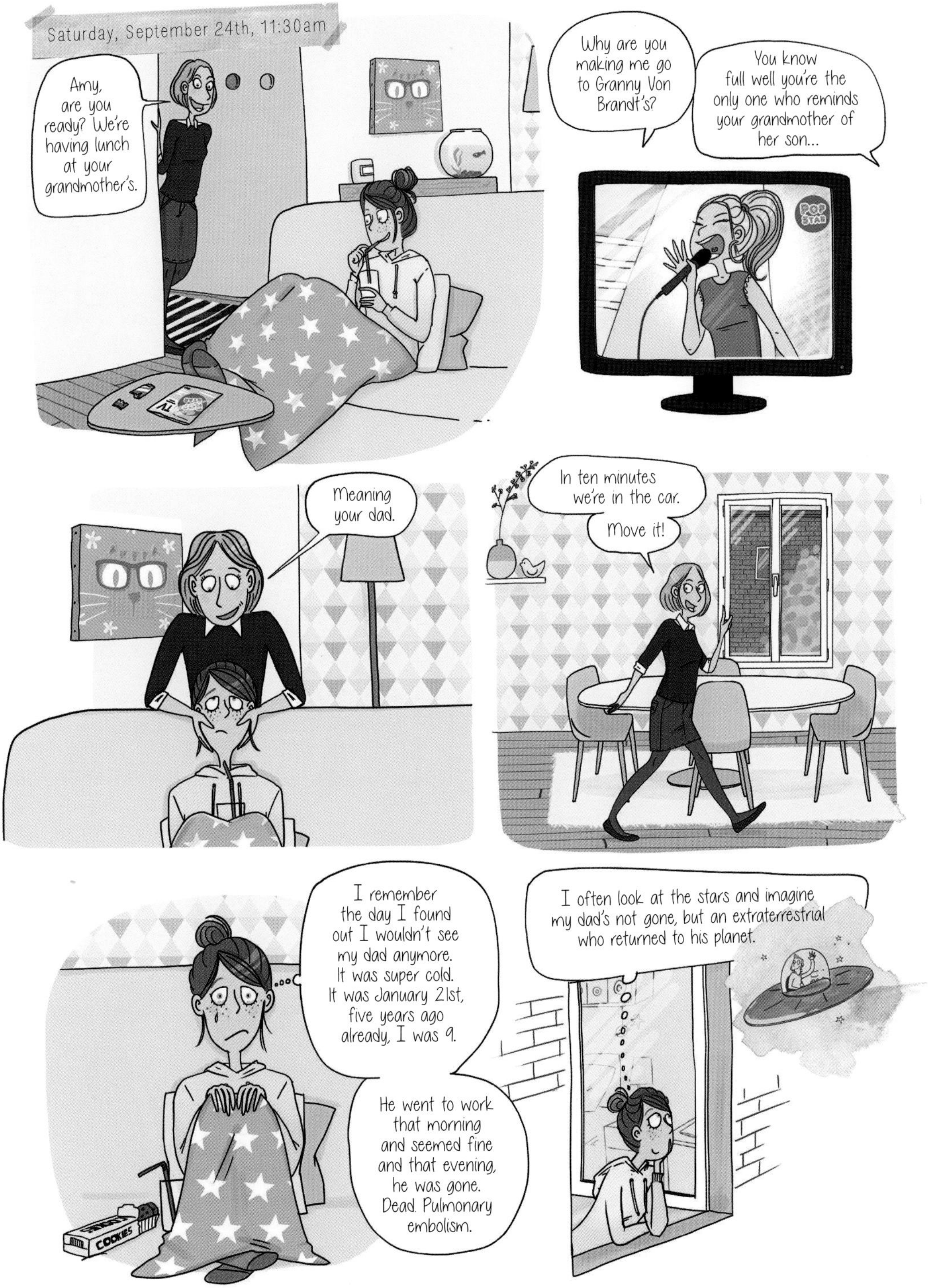
Saturday, September 24th, 11:30am
Amy, are you ready? We're having lunch at your grandmother's.
Why are you making me go to Granny Von Brandt's?
You know full well you're the only one who reminds your grandmother of her son...
POP STAR
Meaning your dad.
In ten minutes we're in the car.
Move it!
I remember the day I found out I wouldn't see my dad anymore. It was super cold. It was January 21st, five years ago already, I was 9.
He went to work that morning and seemed fine and that evening, he was gone. Dead. Pulmonary embolism.
COOKIES
I often look at the stars and imagine my dad's not gone, but an extraterrestrial who returned to his planet.

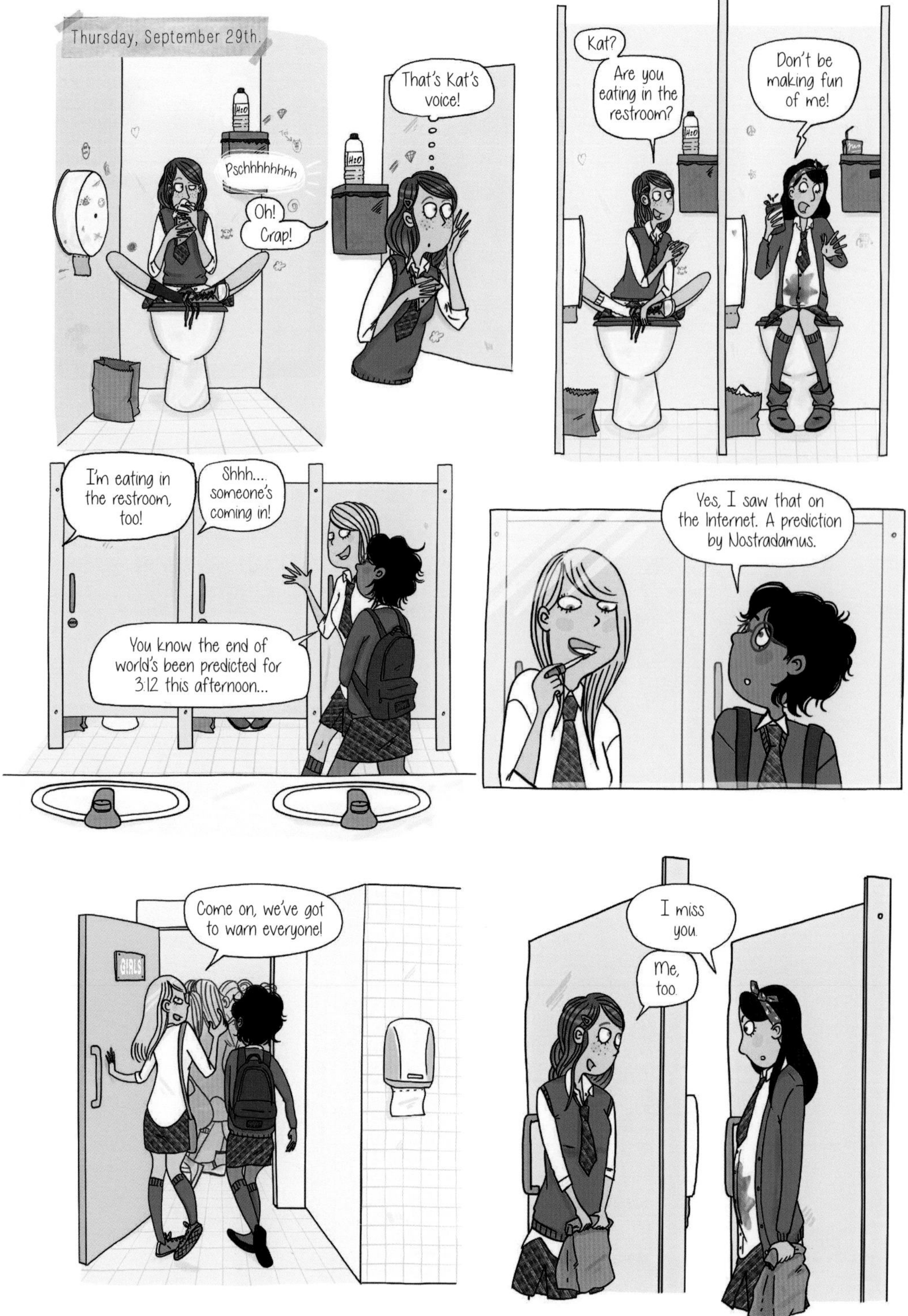
Thursday, September 29th.
Pschhhhhhhh
Oh! Crap!
That's Kat's voice!
Kat?
Are you eating in the restroom?
Don't be making fun of me!
I'm eating in the restroom, too!
Shhh... someone's coming in!
You know the end of world's been predicted for 3:12 this afternoon...
Yes, I saw that on the Internet. A prediction by Nostradamus.
Come on, we've got to warn everyone!
GIRLS
I miss you.
Me, too.

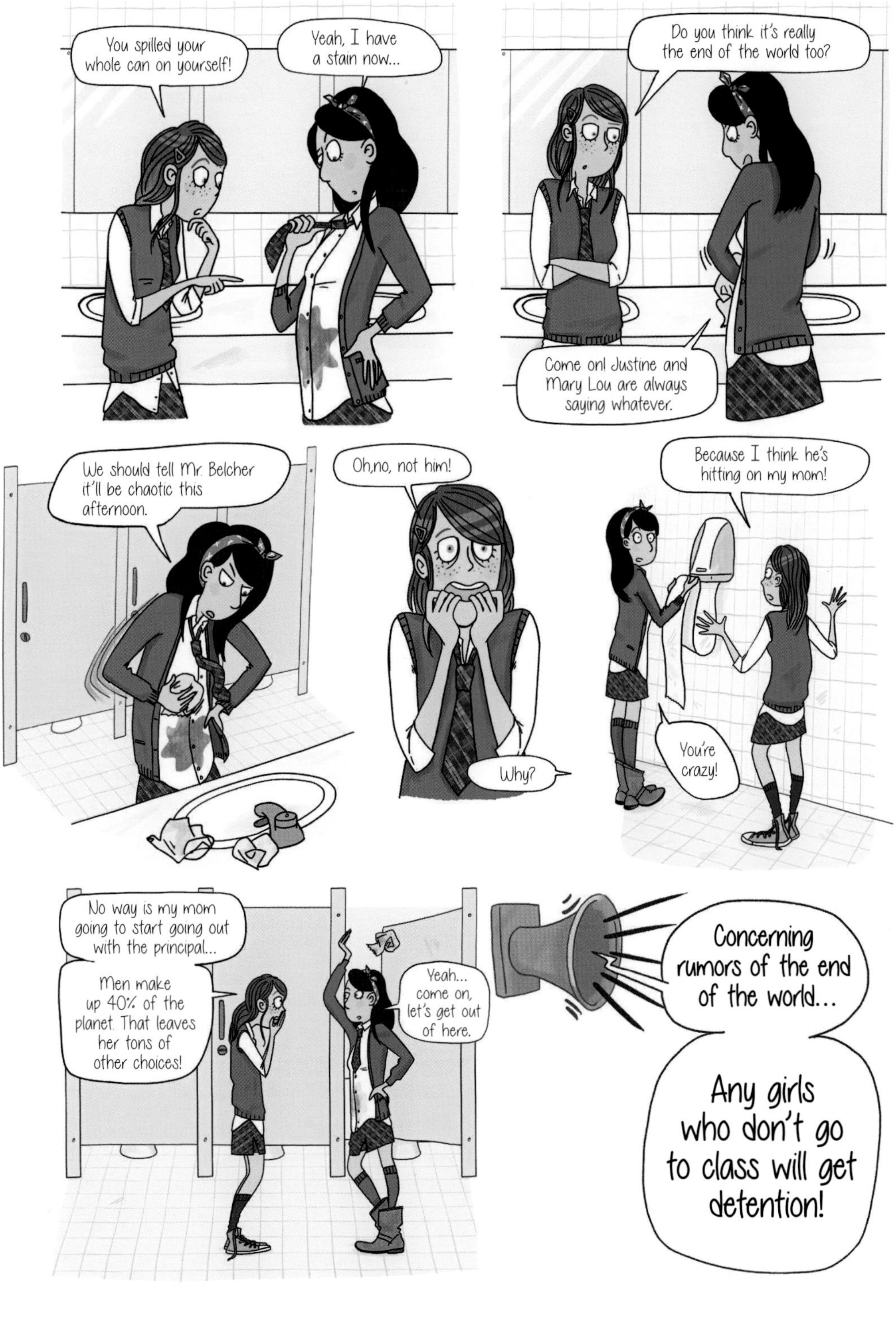

You spilled your whole can on yourself!
Yeah, I have a stain now...
Do you think it's really the end of the world too?
Come on! Justine and Mary Lou are always saying whatever.
We should tell Mr. Belcher it'll be chaotic this afternoon.
Oh,no, not him!
Why?
Because I think he's hitting on my mom!
You're crazy!
No way is my mom going to start going out with the principal...
Men make up 40% of the planet. That leaves her tons of other choices!
Yeah... come on, let's get out of here.
Concerning rumors of the end of the world...
Any girls who don't go to class will get detention!

OCTOBER
Unfavorable stars

If my dad were an alien, I, Amy Von Brandt, may be one too, and one day he'll come get me...

-Saturday, October 1st

9:05am: The end of the world didn't happen!
The real end of the world would've been never making up with Kat (or my mom making me clean the fridge...)

9:10am: Last night, I told my mom about the end of the world thing and afterwards, I told her I'd gotten a C on my grammar test and that I'd gotten the worst grade in the class. With a wink, she said to me: "It's not the end of the world!" We laughed.
But she spoiled it all by adding: "You didn't do the dishes?"

Note to myself:
"I wonder how old my mom was when she started going bonkers over housework."

Note to myself #2:
"Make sure it's not hereditary."

Note to myself #3:
"If it is, try to devote the next years of my life to searching for a vaccine against an obsession with housework."

1:00pm: I'm meeting up with Kat at the arcade in ten minutes. She insisted I dance on the Dance Dance Revolution to "Oops, I Did It Again" by Britney Spears.
To redeem myself... I thought our tiff was a closed case now.
The problem is that Kat is super good at that game...
But not me. It'll be pretty humiliating. Okay, I have to go.
We're meeting in front of the arcade at 1:10pm...

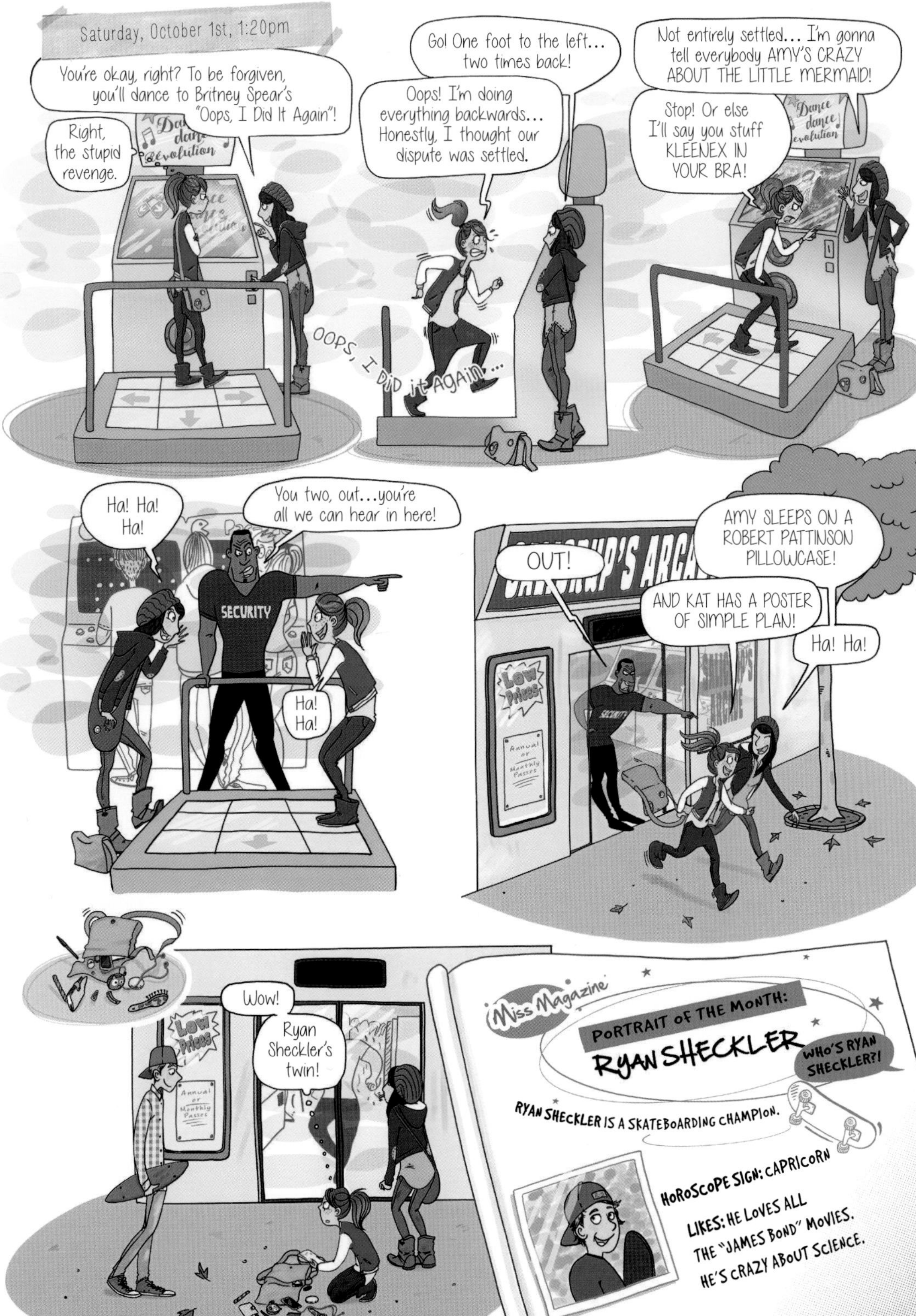

Saturday, October 1st, 1:20pm
You're okay, right? To be forgiven, you'll dance to Britney Spear's "Oops, I Did It Again"!
Right, the stupid revenge.
Go! One foot to the left… two times back!
Oops! I'm doing everything backwards… Honestly, I thought our dispute was settled.
OOPS, I DID it AGAIN…
Not entirely settled… I'm gonna tell everybody AMY'S CRAZY ABOUT THE LITTLE MERMAID!
Stop! Or else I'll say you stuff KLEENEX IN YOUR BRA!
Ha! Ha! Ha!
You two, out…you're all we can hear in here!
SECURITY
Ha! Ha!
OUT!
AMY SLEEPS ON A ROBERT PATTINSON PILLOWCASE!
AND KAT HAS A POSTER OF SIMPLE PLAN!
Ha! Ha!
Low Prices
Annual or Monthly Passes
Wow!
Ryan Sheckler's twin!
Miss Magazine
PORTRAIT OF THE MONTH:
RYAN SHECKLER
WHO'S RYAN SHECKLER?!
RYAN SHECKLER IS A SKATEBOARDING CHAMPION.
HOROSCOPE SIGN: CAPRICORN
LIKES: HE LOVES ALL THE "JAMES BOND" MOVIES.
HE'S CRAZY ABOUT SCIENCE.

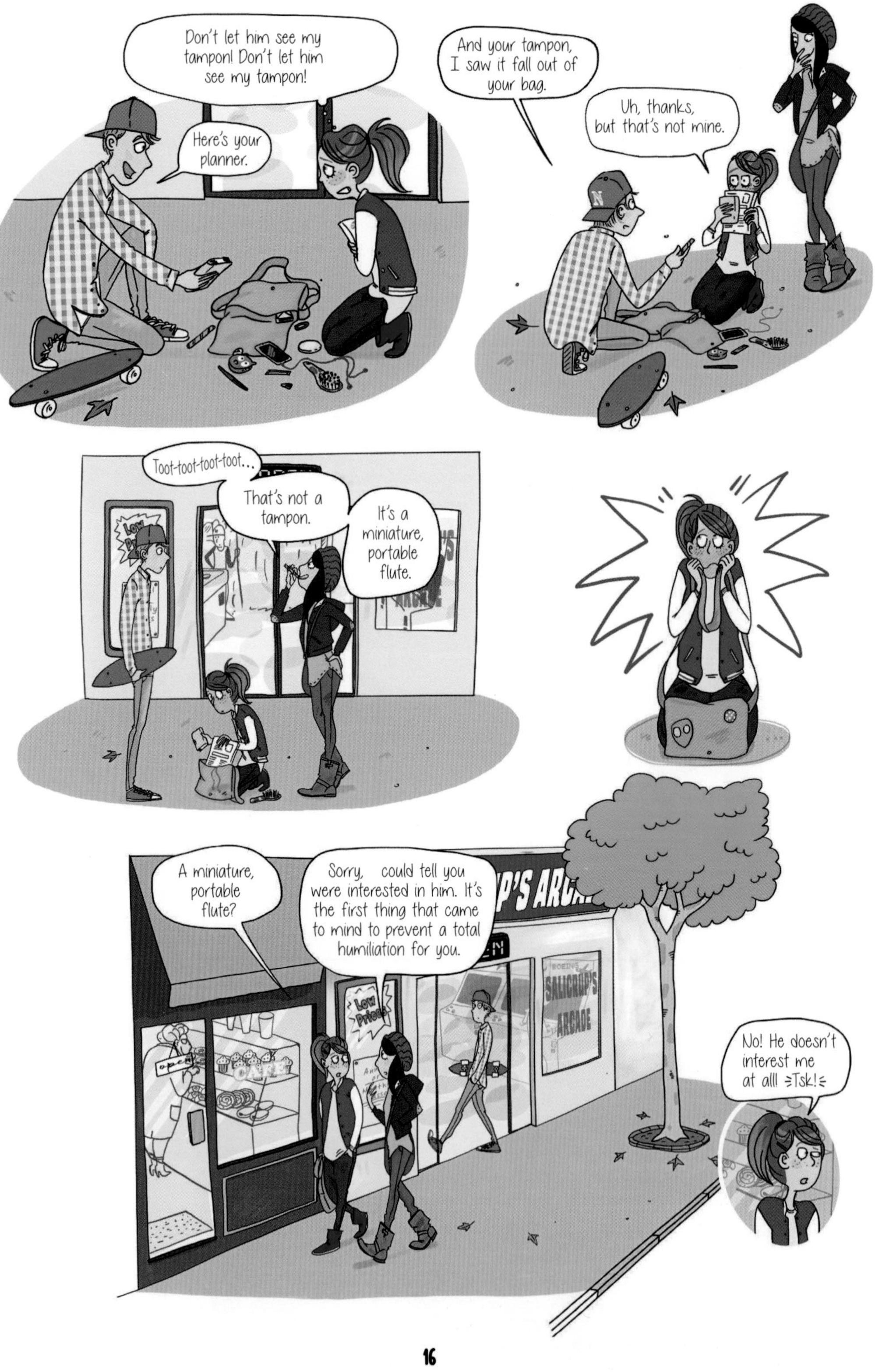
Don't let him see my tampon! Don't let him see my tampon!
Here's your planner.
And your tampon, I saw it fall out of your bag.
Uh, thanks, but that's not mine.
Toot-toot-toot-toot...
That's not a tampon.
It's a miniature, portable flute.
A miniature, portable flute?
Sorry, could tell you were interested in him. It's the first thing that came to mind to prevent a total humiliation for you.
SALICRUP'S ARCADE
No! He doesn't interest me at all! Tsk!

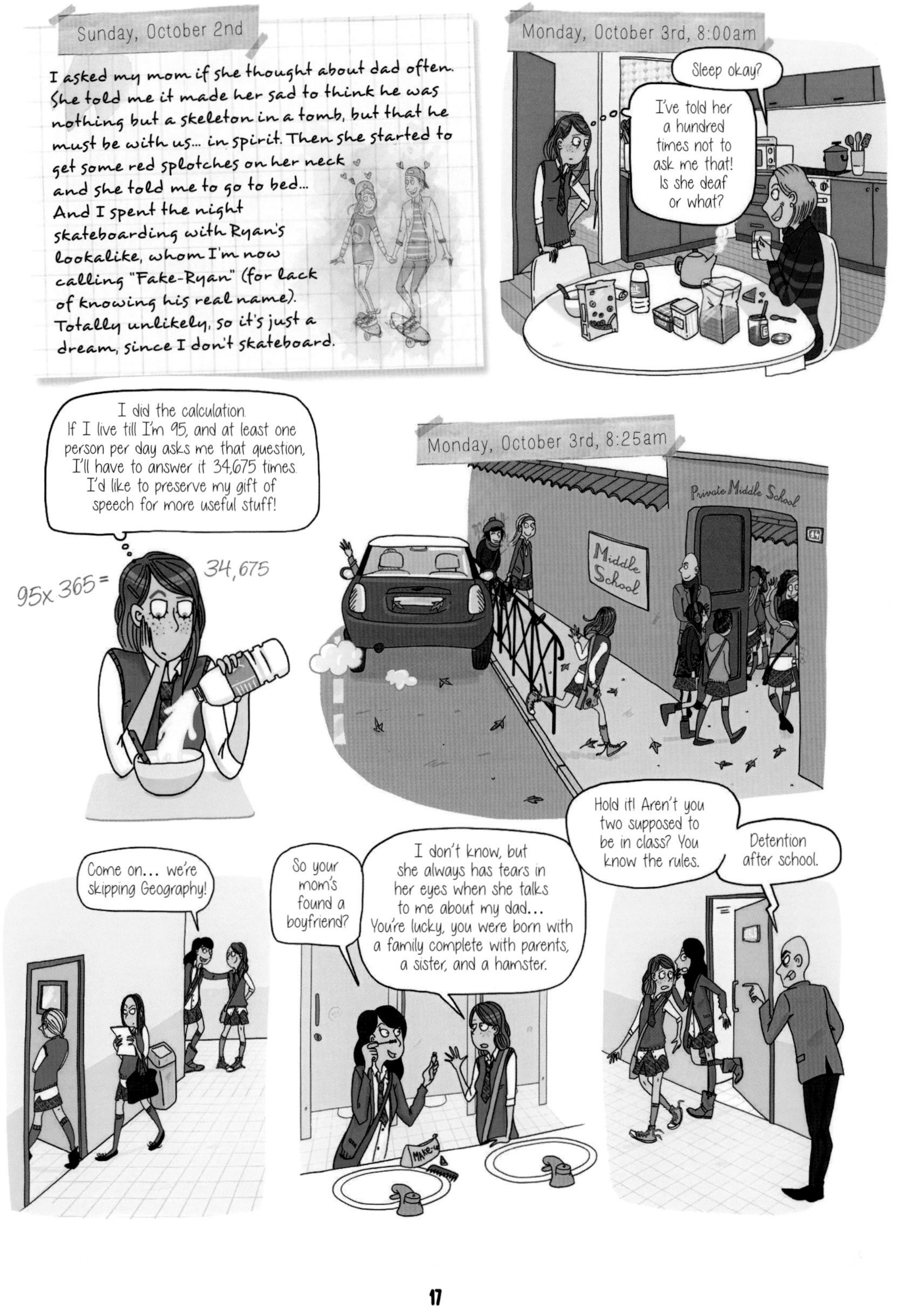
Sunday, October 2nd
I asked my mom if she thought about dad often. She told me it made her sad to think he was nothing but a skeleton in a tomb, but that he must be with us... in spirit. Then she started to get some red splotches on her neck and she told me to go to bed... And I spent the night skateboarding with Ryan's lookalike, whom I'm now calling "Fake-Ryan" (for lack of knowing his real name). Totally unlikely, so it's just a dream, since I don't skateboard.
Monday, October 3rd, 8:00am
Sleep okay?
I've told her a hundred times not to ask me that! Is she deaf or what?
I did the calculation. If I live till I'm 95, and at least one person per day asks me that question, I'll have to answer it 34,675 times. I'd like to preserve my gift of speech for more useful stuff!
95x 365 =
34,675
Monday, October 3rd, 8:25am
Private Middle School
Middle School
Come on... we're skipping Geography!
So your mom's found a boyfriend?
I don't know, but she always has tears in her eyes when she talks to me about my dad... You're lucky, you were born with a family complete with parents, a sister, and a hamster.
Hold it! Aren't you two supposed to be in class? You know the rules.
Detention after school.

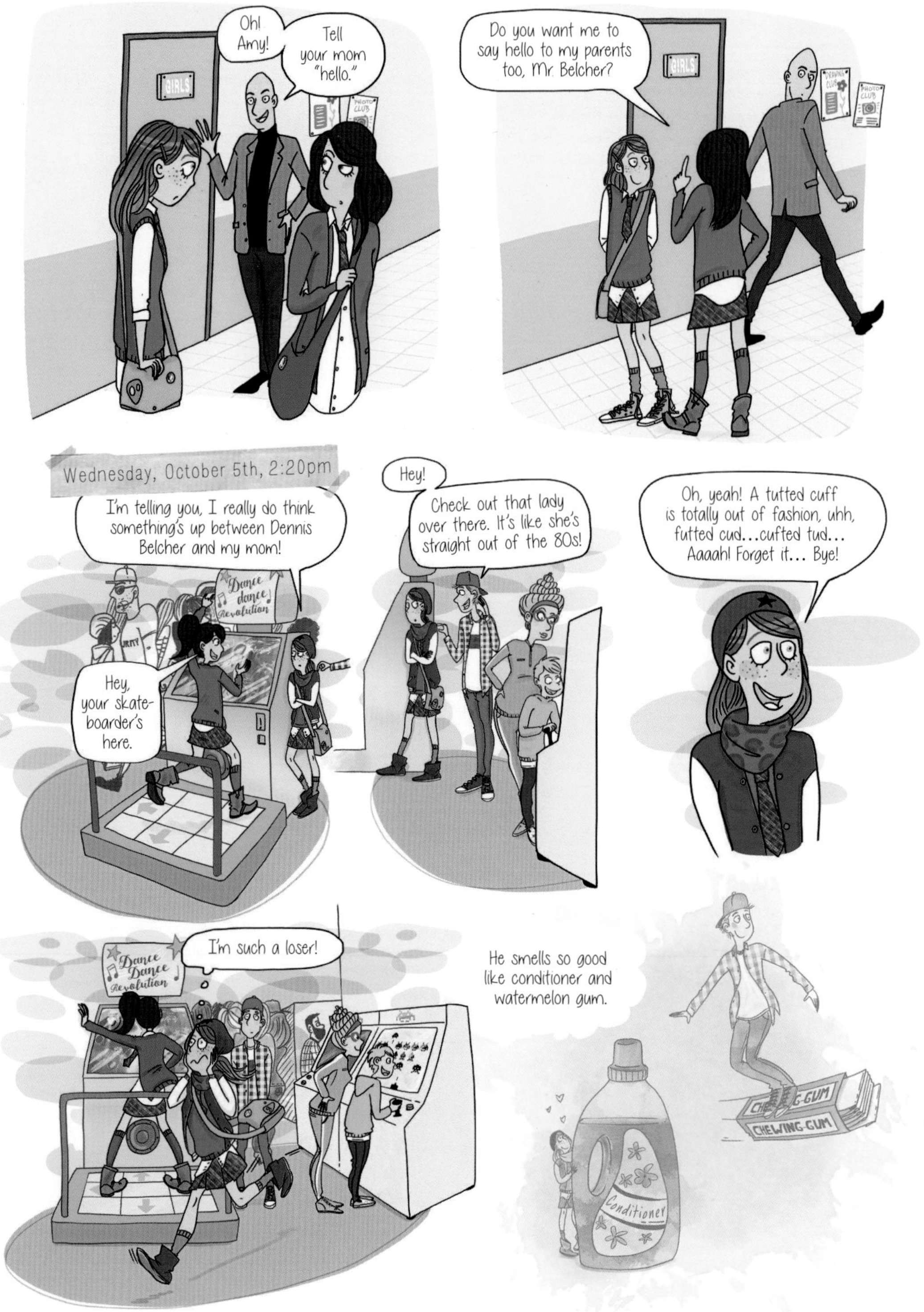
GIRLS
Oh! Amy!
Tell your mom "hello."
Do you want me to say hello to my parents too, Mr. Belcher?
GIRLS
Wednesday, October 5th, 2:20pm
I'm telling you, I really do think something's up between Dennis Belcher and my mom!
Dance dance Revolution
Hey, your skate-boarder's here.
Hey!
Check out that lady over there. It's like she's straight out of the 80s!
Oh, yeah! A tutted cuff is totally out of fashion, uhh, futted cud...cufted tud... Aaaah! Forget it... Bye!
Dance Dance Revolution
I'm such a loser!
He smells so good like conditioner and watermelon gum.
Conditioner
CHEWING-GUM
CHEWING-GUM

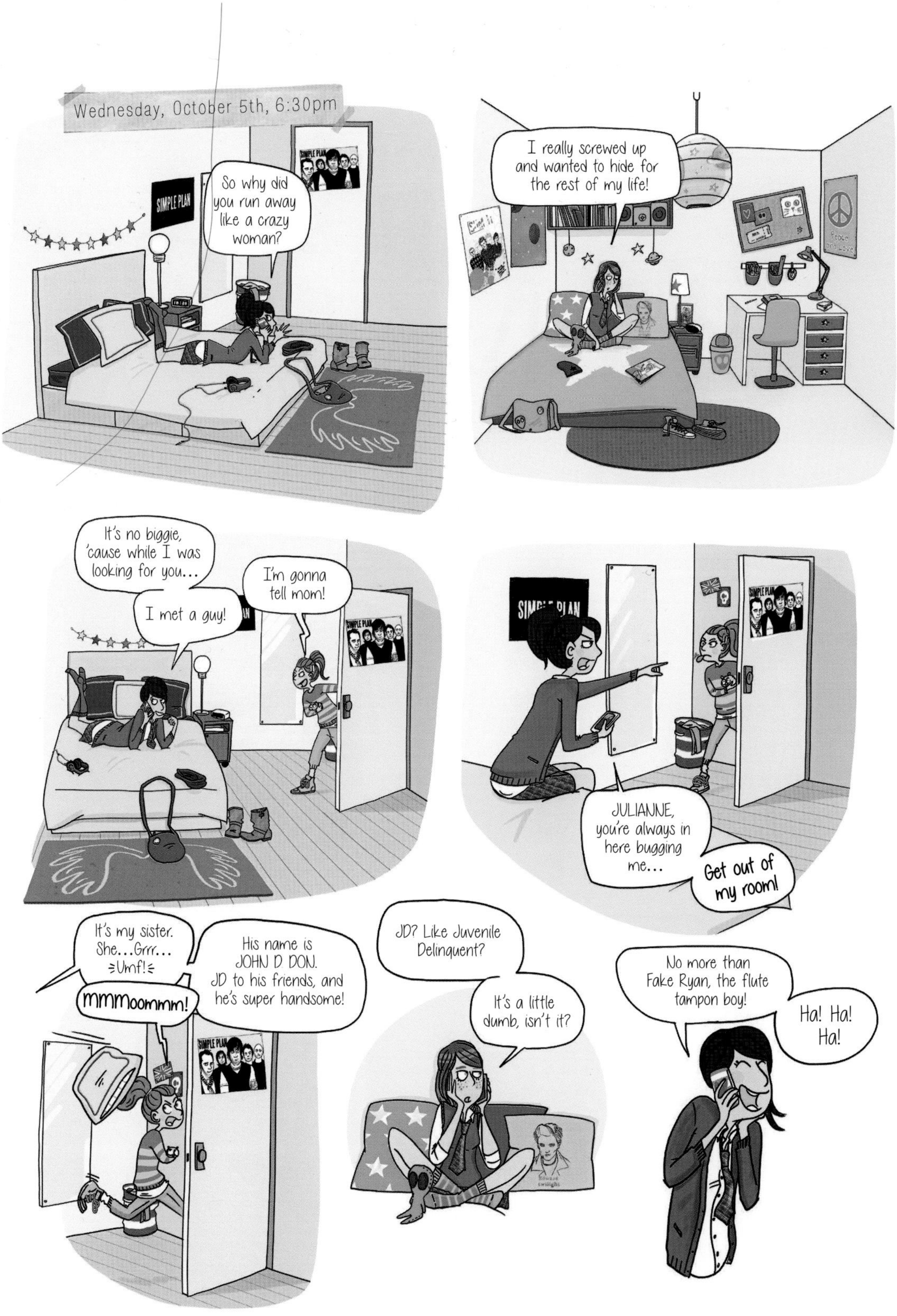
Wednesday, October 5th, 6:30pm
SIMPLE PLAN
So why did you run away like a crazy woman?
I really screwed up and wanted to hide for the rest of my life!
It's no biggie, 'cause while I was looking for you...
I met a guy!
I'm gonna tell mom!
JULIANNE, you're always in here bugging me...
Get out of my room!
It's my sister. She...Grrr... Umf!
MMMoommm!
His name is JOHN D. DON. JD to his friends, and he's super handsome!
JD? Like Juvenile Delinquent?
It's a little dumb, isn't it?
No more than Fake Ryan, the flute tampon boy!
Ha! Ha! Ha!

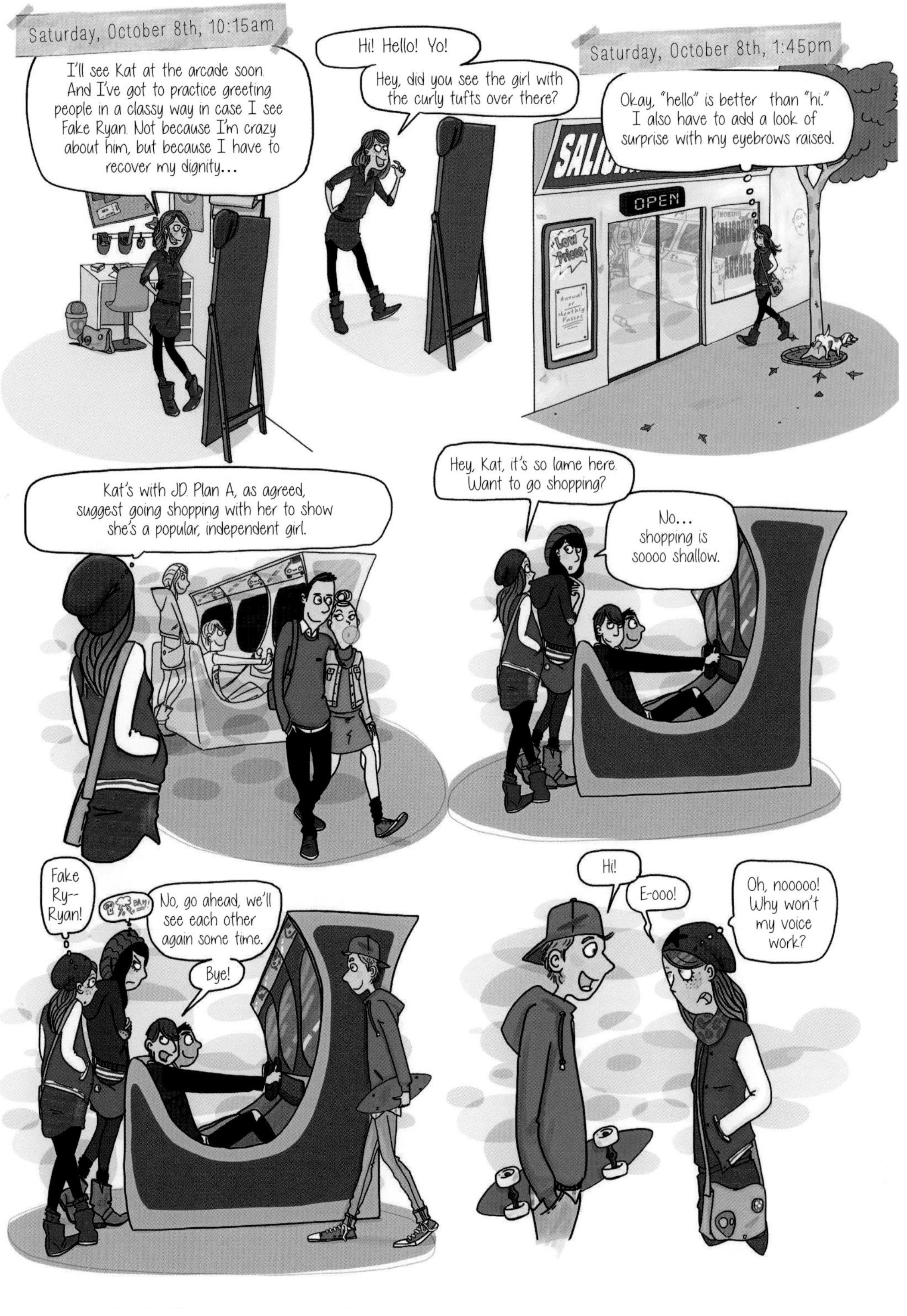

Saturday, October 8th, 10:15am
I'll see Kat at the arcade soon. And I've got to practice greeting people in a classy way in case I see Fake Ryan. Not because I'm crazy about him, but because I have to recover my dignity...
Hi! Hello! Yo!
Hey, did you see the girl with the curly tufts over there?
Saturday, October 8th, 1:45pm
Okay, "hello" is better than "hi." I also have to add a look of surprise with my eyebrows raised.
OPEN
Low Prices
Annual or Monthly Passes
Kat's with JD. Plan A, as agreed, suggest going shopping with her to show she's a popular, independent girl.
Hey, Kat, it's so lame here. Want to go shopping?
No... shopping is soooo shallow.
Fake Ry-- Ryan!
No, go ahead, we'll see each other again some time.
Bye!
Hi!
E-ooo!
Oh, nooooo! Why won't my voice work?

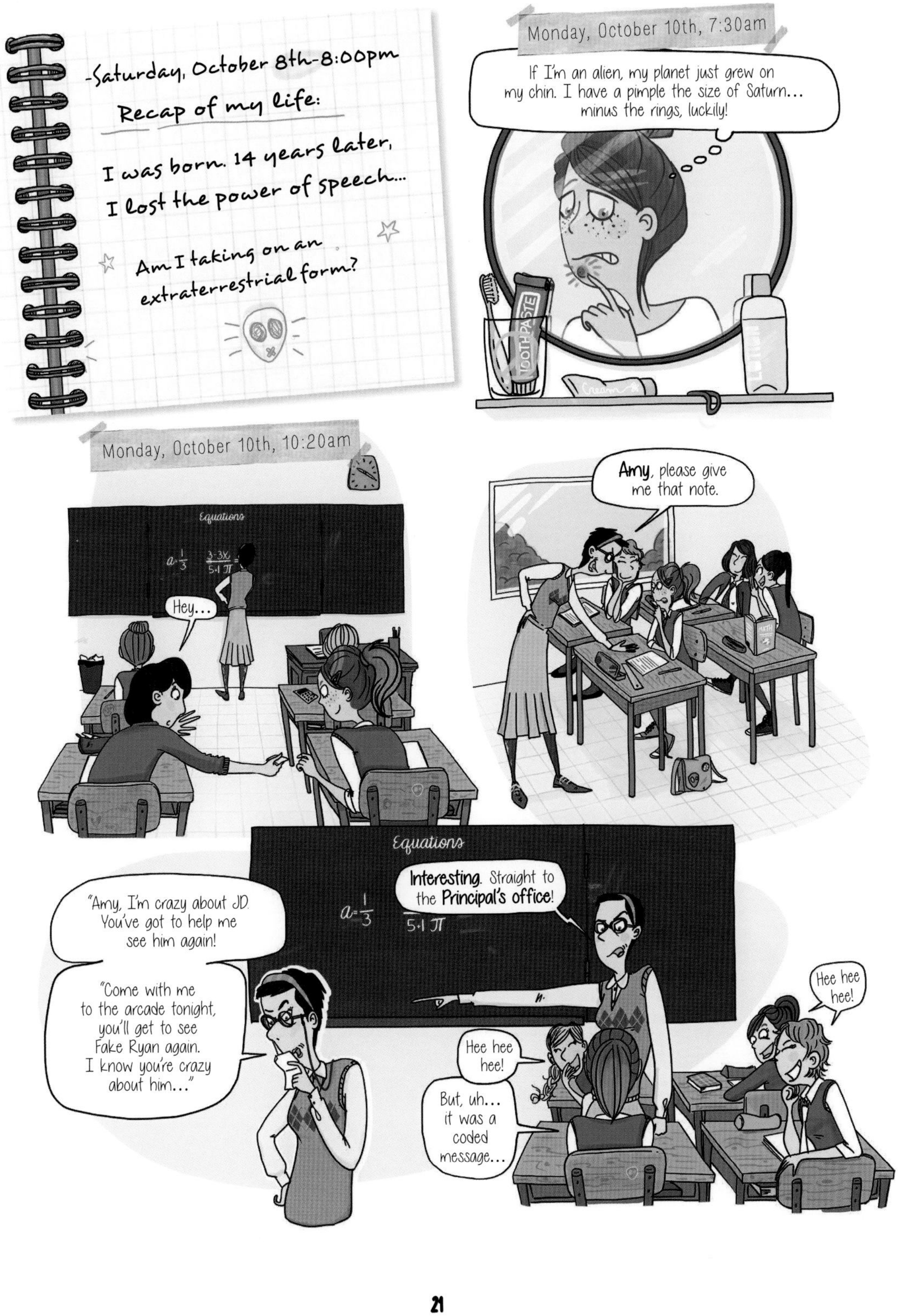
-Saturday, October 8th-8:00pm
Recap of my life:
I was born. 14 years later, I lost the power of speech...
Am I taking on an extraterrestrial form?
Monday, October 10th, 7:30am
If I'm an alien, my planet just grew on my chin. I have a pimple the size of Saturn... minus the rings, luckily!
TOOTHPASTE
LOTION
Monday, October 10th, 10:20am
Equations
Hey...
Amy, please give me that note.
MATH
Equations
Interesting. Straight to the Principal's office!
"Amy, I'm crazy about JD. You've got to help me see him again!
"Come with me to the arcade tonight, you'll get to see Fake Ryan again. I know you're crazy about him..."
Hee hee hee!
Hee hee hee!
But, uh... it was a coded message...

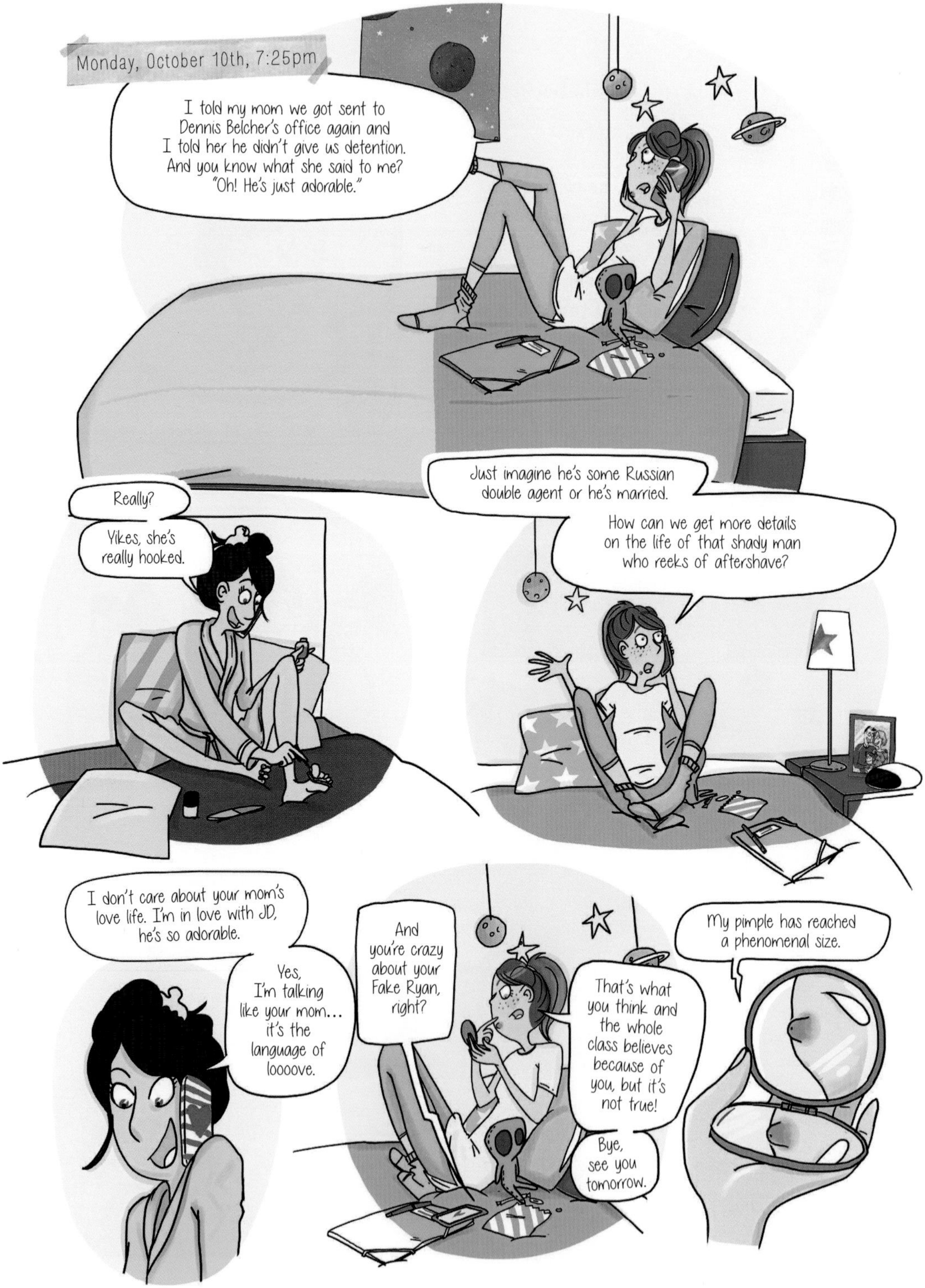
Monday, October 10th, 7:25pm
I told my mom we got sent to Dennis Belcher's office again and I told her he didn't give us detention. And you know what she said to me? "Oh! He's just adorable."
Really?
Yikes, she's really hooked.
Just imagine he's some Russian double agent or he's married.
How can we get more details on the life of that shady man who reeks of aftershave?
I don't care about your mom's love life. I'm in love with JD, he's so adorable.
Yes, I'm talking like your mom... it's the language of looove.
And you're crazy about your Fake Ryan, right?
That's what you think and the whole class believes because of you, but it's not true!
Bye, see you tomorrow.
My pimple has reached a phenomenal size.

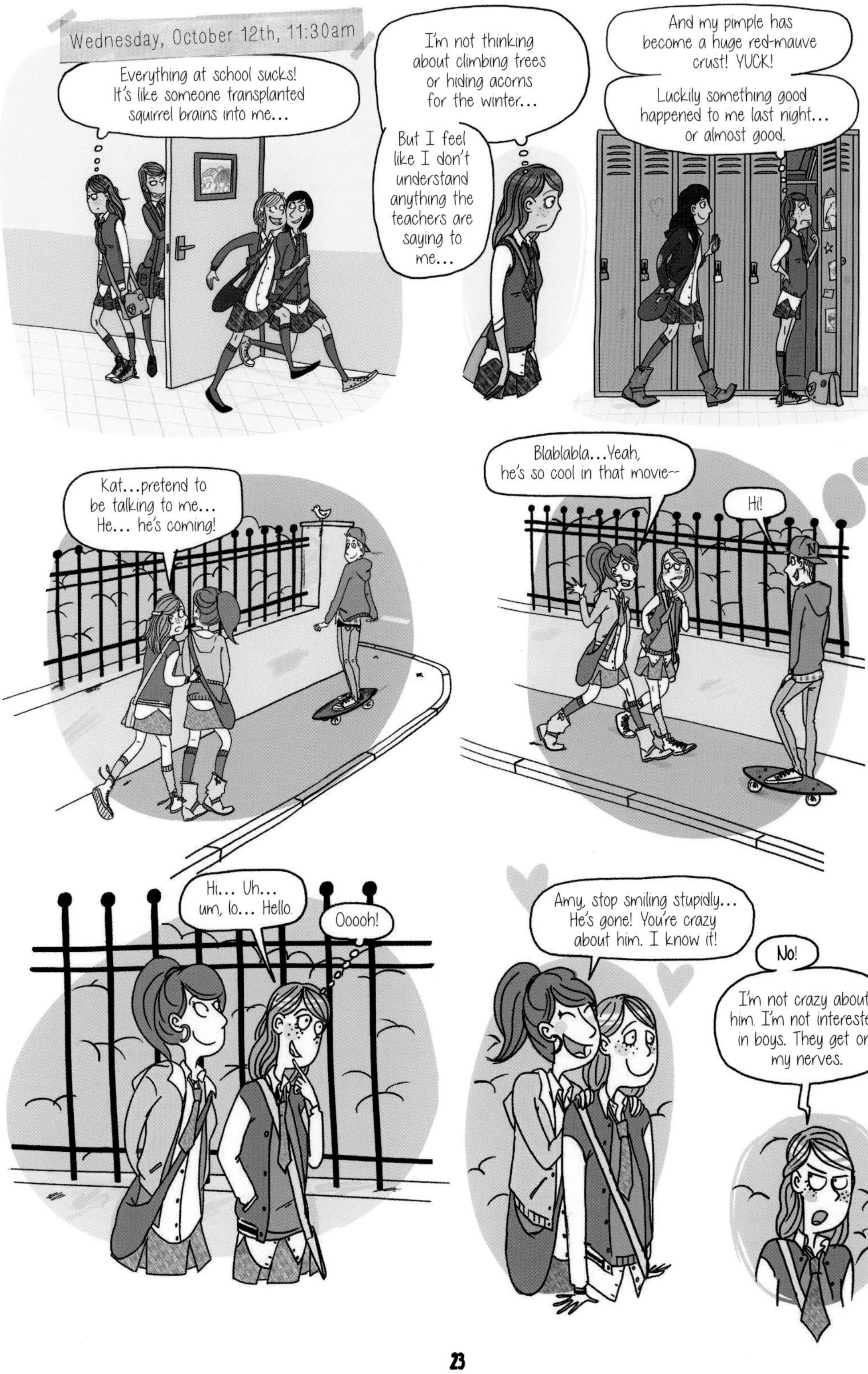

Wednesday, October 12th, 11:30am
Everything at school sucks! It's like someone transplanted squirrel brains into me...
I'm not thinking about climbing trees or hiding acorns for the winter...
But I feel like I don't understand anything the teachers are saying to me...
And my pimple has become a huge red-mauve crust! YUCK!
Luckily something good happened to me last night... or almost good.
Kat...pretend to be talking to me... He... he's coming!
Blablabla...Yeah, he's so cool in that movie--
Hi!
Hi... Uh... um, lo... Hello.
Ooooh!
Amy, stop smiling stupidly... He's gone! You're crazy about him. I know it!
No!
I'm not crazy about him. I'm not interested in boys. They get on my nerves.

-Summary of the month of October (haven't had much time to keep up with my journal lately, too much going on!):

Tuesday, October 18th: Fake Ryan's name is Nick. I found out thanks to Kat. While going to the store for a milkshake, she saw a bunch of guys and heard one of them say, "Hey, Nick!" and Fake Ryan came up. Afterwards, she saw JD and offered him a slurp of her milkshake. It seems he took a drink while looking her in the eyes and asked her for her phone number. According to her, I totally should use this milkshake trick on Fake Ryan. We'll see...

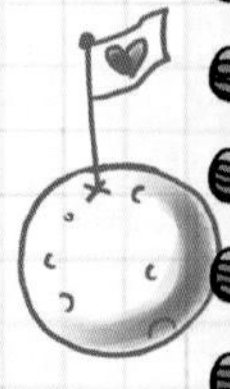

Wednesday, October 19th: My pimple disappeared this Wednesday, thanks to some lemon juice (my grandma's cure), it works! (Probably by chance, according to Mom)

Thursday, October 20th: Today's the day when I got into it with my mom about the mess in the house. She wouldn't stop saying: "Whose is this? Whose is that?" while pointing at my things. I got the idea of putting post-its all around the house with: "This is Amy's" on my stuff and "This is Frances's" on hers. And she really laughed when she saw all those post-its. She's cool, all the same!

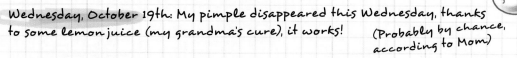

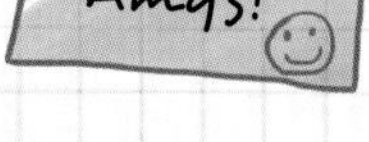

This is Amy's!

Friday, October 21st: Kat got invited to a Halloween party. A friend of JD's is throwing it. Nick, aka Fake Ryan, will be there too, it seems. I'm not too sure I want to go.

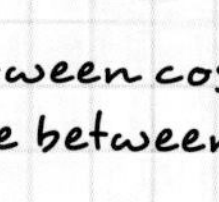

Friday, October 28th: I've waited too long to find a Halloween costume... there were only two kinds left at the store: I had a choice between... a princess and... Zorro. Yeah...Not cool!
Kat had found a Catwoman costume a few days earlier.

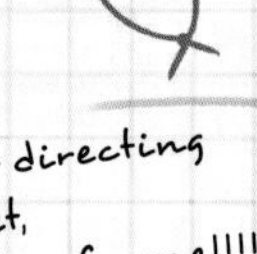

Saturday, October 29th: the Halloween party... Uhh...Pffff!
The evening of the biggest humiliation
of my life because of a milkshake!

If there's some higher power directing human beings on the planet, it's decided it's really got it in for me!!!!

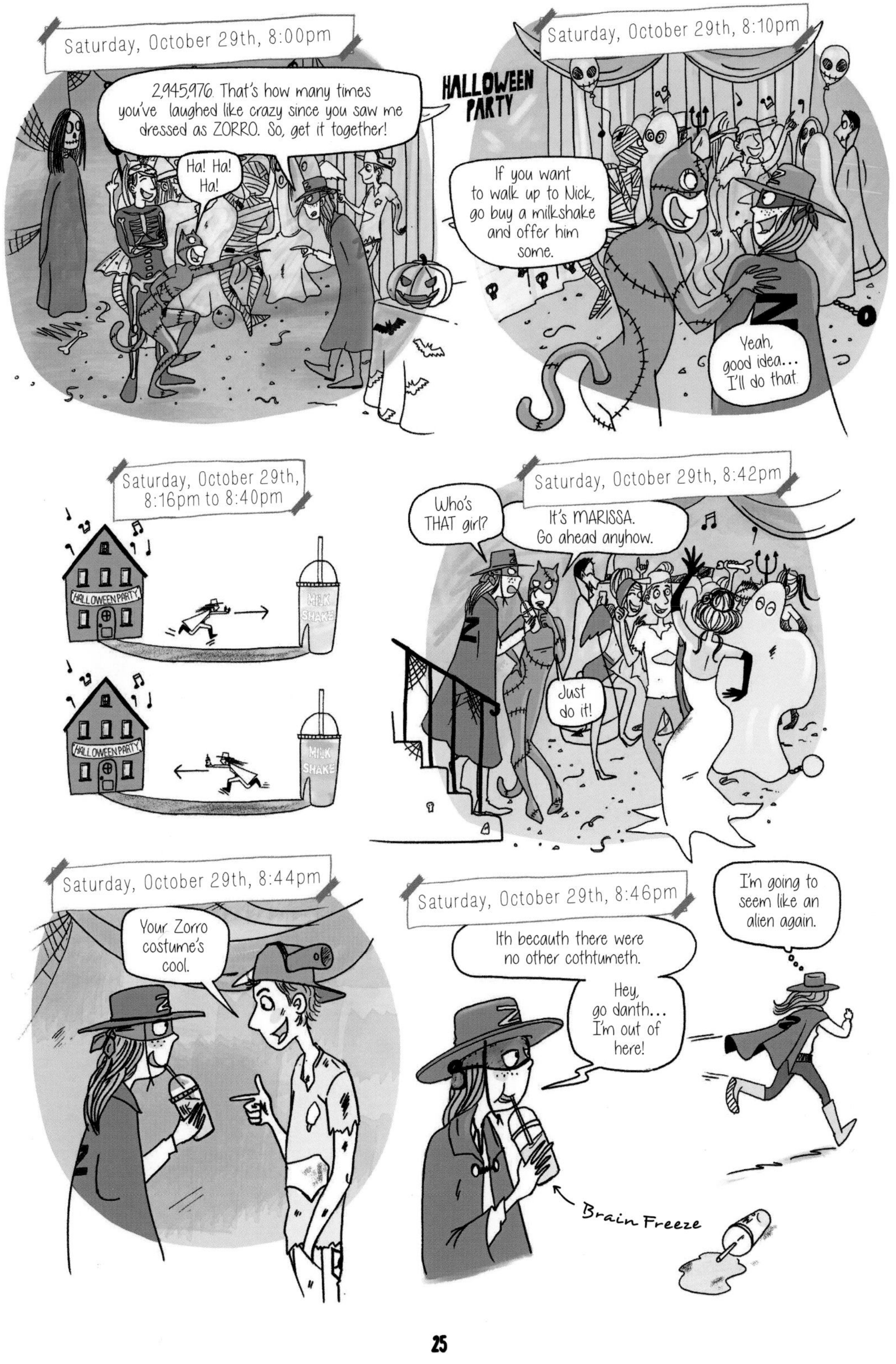
Saturday, October 29th, 8:00pm
2,945,976. That's how many times you've laughed like crazy since you saw me dressed as ZORRO. So, get it together!
Ha! Ha! Ha!
HALLOWEEN PARTY
Saturday, October 29th, 8:10pm
If you want to walk up to Nick, go buy a milkshake and offer him some.
Yeah, good idea... I'll do that.
Saturday, October 29th, 8:16pm to 8:40pm
HALLOWEEN PARTY
MILK SHAKE
HALLOWEEN PARTY
MILK SHAKE
Saturday, October 29th, 8:42pm
Who's THAT girl?
It's MARISSA. Go ahead anyhow.
Just do it!
Saturday, October 29th, 8:44pm
Your Zorro costume's cool.
Saturday, October 29th, 8:46pm
I'm going to seem like an alien again.
Ith becauth there were no other cothtumeth.
Hey, go danth... I'm out of here!
Brain Freeze

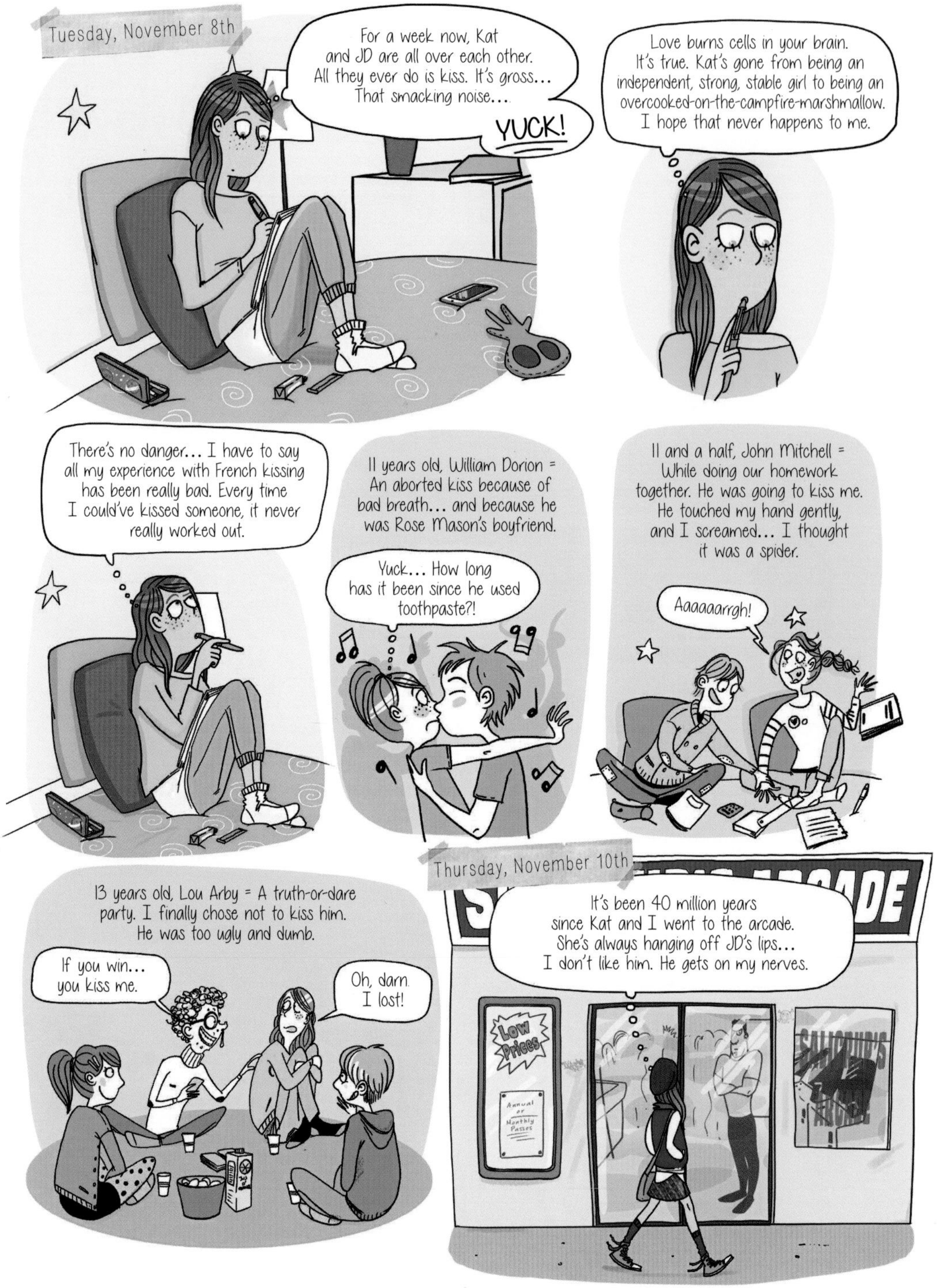
Tuesday, November 8th
For a week now, Kat and JD are all over each other. All they ever do is kiss. It's gross... That smacking noise...
YUCK!
Love burns cells in your brain. It's true. Kat's gone from being an independent, strong, stable girl to being an overcooked-on-the-campfire-marshmallow. I hope that never happens to me.
There's no danger... I have to say all my experience with French kissing has been really bad. Every time I could've kissed someone, it never really worked out.
11 years old, William Dorion = An aborted kiss because of bad breath... and because he was Rose Mason's boyfriend.
Yuck... How long has it been since he used toothpaste?!
11 and a half, John Mitchell = While doing our homework together. He was going to kiss me. He touched my hand gently, and I screamed... I thought it was a spider.
Aaaaaarrgh!
13 years old, Lou Arby = A truth-or-dare party. I finally chose not to kiss him. He was too ugly and dumb.
If you win... you kiss me.
Oh, darn. I lost!
Thursday, November 10th
It's been 40 million years since Kat and I went to the arcade. She's always hanging off JD's lips... I don't like him. He gets on my nerves.
Low Prices
Annual or Monthly Passes

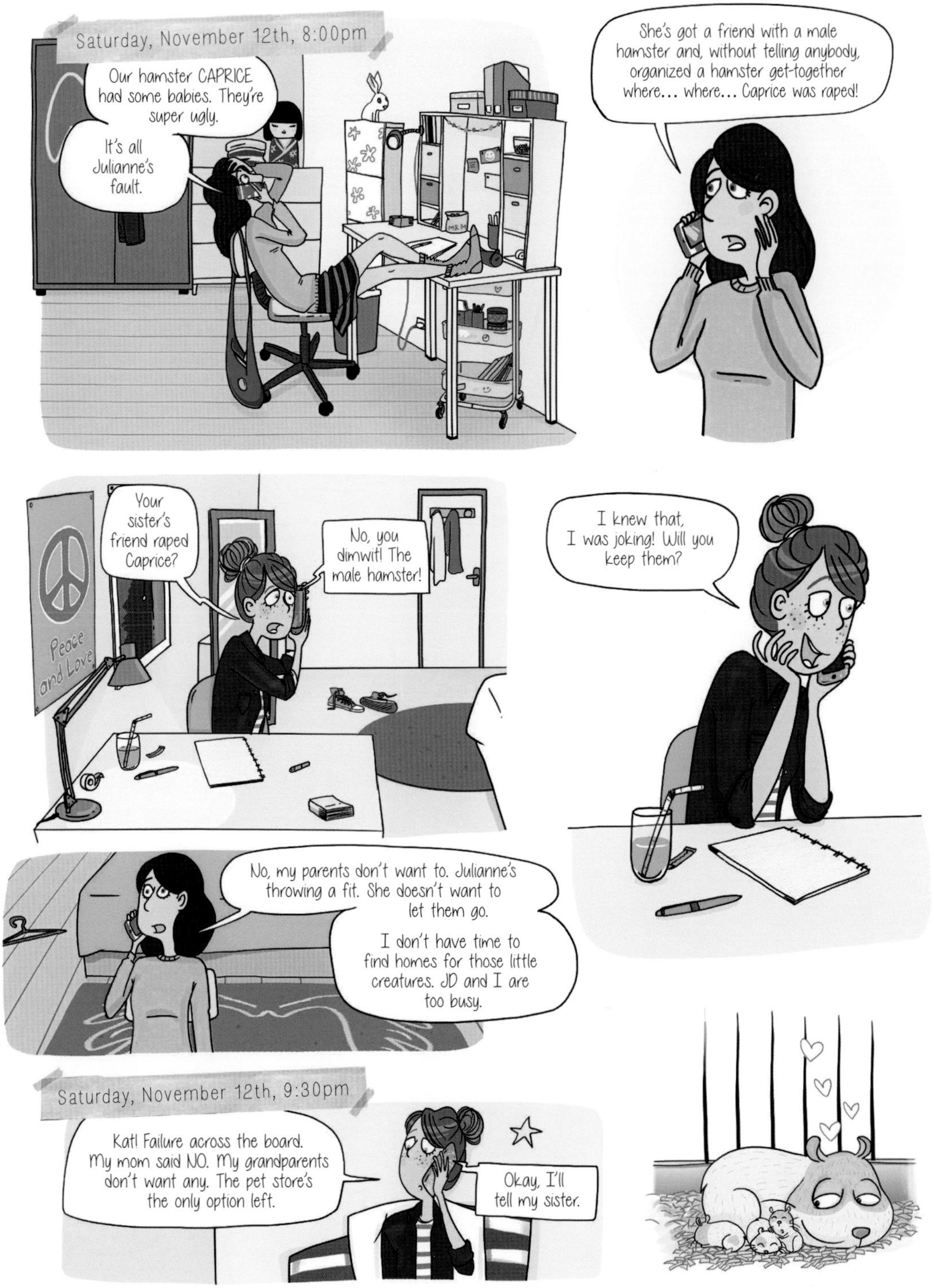
Saturday, November 12th, 8:00pm
Our hamster CAPRICE had some babies. They're super ugly.
It's all Julianne's fault.
She's got a friend with a male hamster and, without telling anybody, organized a hamster get-together where... where... Caprice was raped!
Your sister's friend raped Caprice?
No, you dimwit! The male hamster!
I knew that, I was joking! Will you keep them?
No, my parents don't want to. Julianne's throwing a fit. She doesn't want to let them go.
I don't have time to find homes for those little creatures. JD and I are too busy.
Saturday, November 12th, 9:30pm
Kat! Failure across the board. My mom said NO. My grandparents don't want any. The pet store's the only option left.
Okay, I'll tell my sister.

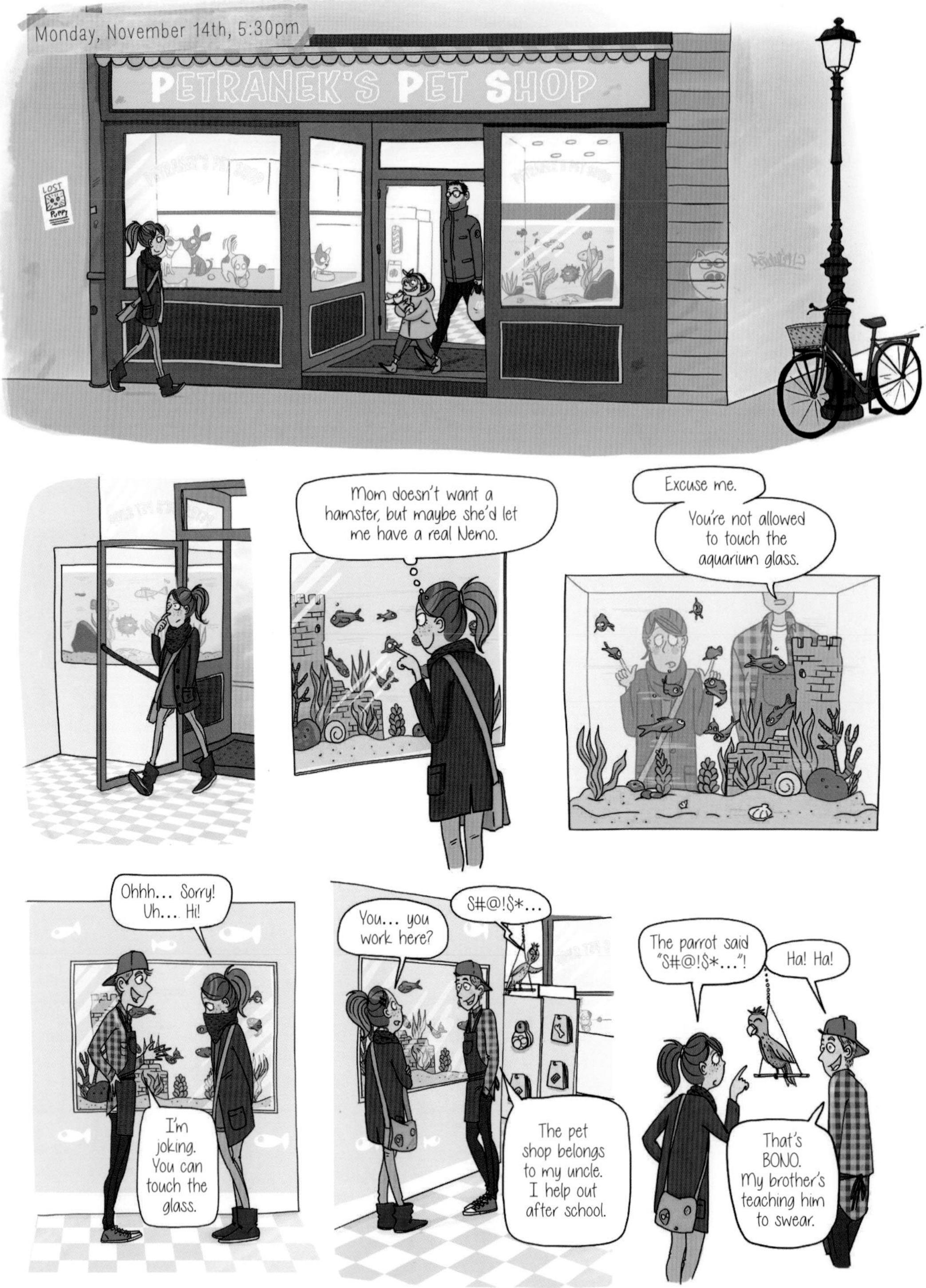

Monday, November 14th, 5:30pm
PETRANEK'S PET SHOP
LOST PUPPY
Mom doesn't want a hamster, but maybe she'd let me have a real Nemo.
Excuse me.
You're not allowed to touch the aquarium glass.
Ohhh... Sorry! Uh... Hi!
I'm joking. You can touch the glass.
You... you work here?
S#@!$*...
The pet shop belongs to my uncle. I help out after school.
The parrot said "S#@!$*..."!
Ha! Ha!
That's BONO. My brother's teaching him to swear.

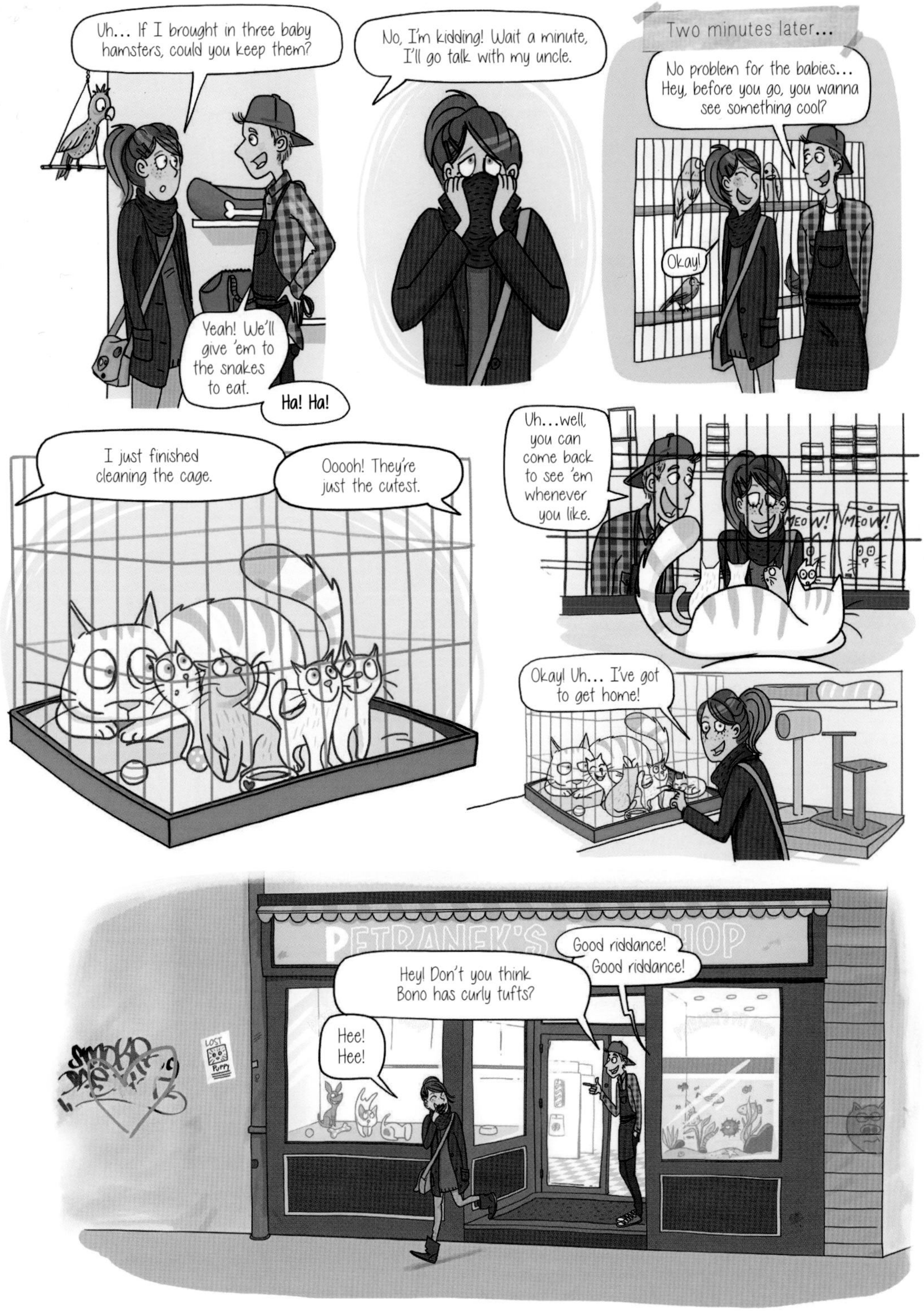

Uh... If I brought in three baby hamsters, could you keep them?
Yeah! We'll give 'em to the snakes to eat.
Ha! Ha!
No, I'm kidding! Wait a minute, I'll go talk with my uncle.
Two minutes later...
No problem for the babies... Hey, before you go, you wanna see something cool?
Okay!
I just finished cleaning the cage.
Ooooh! They're just the cutest.
Uh...well, you can come back to see 'em whenever you like.
MEOW!
MEOW!
Okay! Uh... I've got to get home!
Good riddance! Good riddance!
Hey! Don't you think Bono has curly tufts?
Hee! Hee!
LOST
PUPPY

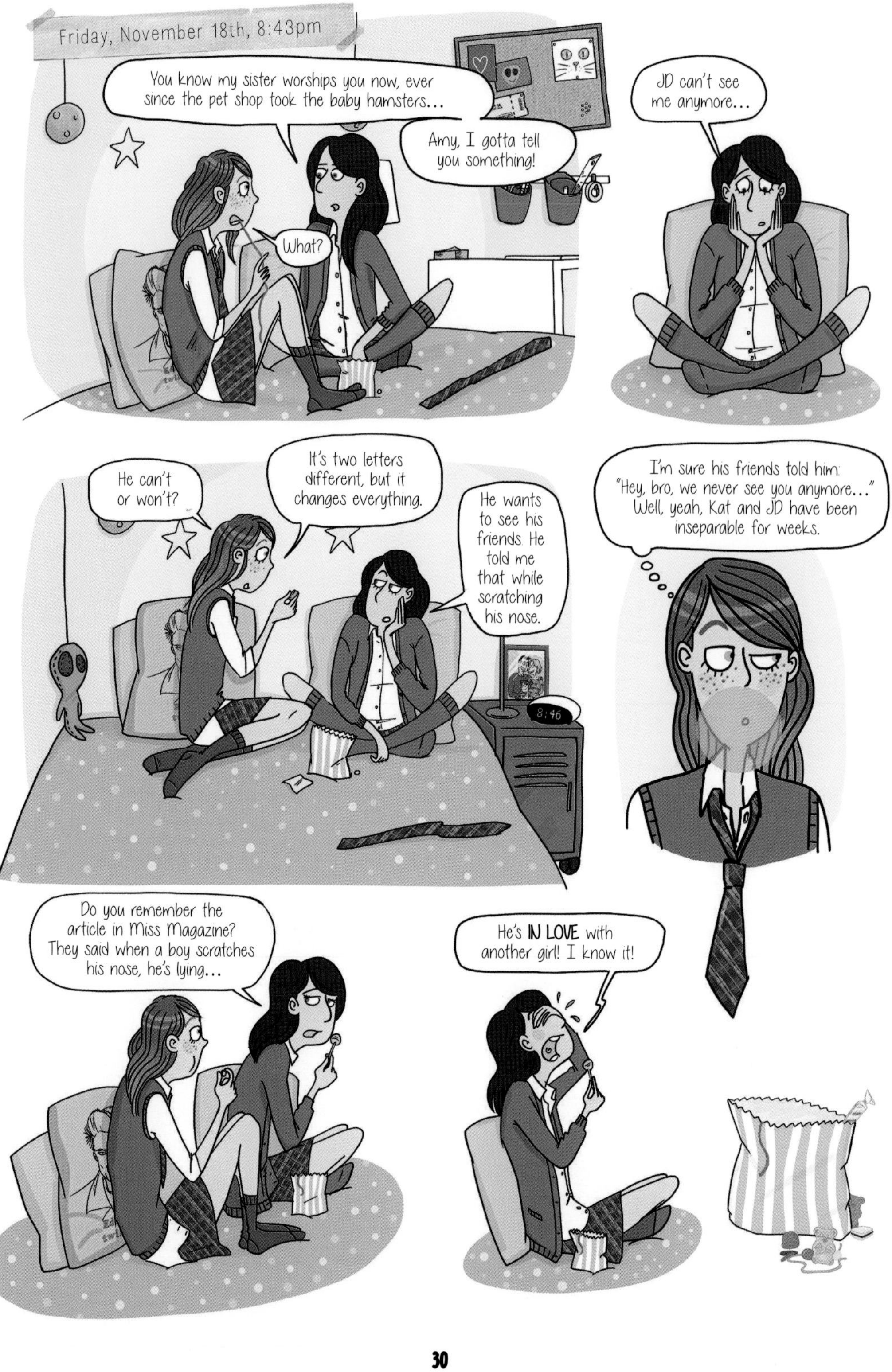
Friday, November 18th, 8:43pm
You know my sister worships you now, ever since the pet shop took the baby hamsters...
Amy, I gotta tell you something!
What?
JD can't see me anymore...
He can't or won't?
It's two letters different, but it changes everything.
He wants to see his friends. He told me that while scratching his nose.
I'm sure his friends told him: "Hey, bro, we never see you anymore..." Well, yeah, Kat and JD have been inseparable for weeks.
Do you remember the article in Miss Magazine? They said when a boy scratches his nose, he's lying...
He's **IN LOVE** with another girl! I know it!

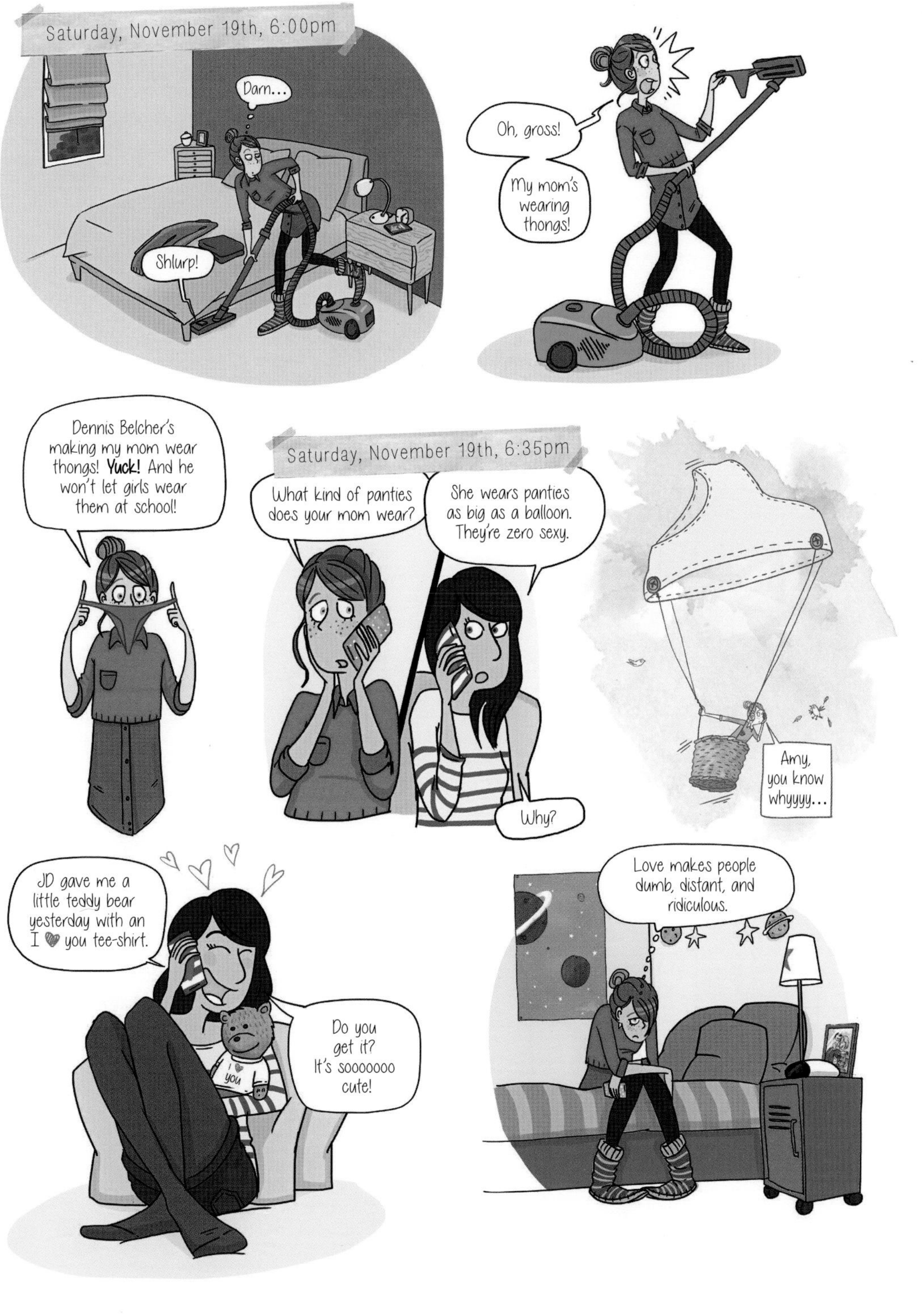
Saturday, November 19th, 6:00pm
Darn...
Shlurp!
Oh, gross!
My mom's wearing thongs!
Dennis Belcher's making my mom wear thongs! Yuck! And he won't let girls wear them at school!
Saturday, November 19th, 6:35pm
What kind of panties does your mom wear?
She wears panties as big as a balloon. They're zero sexy.
Why?
Amy, you know whyyyy...
JD gave me a little teddy bear yesterday with an I ♥ you tee-shirt.
I ♥ you
Do you get it? It's sooooooo cute!
Love makes people dumb, distant, and ridiculous.

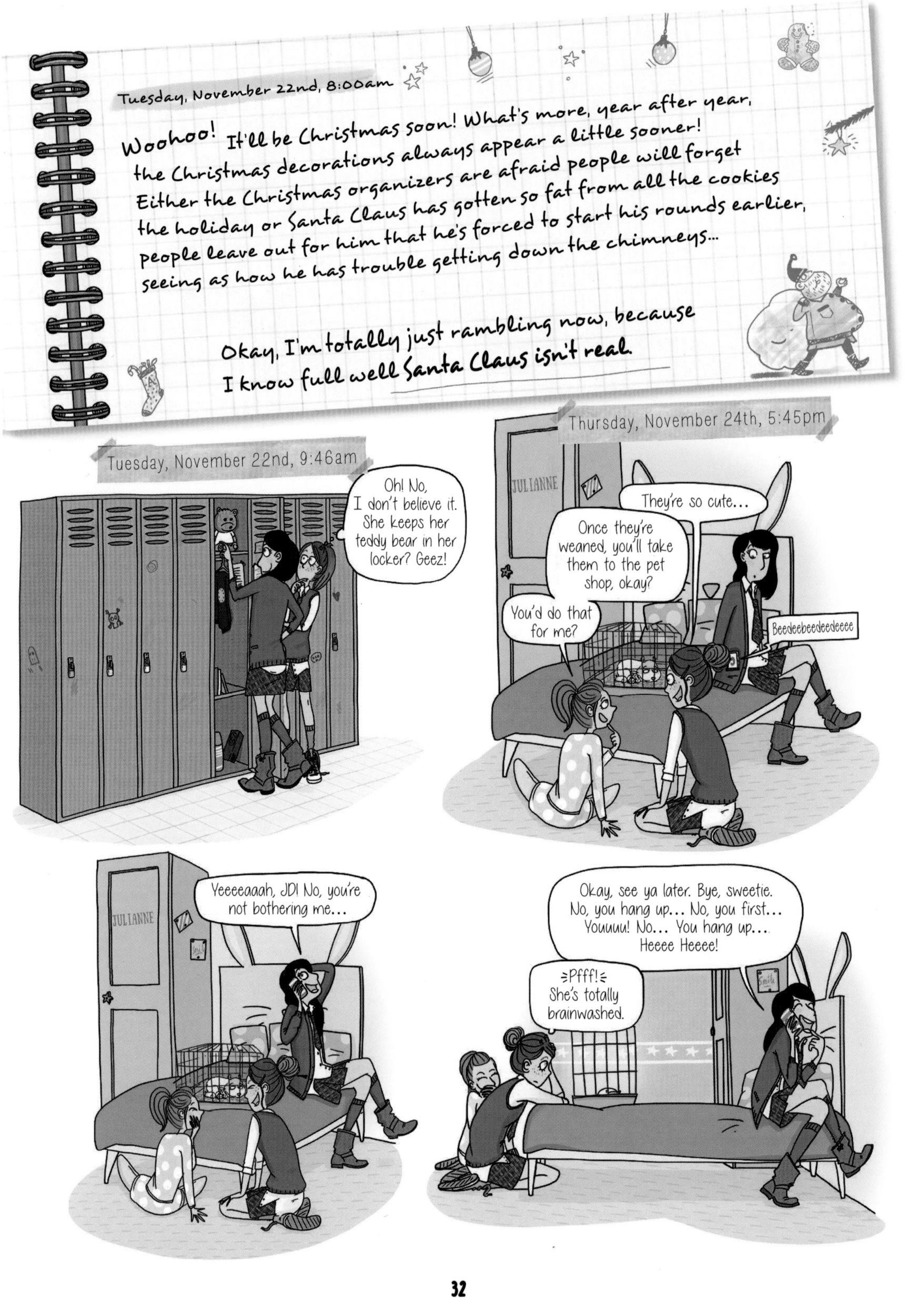
Tuesday, November 22nd, 8:00am
Woohoo! It'll be Christmas soon! What's more, year after year, the Christmas decorations always appear a little sooner! Either the Christmas organizers are afraid people will forget the holiday or Santa Claus has gotten so fat from all the cookies people leave out for him that he's forced to start his rounds earlier, seeing as how he has trouble getting down the chimneys...
Okay, I'm totally just rambling now, because I know full well Santa Claus isn't real.
Tuesday, November 22nd, 9:46am
Oh! No, I don't believe it. She keeps her teddy bear in her locker? Geez!
Thursday, November 24th, 5:45pm
JULIANNE
They're so cute...
Once they're weaned, you'll take them to the pet shop, okay?
You'd do that for me?
Beedeebeedeedeeee
JULIANNE
Yeeeeaaah, JD! No, you're not bothering me...
Okay, see ya later. Bye, sweetie. No, you hang up... No, you first... Youuuu! No... You hang up... Heeee Heeee!
Pfff! She's totally brainwashed.

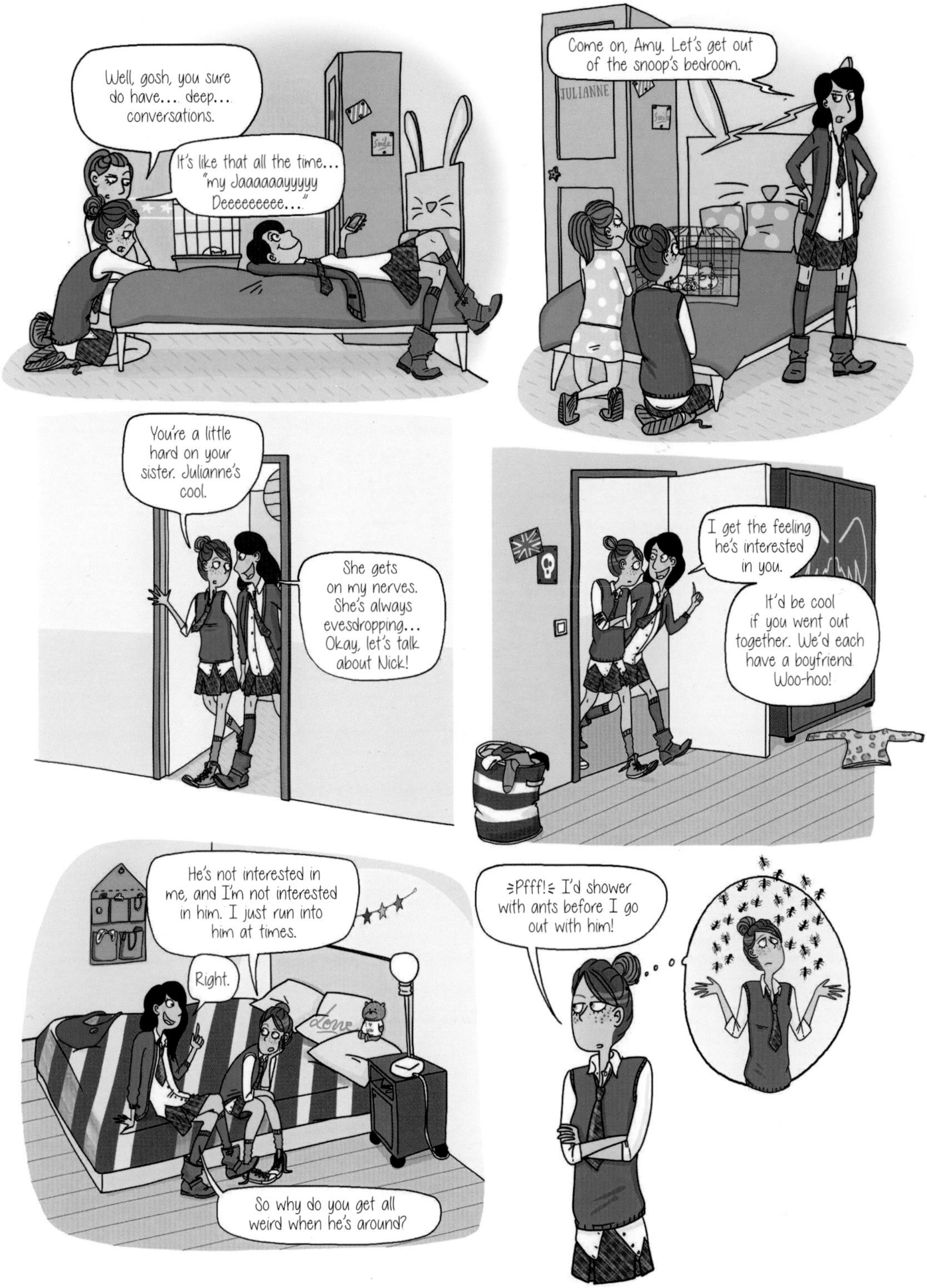
Well, gosh, you sure do have... deep... conversations.
It's like that all the time... "my Jaaaaaayyyyy Deeeeeeeee..."
Come on, Amy. Let's get out of the snoop's bedroom.
JULIANNE
You're a little hard on your sister. Julianne's cool.
She gets on my nerves. She's always evesdropping... Okay, let's talk about Nick!
I get the feeling he's interested in you.
It'd be cool if you went out together. We'd each have a boyfriend. Woo-hoo!
He's not interested in me, and I'm not interested in him. I just run into him at times.
Right.
So why do you get all weird when he's around?
Pfff! I'd shower with ants before I go out with him!

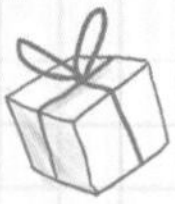

DECEMBER
My lucky star

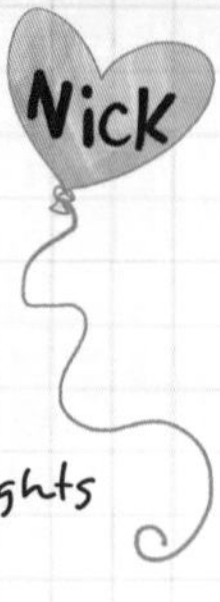
Nick

-Thursday, December 1st - 6:30pm: That's it, there are Christmas lights on the trees and all the houses in the neighborhood! And they've started playing Christmas songs on the radio. Every time I hear them, I have a little pang of sadness in my heart. My mom too.

We miss my dad...

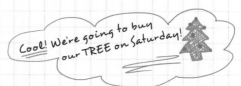

Cool! We're going to buy our TREE on Saturday!

- Friday, December 2nd - 8:30pm: Kat didn't want to come to the pet store with me to drop off the baby hamsters... The Queen was going to the movies with JD. She told me: "JD's so nice! He always buys my popcorn!" Okay, if she wants to get fat, that's her problem. Personally, I think popcorn smells like puke.

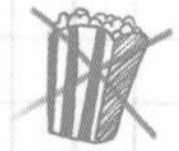

→ The hamsters names are: Bacon Junior, Buffy, and Bono.

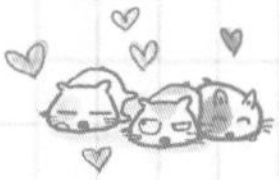

Nick wasn't at the store. Some girl with red hair took care of the baby hamsters. Julianne had put the babies in a shoebox with a little cushion from a Barbie bed... It was kind of embarrassing!

I saw the baby cats again, they're so, so cute! There's a little, white kitten with a gray mark down her face... she's so adorable. I named her "Sybil." She's so beautiful! But... Total failure...

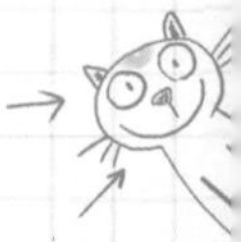

My mom won't let me have a cat! According to her, it's too much work. She says I wouldn't be responsible enough and blah blah blah... I wonder if she's capable of thinking about anything besides cleanliness... and thongs!

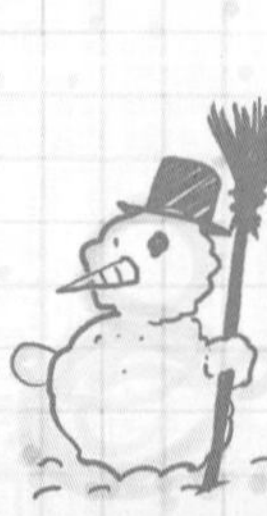

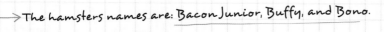

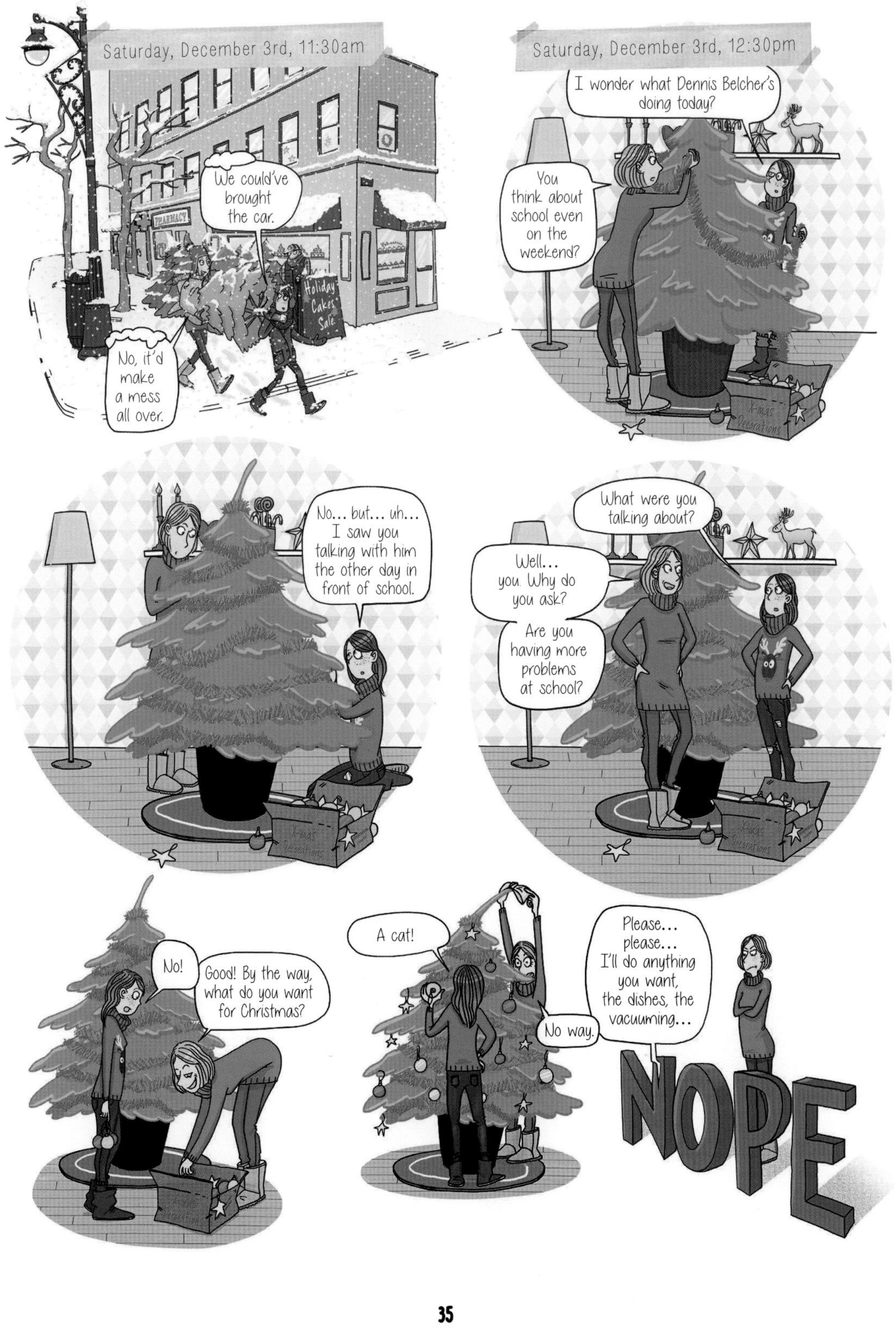

Saturday, December 3rd, 11:30am
PHARMACY
Holiday Cakes Sale
We could've brought the car.
No, it'd make a mess all over.
Saturday, December 3rd, 12:30pm
I wonder what Dennis Belcher's doing today?
You think about school even on the weekend?
X-mas Decorations
No... but... uh... I saw you talking with him the other day in front of school.
X-mas Decorations
What were you talking about?
Well... you. Why do you ask?
Are you having more problems at school?
X-mas Decorations
No!
Good! By the way, what do you want for Christmas?
A cat!
No way.
Please... please... I'll do anything you want, the dishes, the vacuuming...
NOPE

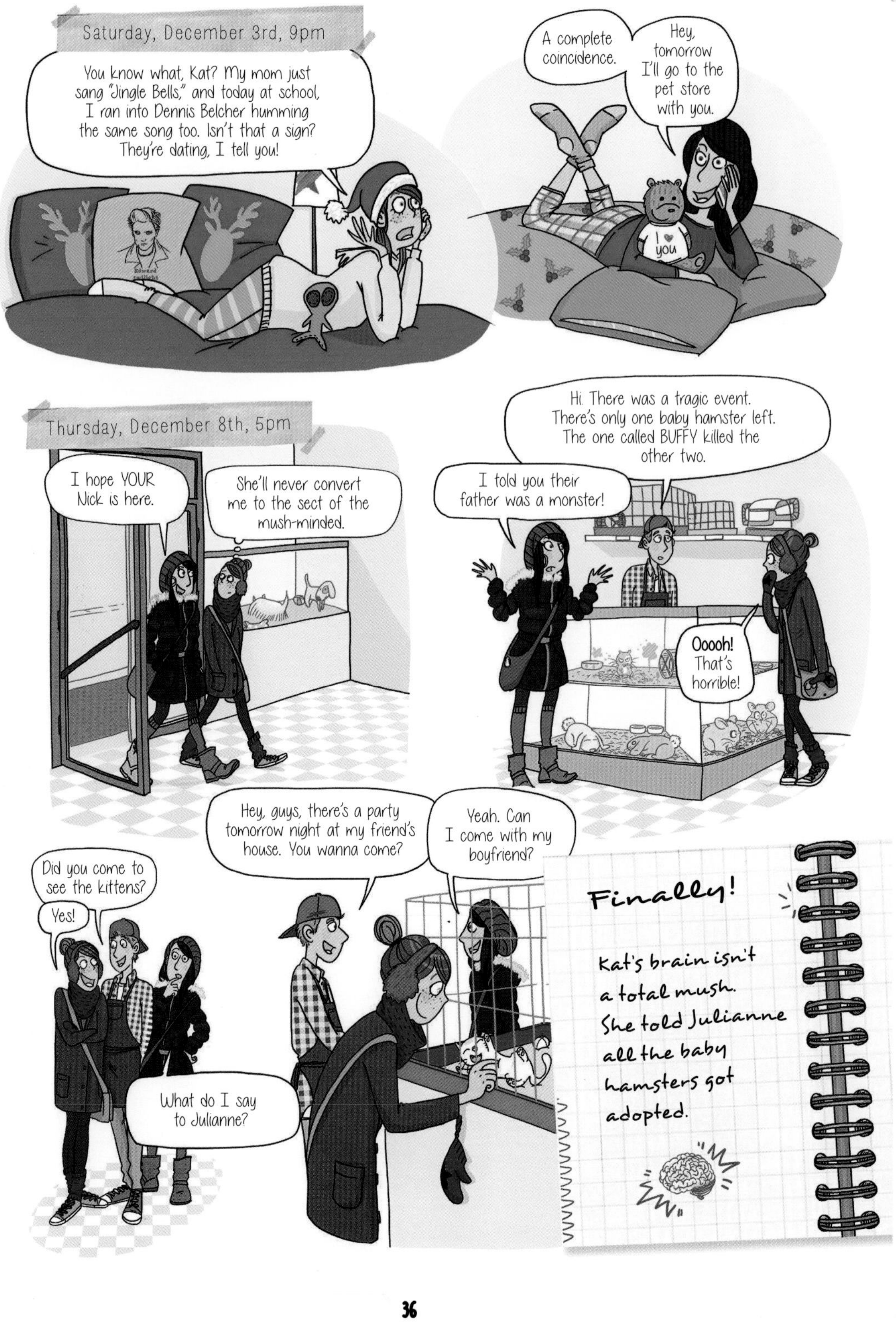
Saturday, December 3rd, 9pm
You know what, Kat? My mom just sang "Jingle Bells," and today at school, I ran into Dennis Belcher humming the same song too. Isn't that a sign? They're dating, I tell you!
A complete coincidence.
Hey, tomorrow I'll go to the pet store with you.
I ♥ you
Thursday, December 8th, 5pm
I hope YOUR Nick is here.
She'll never convert me to the sect of the mush-minded.
Hi. There was a tragic event. There's only one baby hamster left. The one called BUFFY killed the other two.
I told you their father was a monster!
Ooooh! That's horrible!
Did you come to see the kittens?
Yes!
Hey, guys, there's a party tomorrow night at my friend's house. You wanna come?
Yeah. Can I come with my boyfriend?
What do I say to Julianne?
Finally!
Kat's brain isn't a total mush. She told Julianne all the baby hamsters got adopted.

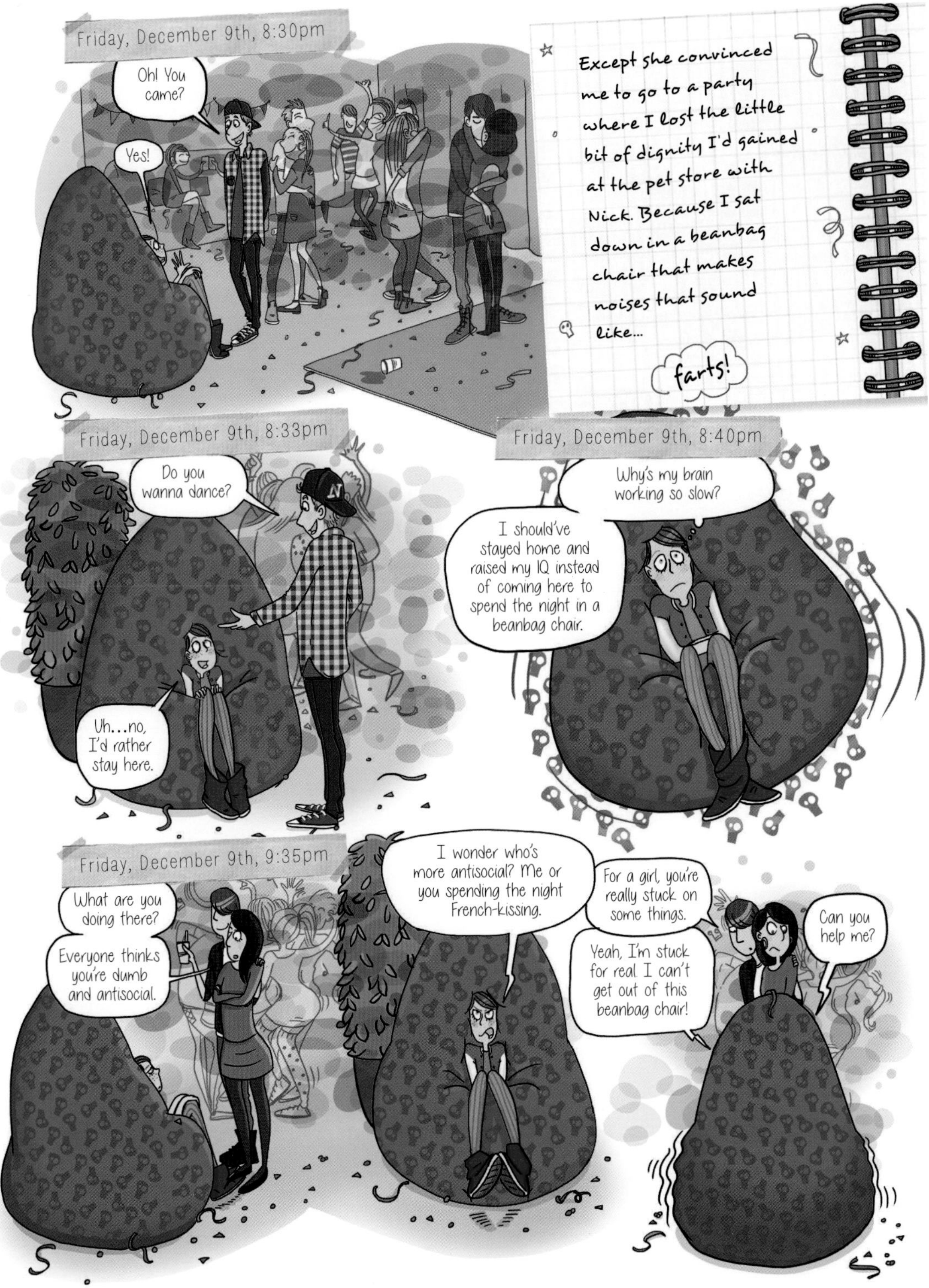

Friday, December 9th, 8:30pm
Oh! You came?
Yes!
Except she convinced me to go to a party where I lost the little bit of dignity I'd gained at the pet store with Nick. Because I sat down in a beanbag chair that makes noises that sound like...
farts!
Friday, December 9th, 8:33pm
Do you wanna dance?
Uh...no, I'd rather stay here.
Friday, December 9th, 8:40pm
Why's my brain working so slow?
I should've stayed home and raised my IQ instead of coming here to spend the night in a beanbag chair.
Friday, December 9th, 9:35pm
What are you doing there?
Everyone thinks you're dumb and antisocial.
I wonder who's more antisocial? Me or you spending the night French-kissing.
For a girl, you're really stuck on some things.
Yeah, I'm stuck for real. I can't get out of this beanbag chair!
Can you help me?

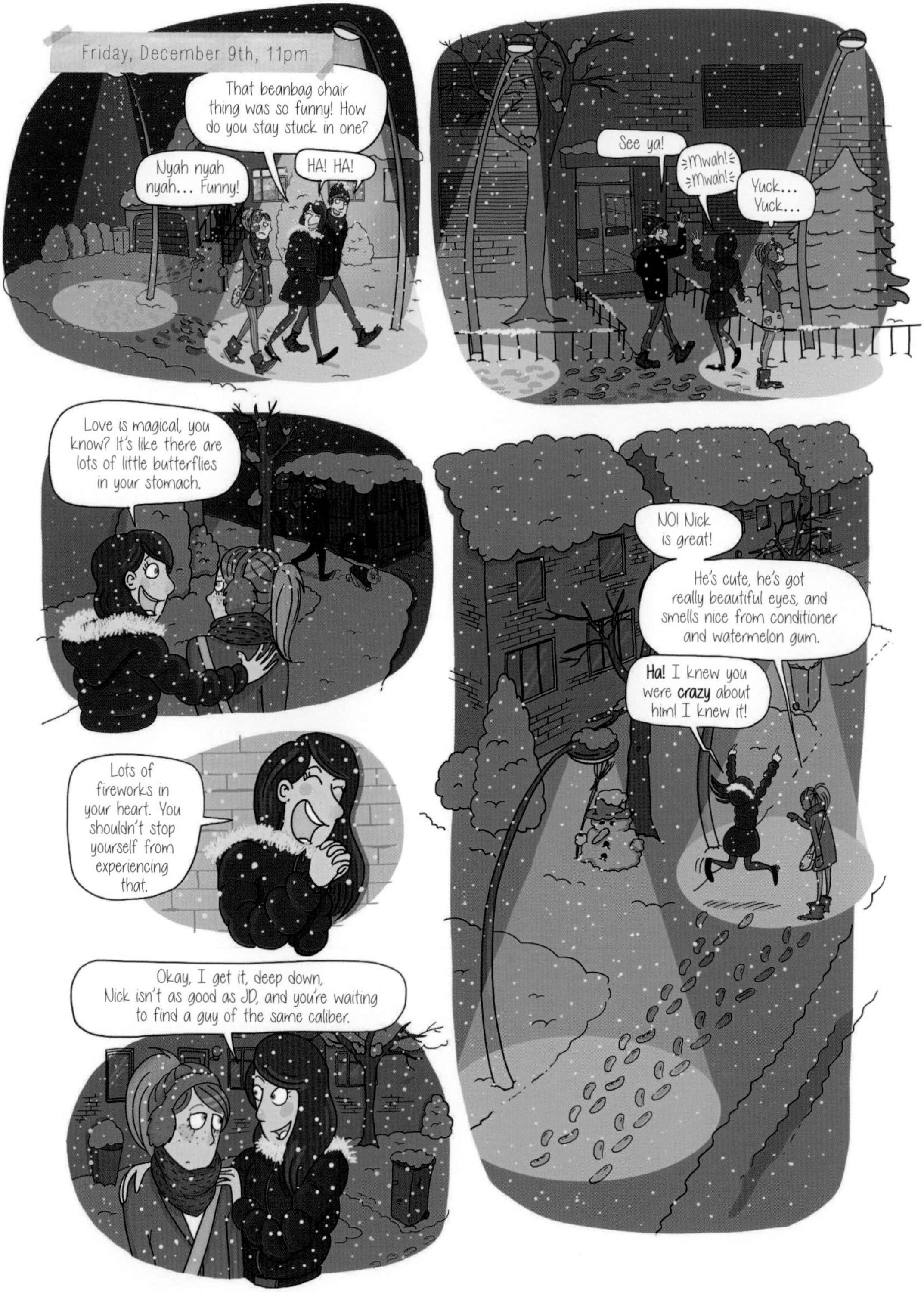
Friday, December 9th, 11pm
That beanbag chair thing was so funny! How do you stay stuck in one?
Nyah nyah nyah... Funny!
HA! HA!
See ya!
Mwah! Mwah!
Yuck... Yuck...
Love is magical, you know? It's like there are lots of little butterflies in your stomach.
Lots of fireworks in your heart. You shouldn't stop yourself from experiencing that.
Okay, I get it, deep down, Nick isn't as good as JD, and you're waiting to find a guy of the same caliber.
NO! Nick is great!
He's cute, he's got really beautiful eyes, and smells nice from conditioner and watermelon gum.
Ha! I knew you were crazy about him! I knew it!

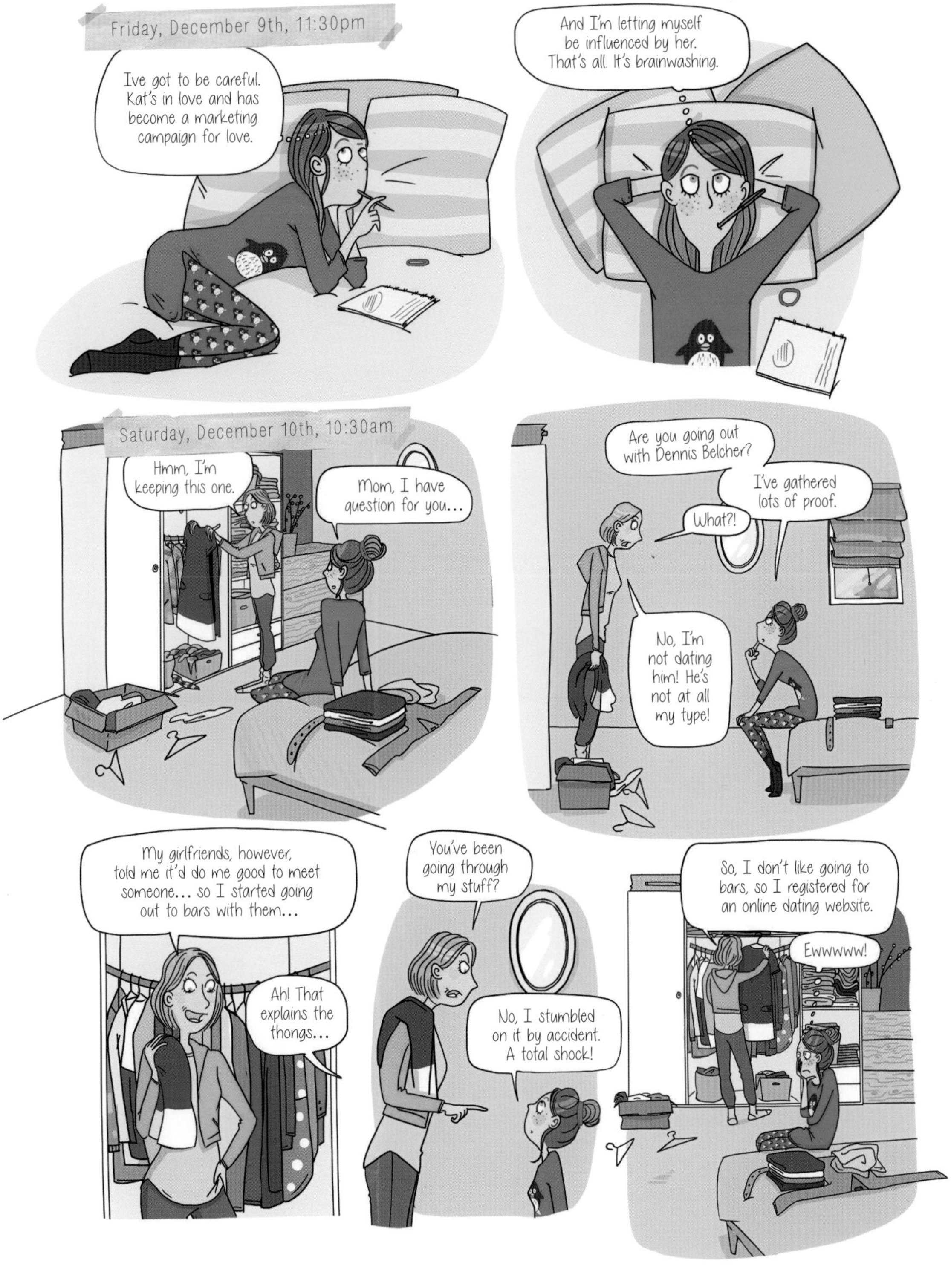
Friday, December 9th, 11:30pm
Ive got to be careful. Kat's in love and has become a marketing campaign for love.
And I'm letting myself be influenced by her. That's all. It's brainwashing.
Saturday, December 10th, 10:30am
Hmm, I'm keeping this one.
Mom, I have question for you...
Are you going out with Dennis Belcher?
I've gathered lots of proof.
What?!
No, I'm not dating him! He's not at all my type!
My girlfriends, however, told me it'd do me good to meet someone... so I started going out to bars with them...
Ah! That explains the thongs...
You've been going through my stuff?
No, I stumbled on it by accident. A total shock!
So, I don't like going to bars, so I registered for an online dating website.
Ewwwww!

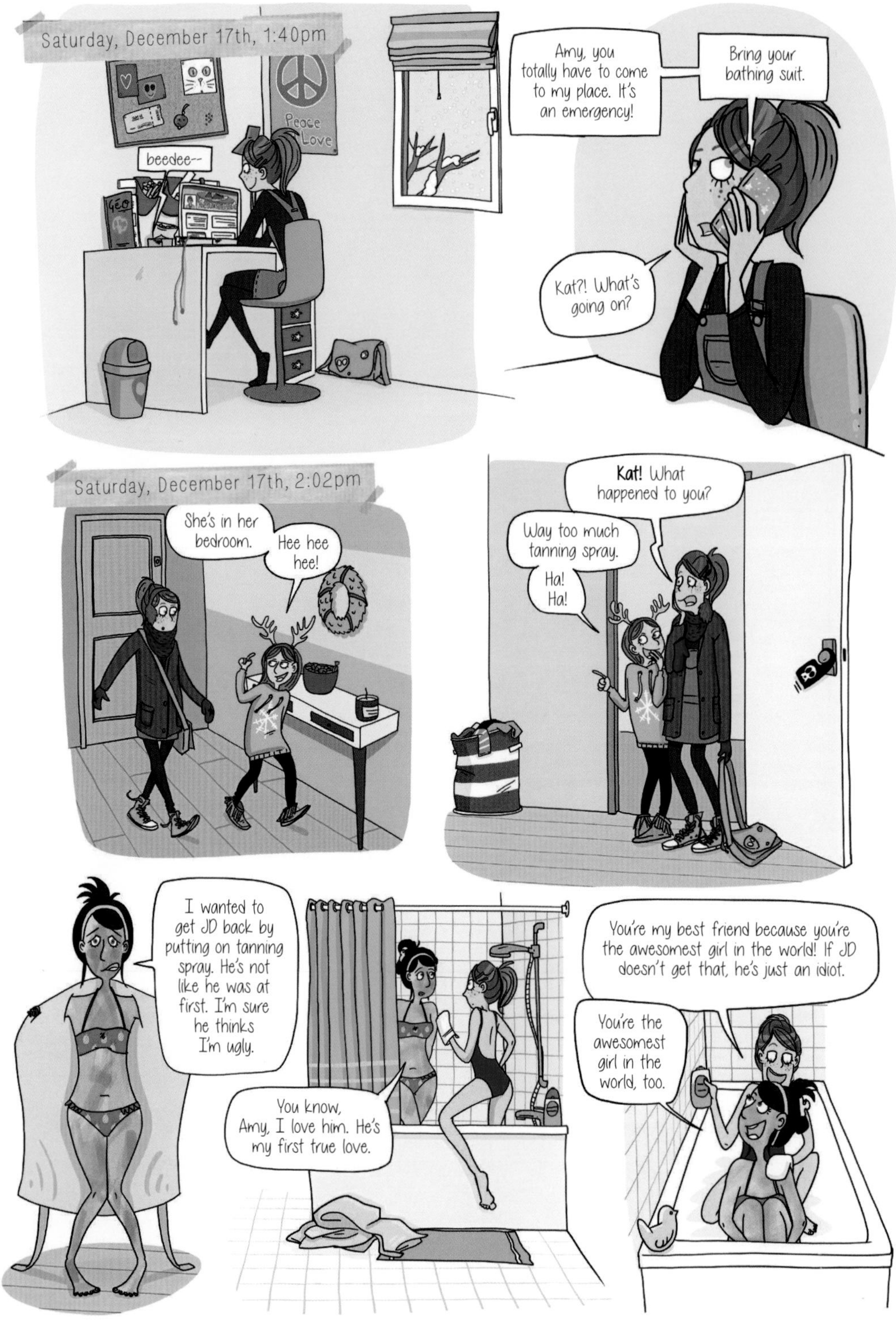

Saturday, December 17th, 1:40pm
Peace Love
beedee--
Amy, you totally have to come to my place. It's an emergency!
Bring your bathing suit.
Kat?! What's going on?
Saturday, December 17th, 2:02pm
She's in her bedroom.
Hee hee hee!
Kat! What happened to you?
Way too much tanning spray.
Ha! Ha!
I wanted to get JD back by putting on tanning spray. He's not like he was at first. I'm sure he thinks I'm ugly.
You know, Amy, I love him. He's my first true love.
You're my best friend because you're the awesomest girl in the world! If JD doesn't get that, he's just an idiot.
You're the awesomest girl in the world, too.

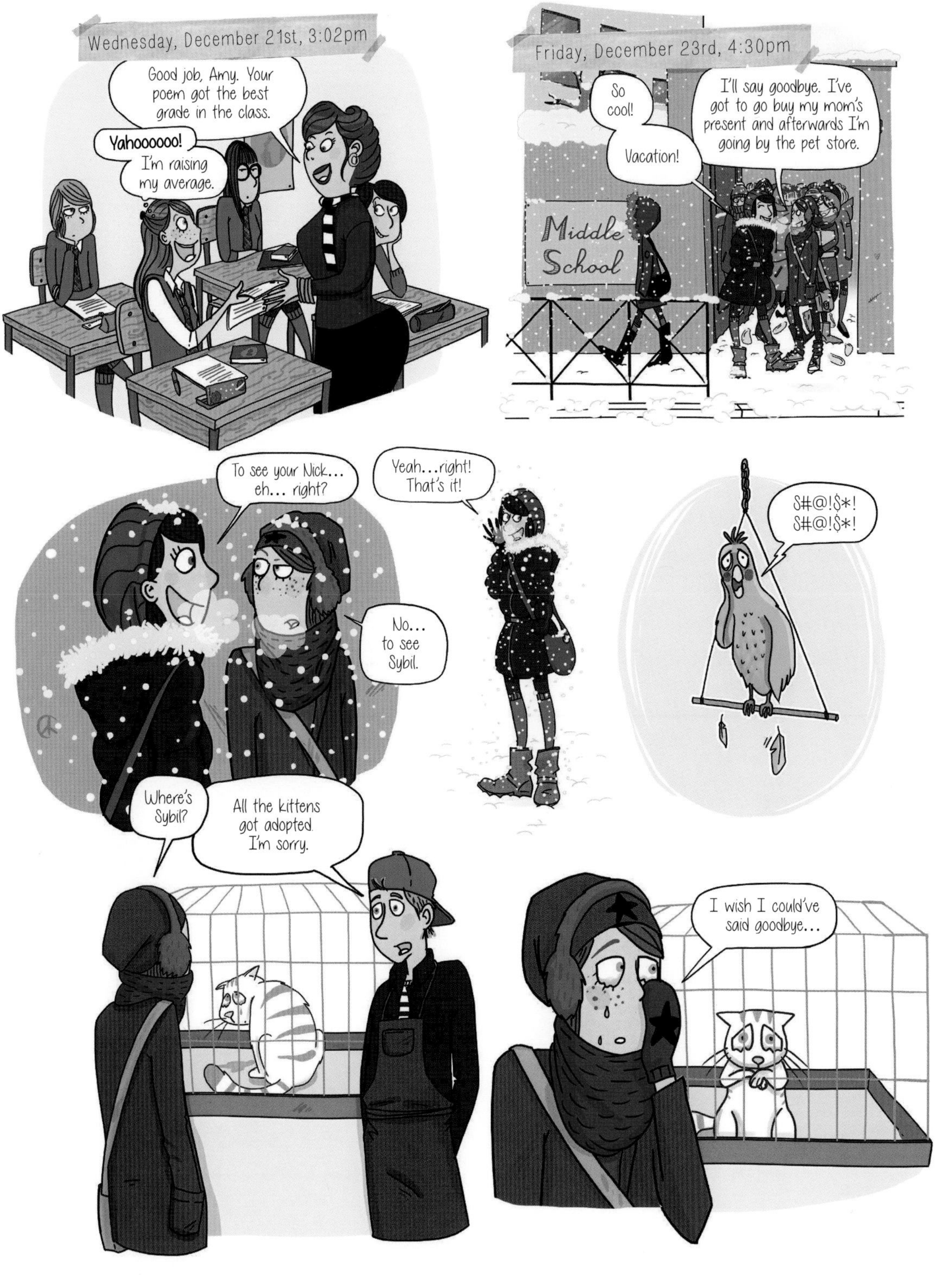

Wednesday, December 21st, 3:02pm
Good job, Amy. Your poem got the best grade in the class.
Yahoooooo! I'm raising my average.
Friday, December 23rd, 4:30pm
So cool!
Vacation!
I'll say goodbye. I've got to go buy my mom's present and afterwards I'm going by the pet store.
Middle School
To see your Nick... eh... right?
No... to see Sybil.
Yeah...right! That's it!
S#@!$*! S#@!$*!
Where's Sybil?
All the kittens got adopted. I'm sorry.
I wish I could've said goodbye...

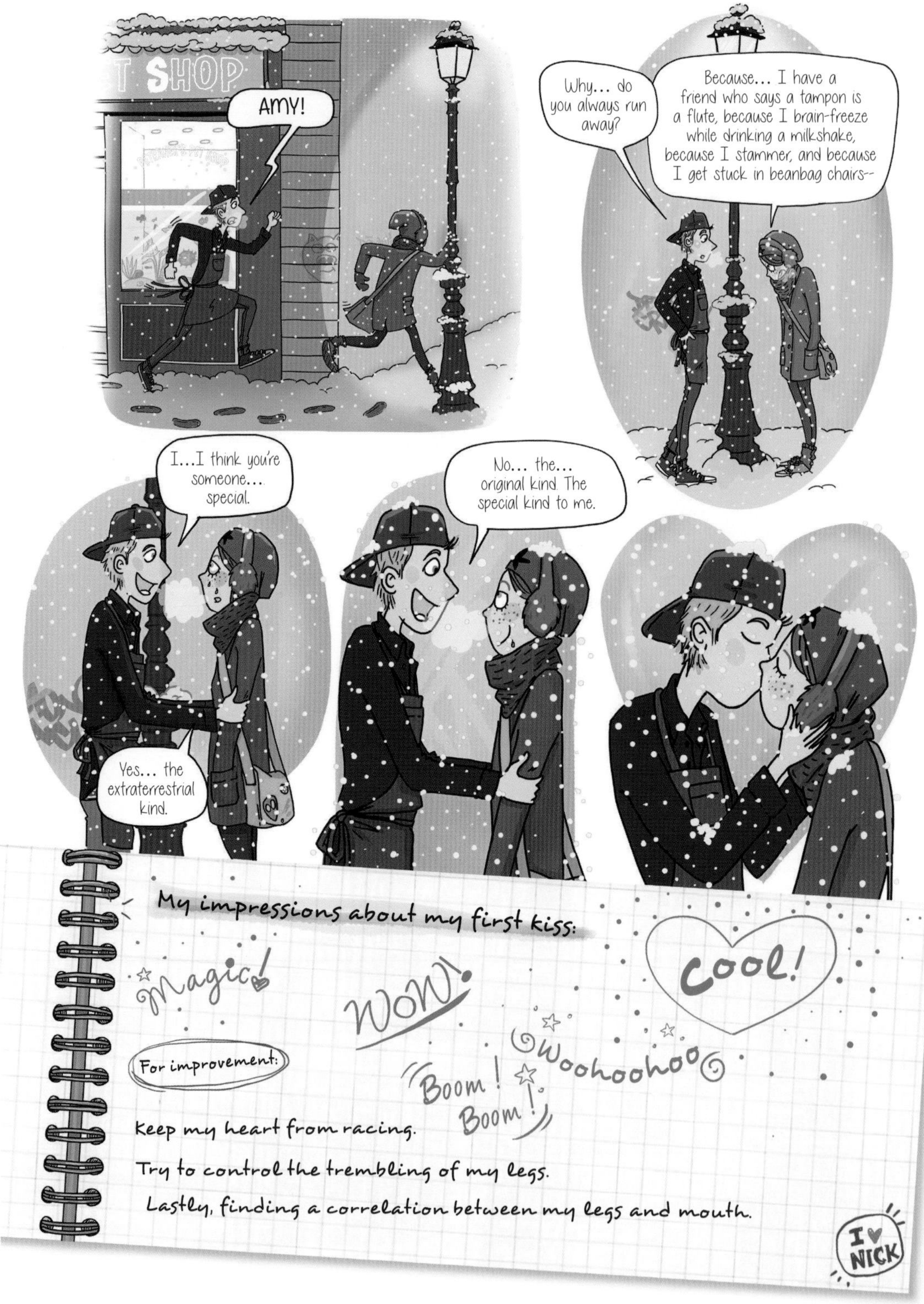
T SHOP
AMY!
Why... do you always run away?
Because... I have a friend who says a tampon is a flute, because I brain-freeze while drinking a milkshake, because I stammer, and because I get stuck in beanbag chairs--
I...I think you're someone... special.
Yes... the extraterrestrial kind.
No... the... original kind. The special kind to me.
My impressions about my first kiss:
Magic!
WOW!
Cool!
Woohoohoo
Boom! Boom!
For improvement:
Keep my heart from racing.
Try to control the trembling of my legs.
Lastly, finding a correlation between my legs and mouth.
I ♥ NICK

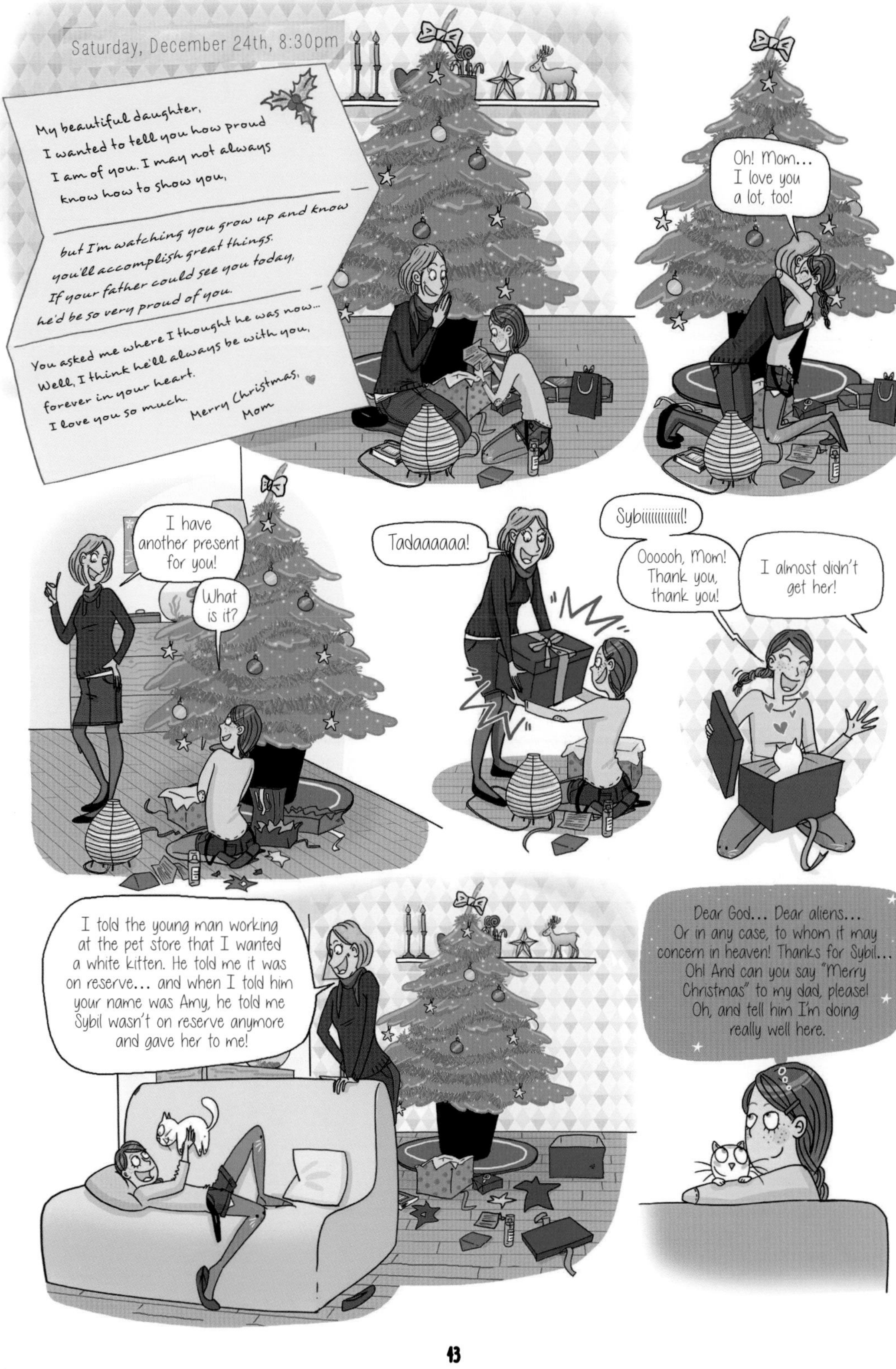
Saturday, December 24th, 8:30pm
My beautiful daughter,
I wanted to tell you how proud I am of you. I may not always know how to show you,
but I'm watching you grow up and know you'll accomplish great things. If your father could see you today, he'd be so very proud of you.
You asked me where I thought he was now... Well, I think he'll always be with you, forever in your heart. I love you so much.
Merry Christmas, Mom
Oh! Mom... I love you a lot, too!
I have another present for you!
What is it?
Tadaaaaaa!
Sybiiiiiiiiiiiil!
Oooooh, Mom! Thank you, thank you!
I almost didn't get her!
I told the young man working at the pet store that I wanted a white kitten. He told me it was on reserve... and when I told him your name was Amy, he told me Sybil wasn't on reserve anymore and gave her to me!
Dear God... Dear aliens... Or in any case, to whom it may concern in heaven! Thanks for Sybil... Oh! And can you say "Merry Christmas" to my dad, please! Oh, and tell him I'm doing really well here.

JANUARY
Total lethargy

My New Year's resolutions...

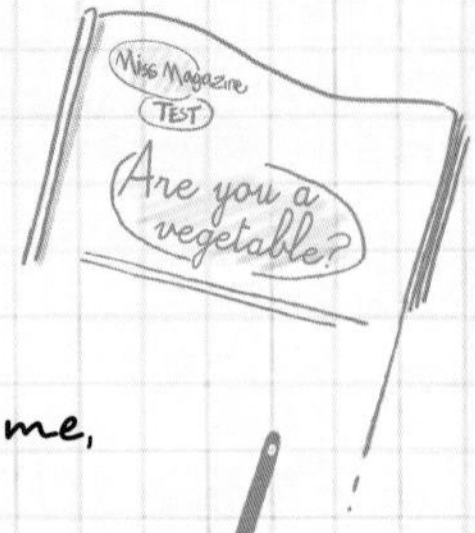
Miss Magazine
TEST
Are you a vegetable?

1. Help my mom more with the housework. She often asks me, and I admit I could be a bit more coperative... cooperative?

Come on, how's that spelled?

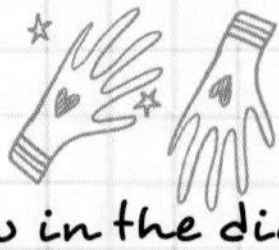

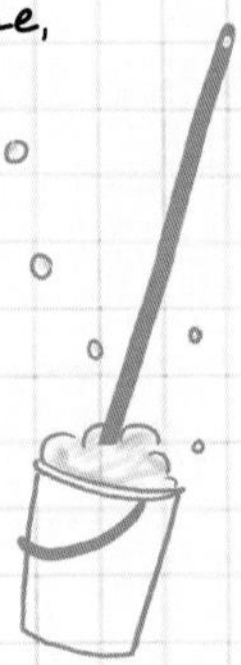

2. Find words I don't know in the dictionary.

(Cooperative, there! One resolution already kept!)

3. No more bickering with Kat.

4. Don't tell Kat I think JD is pretentious, fake, pompous, arrogant, big-headed, hoity-toity, awkward, full of himself, inaccessible, insolent, a show-off, affected, proud, over-confident, arrogant, pontificating, a poseur, flashy, presumptuous, self-aggrandizing, condescending, vain, conceited, and empty.

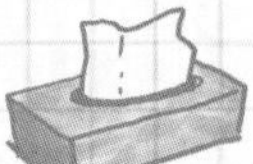

(My new resolution to look in the dictionary is a great resolution! There really are lots of synonyms to describe JD!)

5. To get better grades.

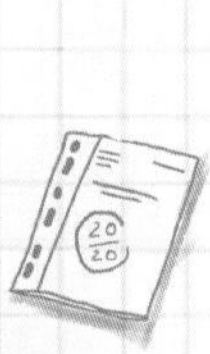

BONUS:
Don't think too much about Nick or let love turn my brain to mush.

P.S.:
Nick and I haven't heard from each other since December 23rd!
Arrrrgh!

P.P.S. Maybe he's as shy as I am.

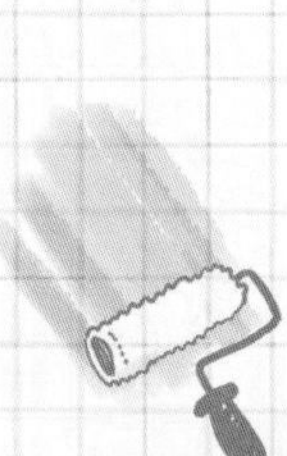

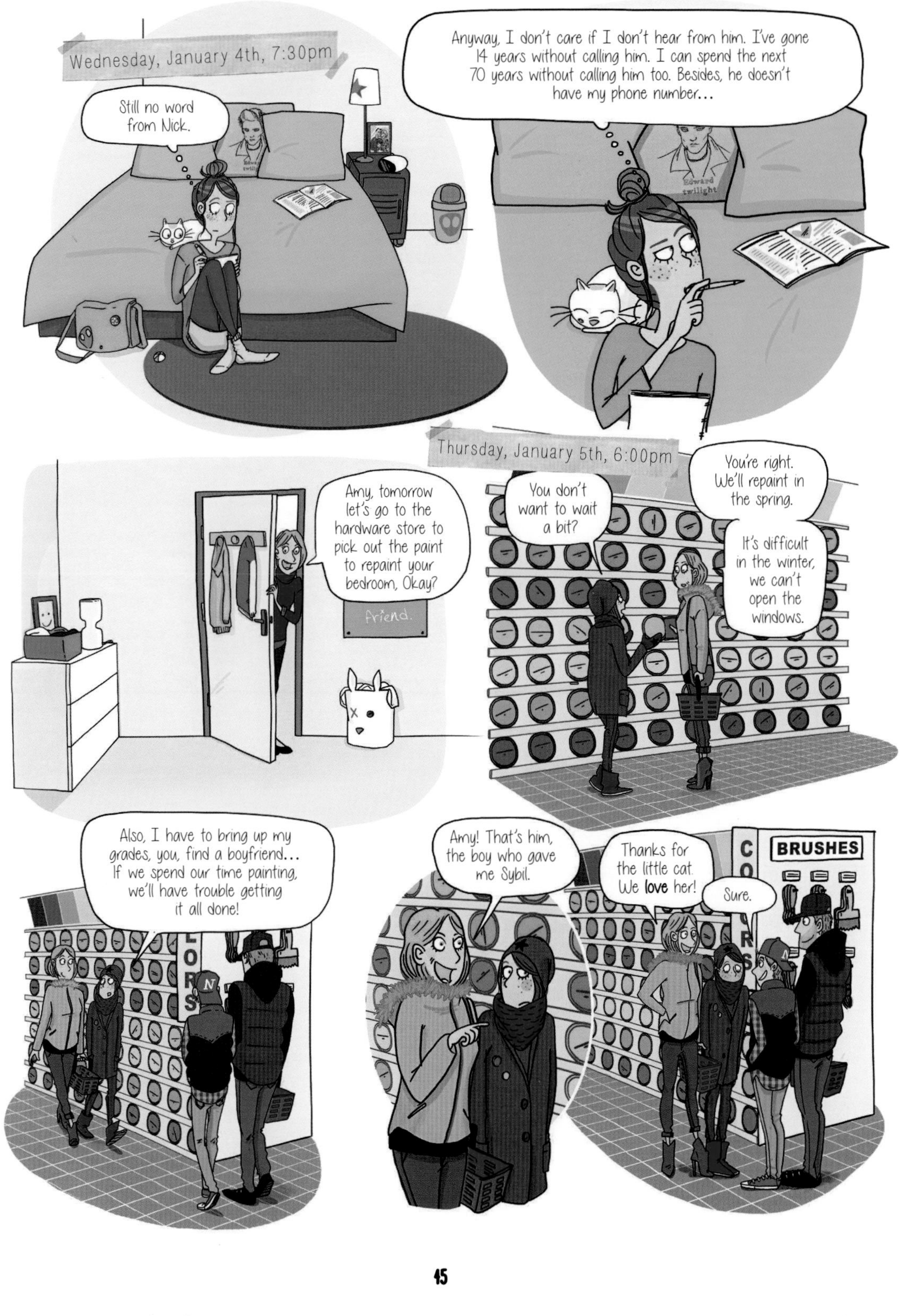
Wednesday, January 4th, 7:30pm
Still no word from Nick.
Edward twilight
Anyway, I don't care if I don't hear from him. I've gone 14 years without calling him. I can spend the next 70 years without calling him too. Besides, he doesn't have my phone number...
Edward twilight
Amy, tomorrow let's go to the hardware store to pick out the paint to repaint your bedroom, Okay?
Friend.
Thursday, January 5th, 6:00pm
You don't want to wait a bit?
You're right. We'll repaint in the spring.
It's difficult in the winter, we can't open the windows.
Also, I have to bring up my grades, you, find a boyfriend... If we spend our time painting, we'll have trouble getting it all done!
Amy! That's him, the boy who gave me Sybil.
Thanks for the little cat. We **love** her!
Sure.
BRUSHES

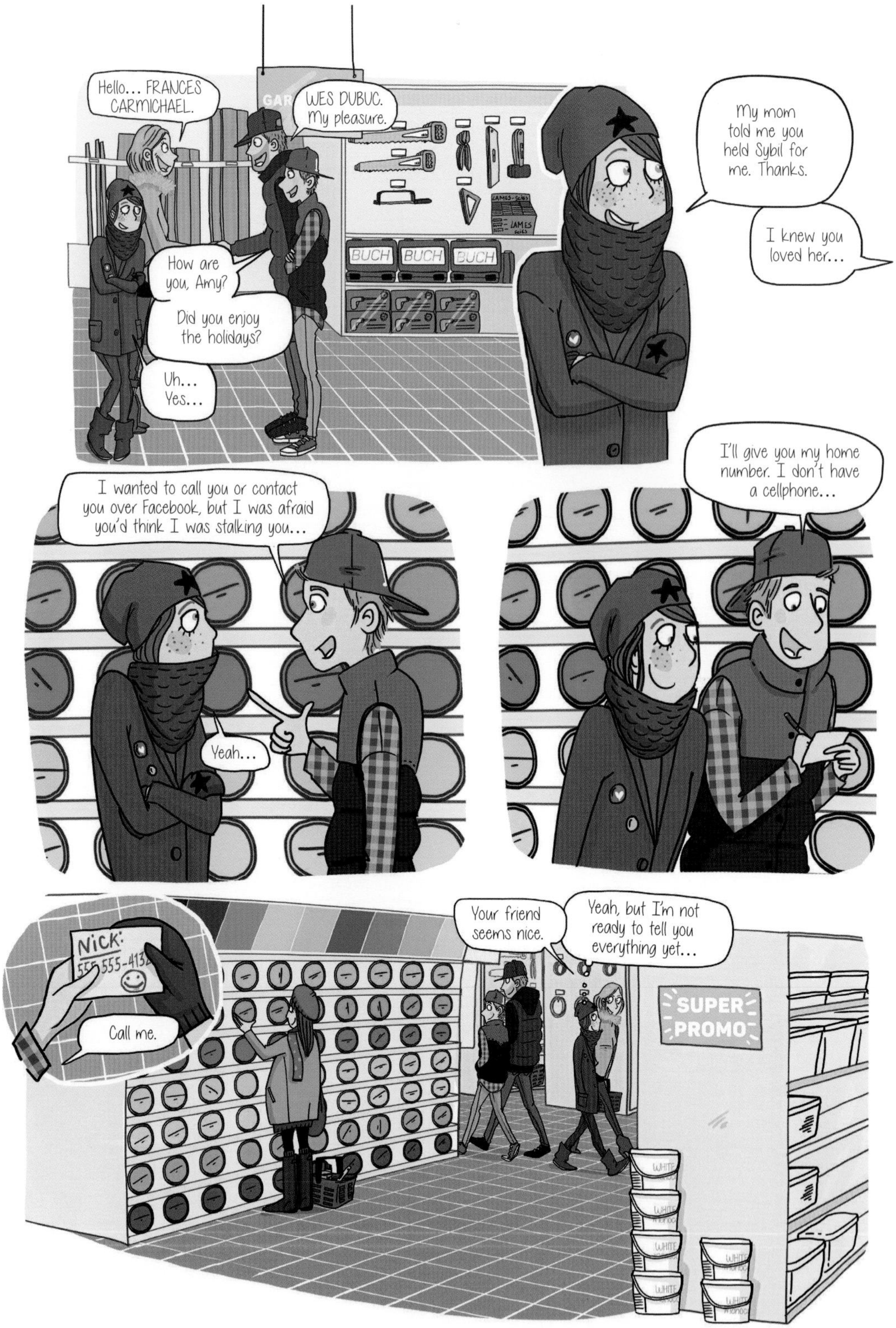

Hello... FRANCES CARMICHAEL.
WES DUBUC. My pleasure.
How are you, Amy?
Did you enjoy the holidays?
Uh... Yes...
My mom told me you held Sybil for me. Thanks.
I knew you loved her...
I wanted to call you or contact you over Facebook, but I was afraid you'd think I was stalking you...
Yeah...
I'll give you my home number. I don't have a cellphone...
NICK:
Call me.
Your friend seems nice.
Yeah, but I'm not ready to tell you everything yet...
SUPER PROMO

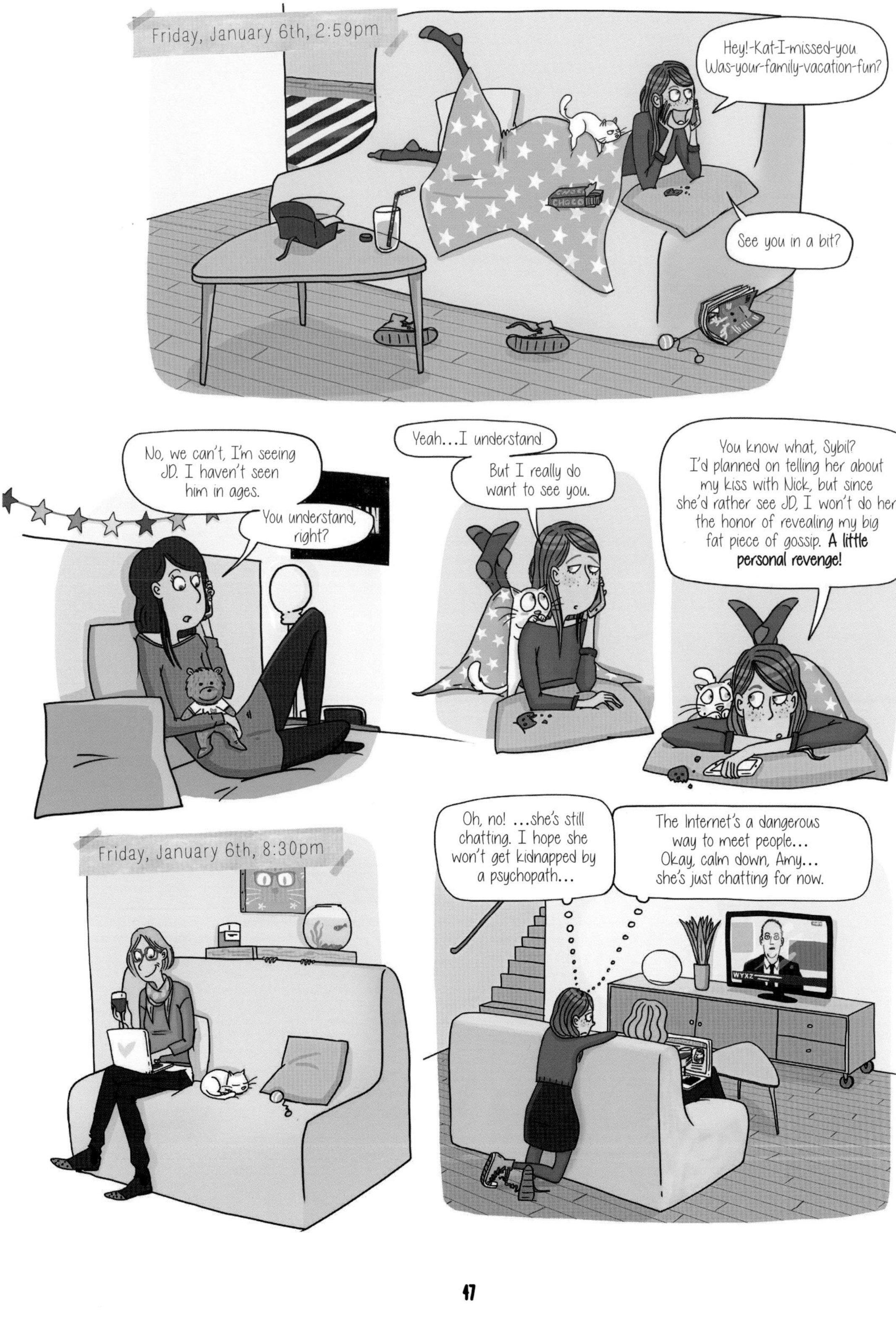
Friday, January 6th, 2:59pm
Hey!-Kat-I-missed-you. Was-your-family-vacation-fun?
See you in a bit?
No, we can't, I'm seeing JD. I haven't seen him in ages.
You understand, right?
Yeah... I understand.
But I really do want to see you.
You know what, Sybil? I'd planned on telling her about my kiss with Nick, but since she'd rather see JD, I won't do her the honor of revealing my big fat piece of gossip. **A little personal revenge!**
Friday, January 6th, 8:30pm
Oh, no! ...she's still chatting. I hope she won't get kidnapped by a psychopath...
The Internet's a dangerous way to meet people... Okay, calm down, Amy... she's just chatting for now.
WYXZ

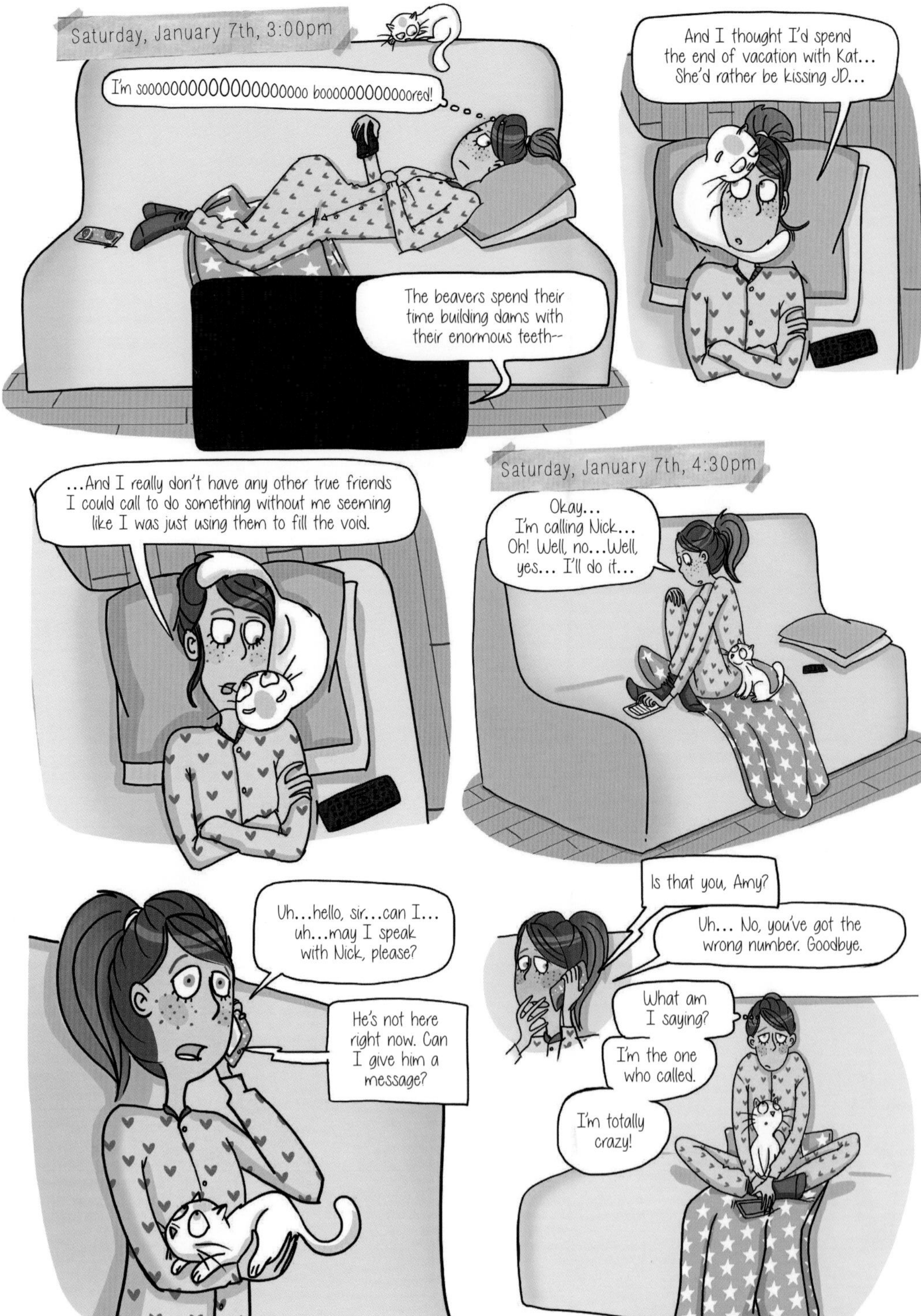

Saturday, January 7th, 3:00pm
I'm soooooOOOOOOOOOOOOOOOoooo boooooOOOOOOOOored!
The beavers spend their time building dams with their enormous teeth--
And I thought I'd spend the end of vacation with Kat... She'd rather be kissing JD...
...And I really don't have any other true friends I could call to do something without me seeming like I was just using them to fill the void.
Saturday, January 7th, 4:30pm
Okay... I'm calling Nick... Oh! Well, no...Well, yes... I'll do it...
Uh...hello, sir...can I... uh...may I speak with Nick, please?
He's not here right now. Can I give him a message?
Is that you, Amy?
Uh... No, you've got the wrong number. Goodbye.
What am I saying?
I'm the one who called.
I'm totally crazy!

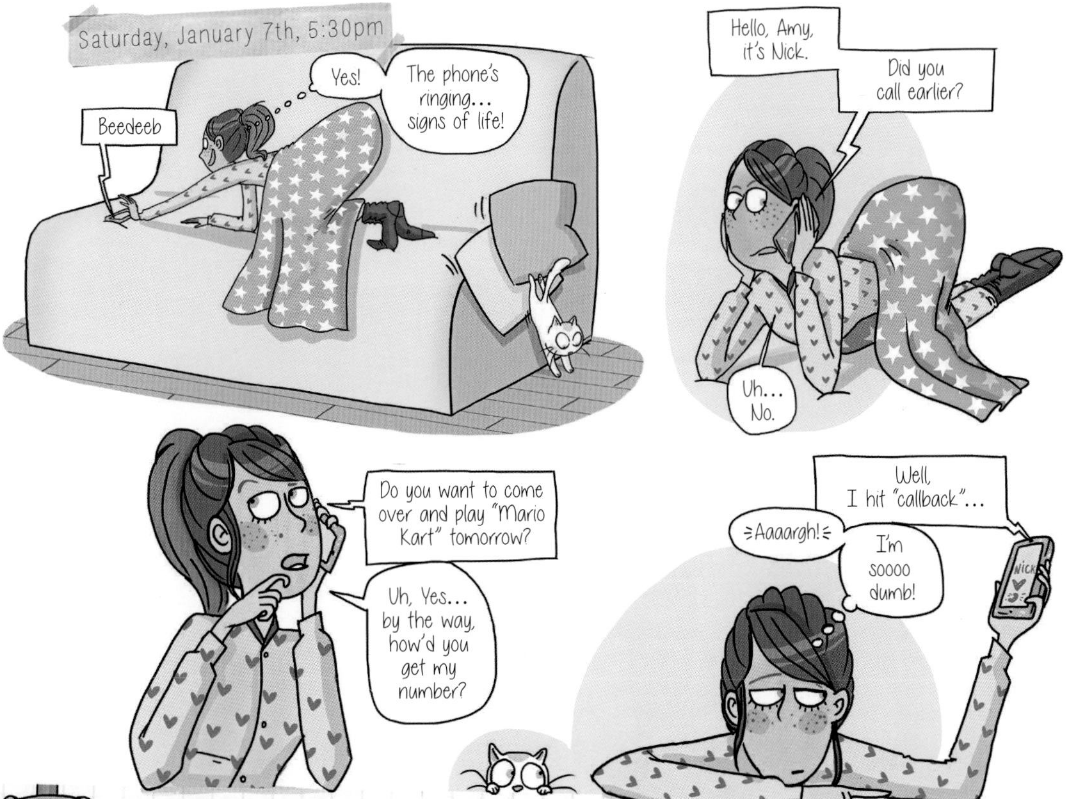
Saturday, January 7th, 5:30pm
Beedeeb
Yes!
The phone's ringing… signs of life!
Hello, Amy, it's Nick.
Did you call earlier?
Uh… No.
Do you want to come over and play "Mario Kart" tomorrow?
Uh, Yes… by the way, how'd you get my number?
Well, I hit "callback"…
Aaaargh!
I'm soooo dumb!
NICK

When Nick asked me to come to his house to play "Mario Kart,"
I thought it was a roundabout way of telling me we'd kiss again...
I didn't think we'd actually play Mario Kart.

Nick won... I hate losing!

I think I said: "Play another game?" and Nick said: "OK!"...
And instead of playing, we started kissing. Then his brother came into the room...and then I got uncomfortable. I left, claiming I had a dentist appointment... Nick didn't believe me.

Who has a dentist appointment on Sunday?

As I was leaving, I said to him while stammering (like usual) that I didn't know how to act around him... Do we kiss every time we see each other? Are we going out? It's like I don't even know if I want to have a boyfriend. So, I told him that I just wanted us to be friends.
And he answered: "Whatever you want!"

I'm sooooooo stupid!

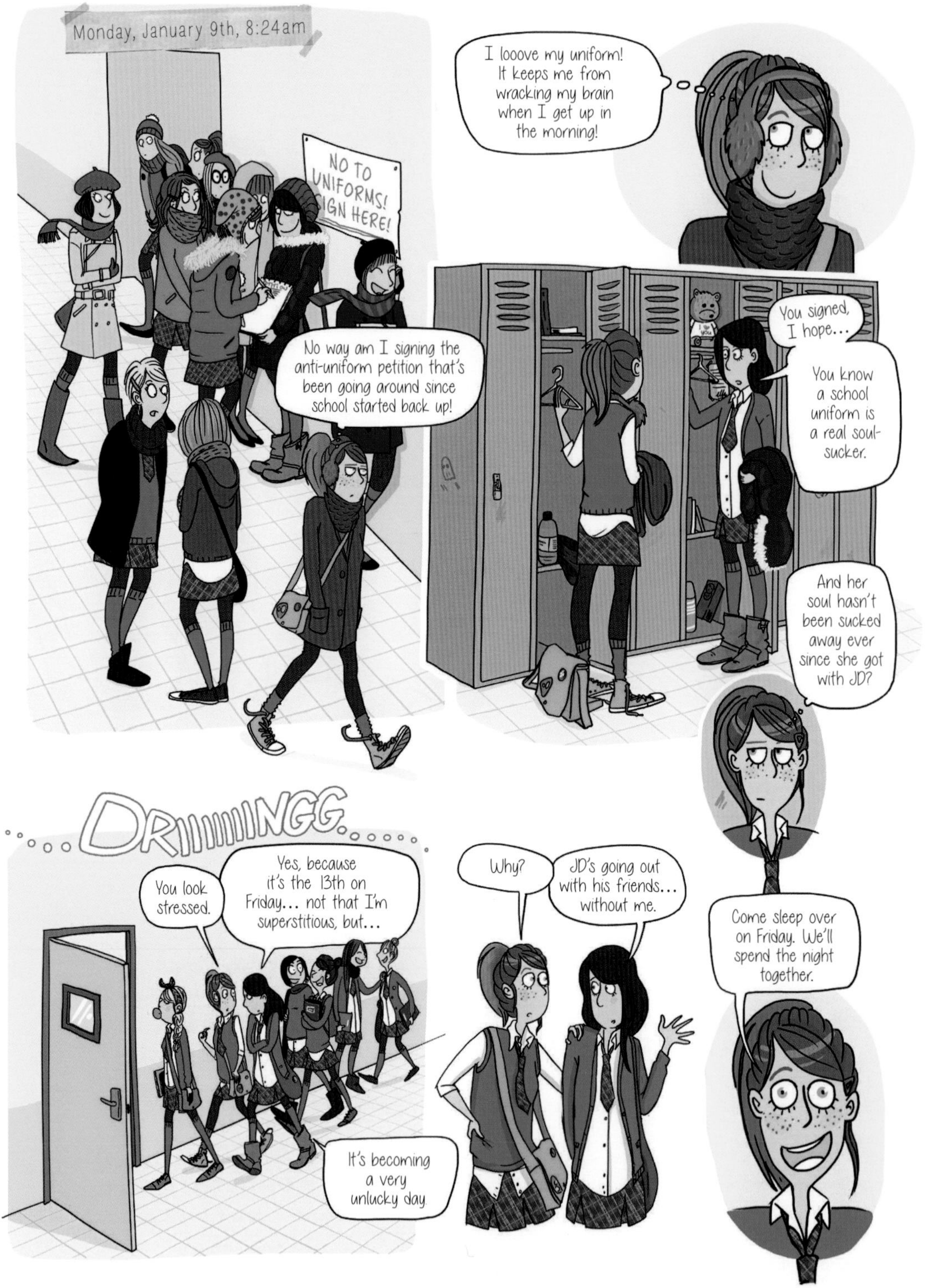
Monday, January 9th, 8:24am
NO TO UNIFORMS! SIGN HERE!
No way am I signing the anti-uniform petition that's been going around since school started back up!
I looove my uniform! It keeps me from wracking my brain when I get up in the morning!
You signed, I hope...
You know a school uniform is a real soul-sucker.
And her soul hasn't been sucked away ever since she got with JD?
DRIIIIIIINGG...
You look stressed.
Yes, because it's the 13th on Friday... not that I'm superstitious, but...
It's becoming a very unlucky day
Why?
JD's going out with his friends... without me.
Come sleep over on Friday. We'll spend the night together.

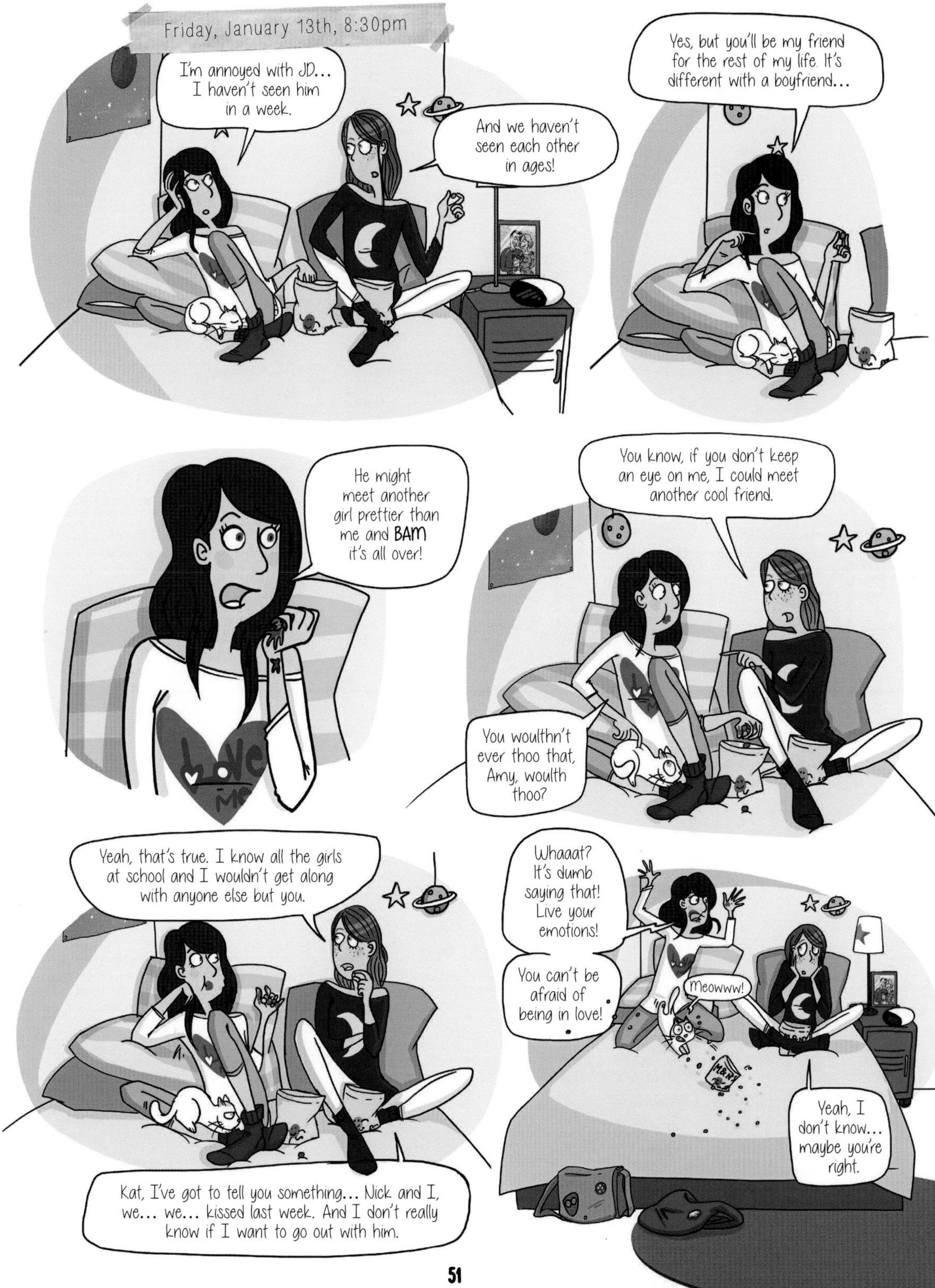
Friday, January 13th, 8:30pm
I'm annoyed with JD... I haven't seen him in a week.
And we haven't seen each other in ages!
Yes, but you'll be my friend for the rest of my life. It's different with a boyfriend...
He might meet another girl prettier than me and BAM it's all over!
You know, if you don't keep an eye on me, I could meet another cool friend.
You woulthn't ever thoo that, Amy, woulth thoo?
Yeah, that's true. I know all the girls at school and I wouldn't get along with anyone else but you.
Kat, I've got to tell you something... Nick and I, we... we... kissed last week. And I don't really know if I want to go out with him.
Whaaat? It's dumb saying that! Live your emotions!
You can't be afraid of being in love!
Meowww!
Yeah, I don't know... maybe you're right.

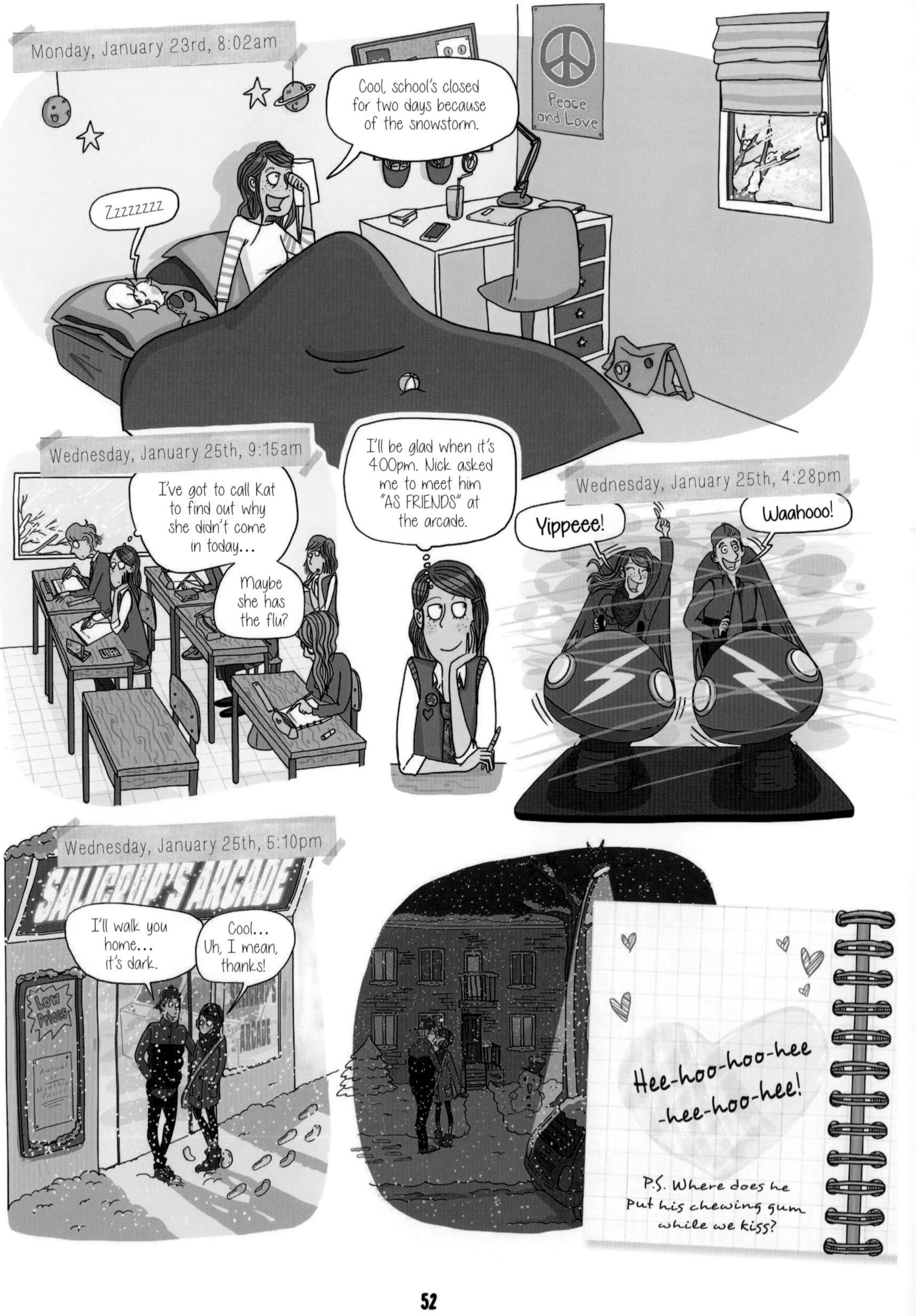
Monday, January 23rd, 8:02am
Cool, school's closed for two days because of the snowstorm.
Zzzzzzzz
Peace and Love
Wednesday, January 25th, 9:15am
I've got to call Kat to find out why she didn't come in today...
Maybe she has the flu?
I'll be glad when it's 4:00pm. Nick asked me to meet him "AS FRIENDS" at the arcade.
Wednesday, January 25th, 4:28pm
Yippeee!
Waahooo!
Wednesday, January 25th, 5:10pm
I'll walk you home... it's dark.
Cool... Uh, I mean, thanks!
Low Prices
ARCADE
Hee-hoo-hoo-hee -hee-hoo-hee!
P.S. Where does he put his chewing gum while we kiss?

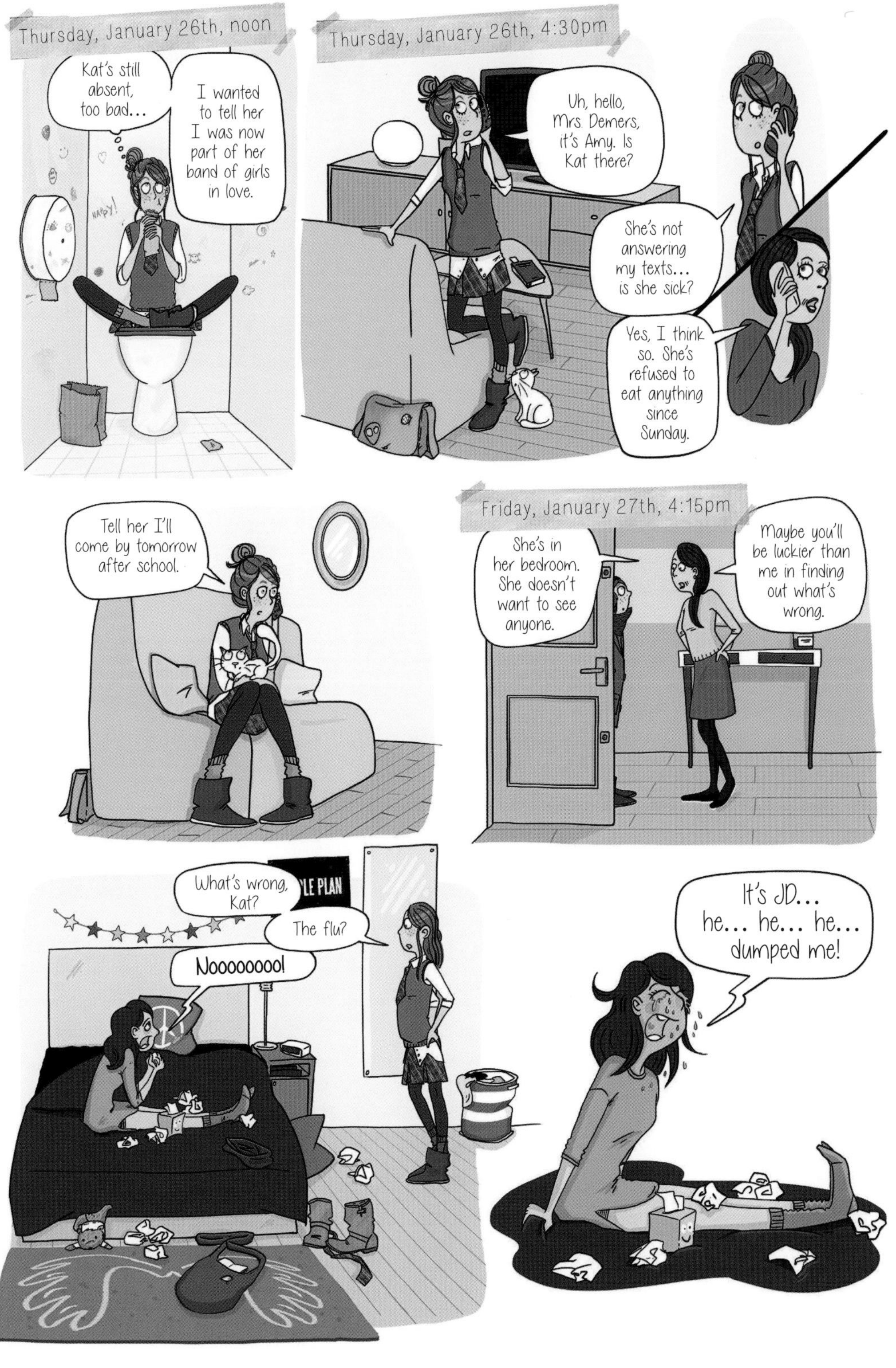

Thursday, January 26th, noon
Kat's still absent, too bad...
I wanted to tell her I was now part of her band of girls in love.
HAPPY!
Thursday, January 26th, 4:30pm
Uh, hello, Mrs. Demers, it's Amy. Is Kat there?
She's not answering my texts... is she sick?
Yes, I think so. She's refused to eat anything since Sunday.
Tell her I'll come by tomorrow after school.
Friday, January 27th, 4:15pm
She's in her bedroom. She doesn't want to see anyone.
Maybe you'll be luckier than me in finding out what's wrong.
LE PLAN
What's wrong, Kat?
The flu?
Noooooooo!
It's JD... he... he... he... dumped me!

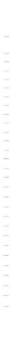

FEBRUARY

Losing my grip

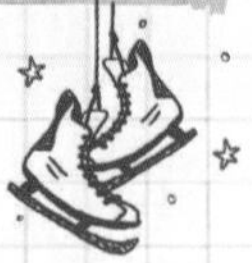

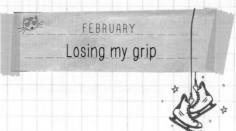

-Wednesday, February 1st:
What do I do now? Kat and JD are through and Kat thinks I don't want to go out with Nick! Pffff!
The other night she told me: "You're the one who's right, guys are jerks. I'm gonna be like you! I don't WANT a boyfriend! Love hurts!"

Yeah, I'm the one this time who's being a bad person...
If Kat doesn't realize I'm going out with Nick, everything'll be fine...
Yeah!... But I feel like I'm being a fake friend with her.

-Friday, February 3rd:
During math class, Kat sent me a drawing of JD with skulls and arrows and written (at least 25 times): "I hate him!"
She was sad, so I tried to make her laugh... and Bing!

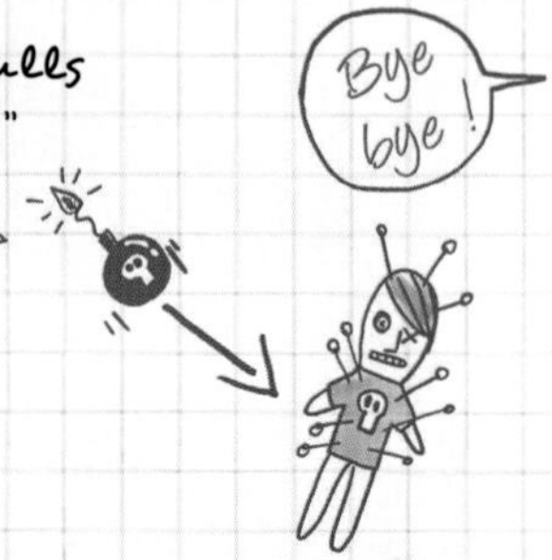
Bye bye!

I got sent to Dennis Belcher's office AGAIN!

Kat and I had lunch together at the cafeteria, that's a lot better than the restroom!

Kat's really unhappy since the break-up.

I feel guilty, but...
Teeteeleeteeteeeeeeeeeeeeeeeeeee = brain malfunction in Nick's presence.

Nick. Nick. Nick. Nick.
Nick. Nick. Nick. Nick.
Nick. Nick. Nick. Nick.
Nick. Nick. Nick. Nick.
Nick. Nick. Nick. Nick...

Note: Try not to have my head in the clouds during Language Arts.

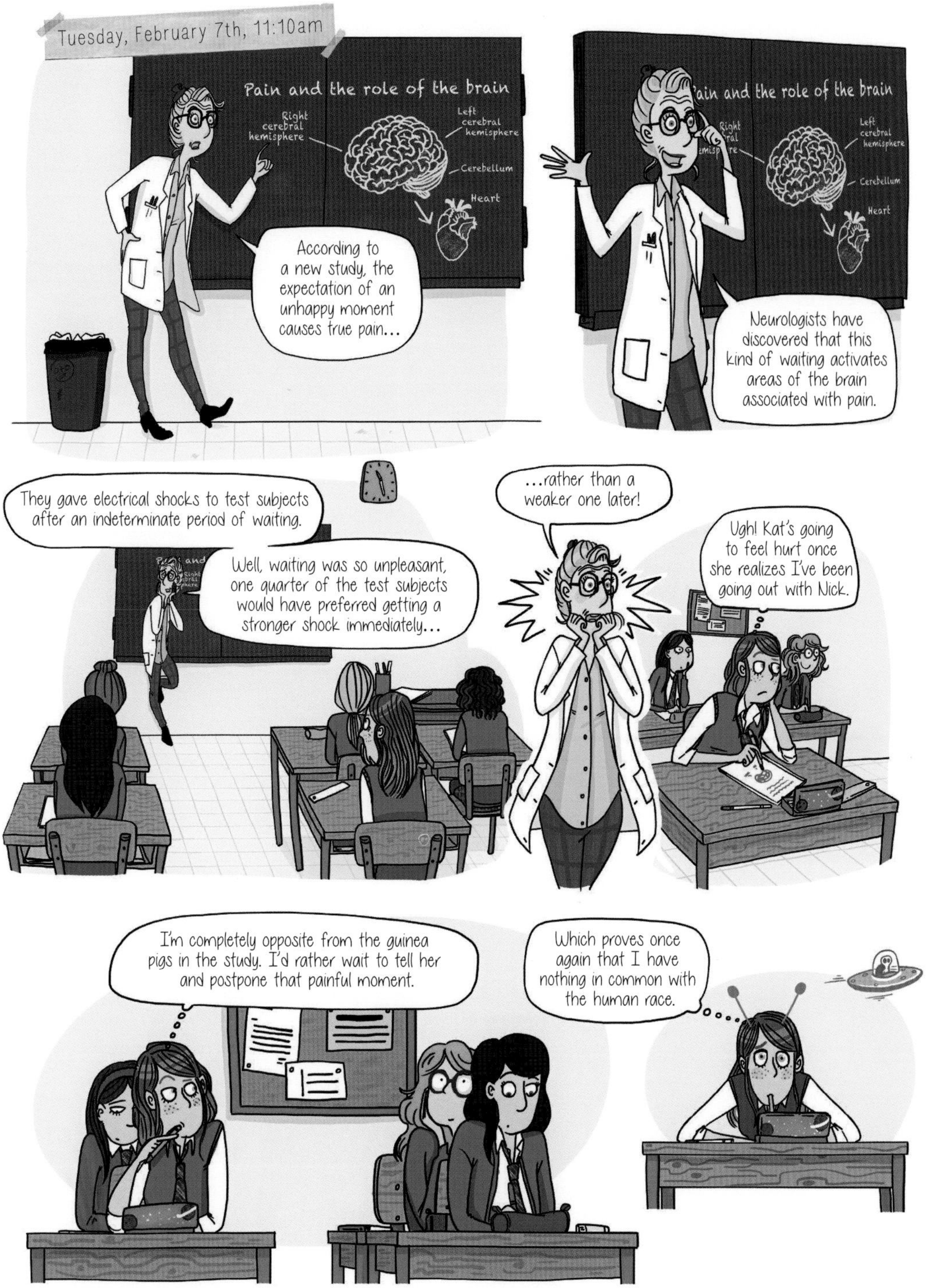
Tuesday, February 7th, 11:10am
Pain and the role of the brain
Right cerebral hemisphere
Left cerebral hemisphere
Cerebellum
Heart
According to a new study, the expectation of an unhappy moment causes true pain...
Neurologists have discovered that this kind of waiting activates areas of the brain associated with pain.
They gave electrical shocks to test subjects after an indeterminate period of waiting.
Well, waiting was so unpleasant, one quarter of the test subjects would have preferred getting a stronger shock immediately...
...rather than a weaker one later!
Ugh! Kat's going to feel hurt once she realizes I've been going out with Nick.
I'm completely opposite from the guinea pigs in the study. I'd rather wait to tell her and postpone that painful moment.
Which proves once again that I have nothing in common with the human race.

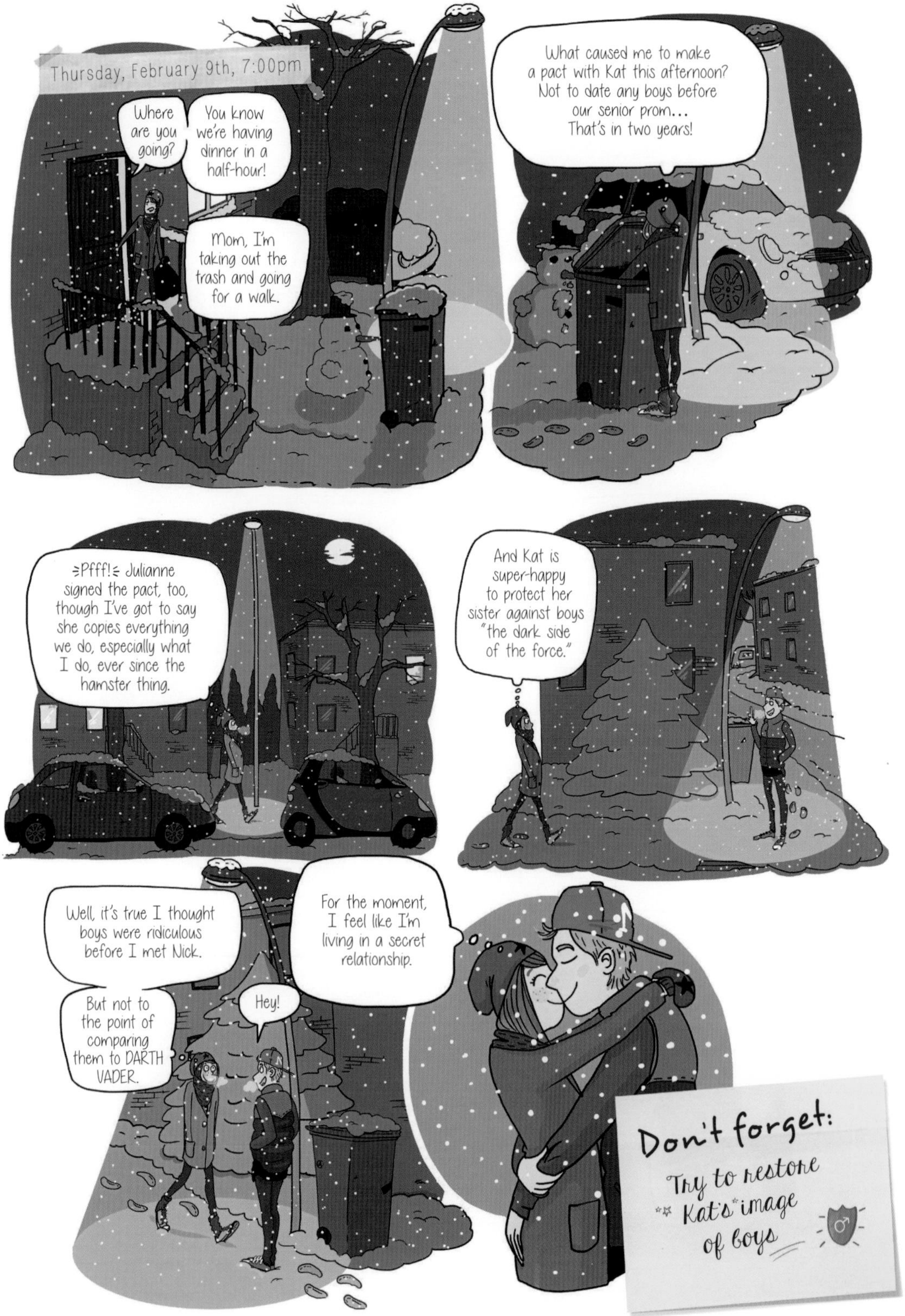
Thursday, February 9th, 7:00pm
Where are you going?
You know we're having dinner in a half-hour!
Mom, I'm taking out the trash and going for a walk.
What caused me to make a pact with Kat this afternoon? Not to date any boys before our senior prom... That's in two years!
Pfff! Julianne signed the pact, too, though I've got to say she copies everything we do, especially what I do, ever since the hamster thing.
And Kat is super-happy to protect her sister against boys "the dark side of the force."
Well, it's true I thought boys were ridiculous before I met Nick.
For the moment, I feel like I'm living in a secret relationship.
But not to the point of comparing them to DARTH VADER.
Hey!
Don't forget:
Try to restore Kat's image of boys

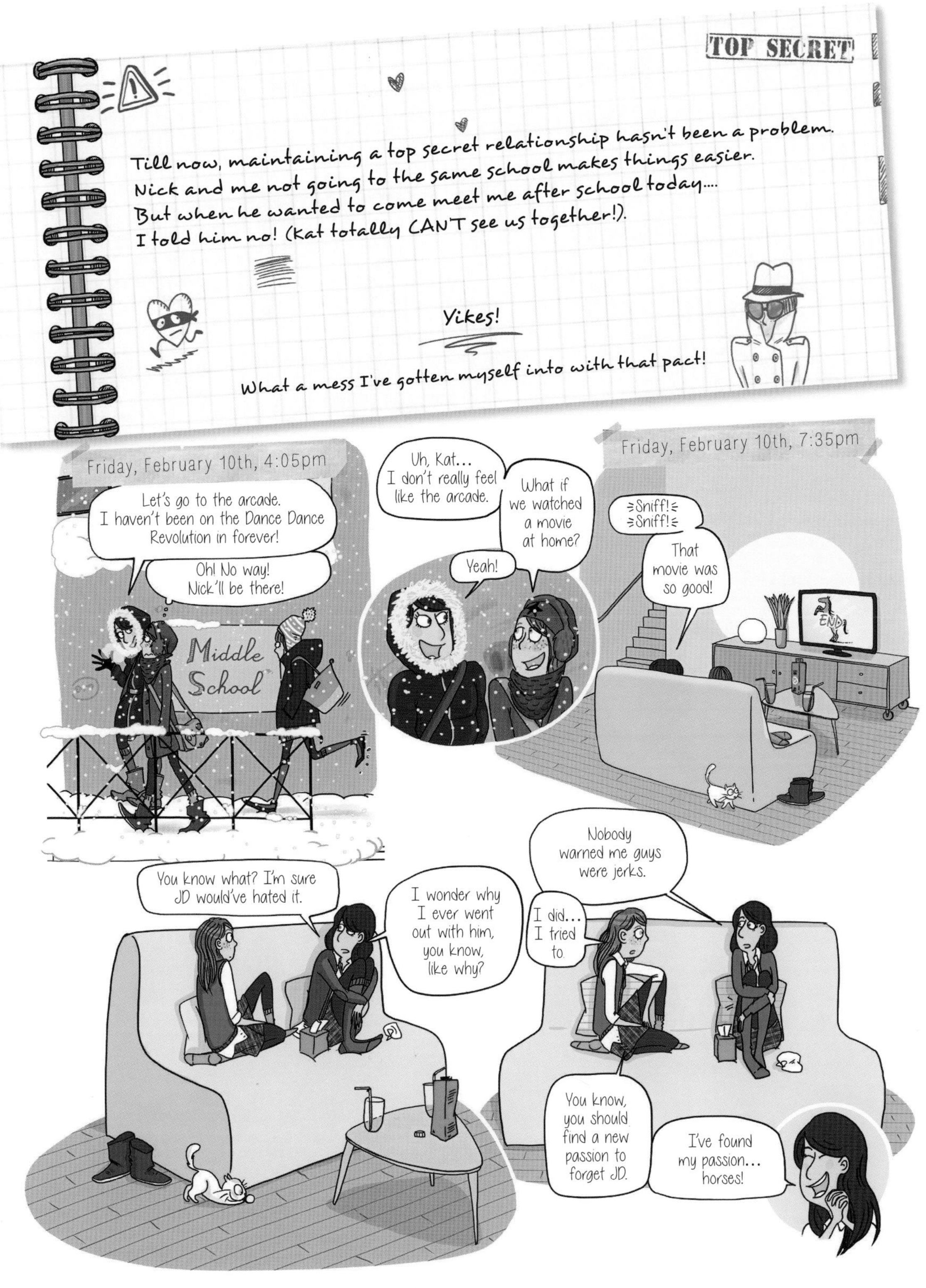
TOP SECRET
Till now, maintaining a top secret relationship hasn't been a problem.
Nick and me not going to the same school makes things easier.
But when he wanted to come meet me after school today....
I told him no! (Kat totally CAN'T see us together!).
Yikes!
What a mess I've gotten myself into with that pact!
Friday, February 10th, 4:05pm
Let's go to the arcade. I haven't been on the Dance Dance Revolution in forever!
Oh! No way! Nick'll be there!
Middle School
Uh, Kat... I don't really feel like the arcade.
What if we watched a movie at home?
Yeah!
Friday, February 10th, 7:35pm
Sniff! Sniff!
That movie was so good!
END
You know what? I'm sure JD would've hated it.
I wonder why I ever went out with him, you know, like why?
Nobody warned me guys were jerks.
I did... I tried to.
You know, you should find a new passion to forget JD.
I've found my passion... horses!

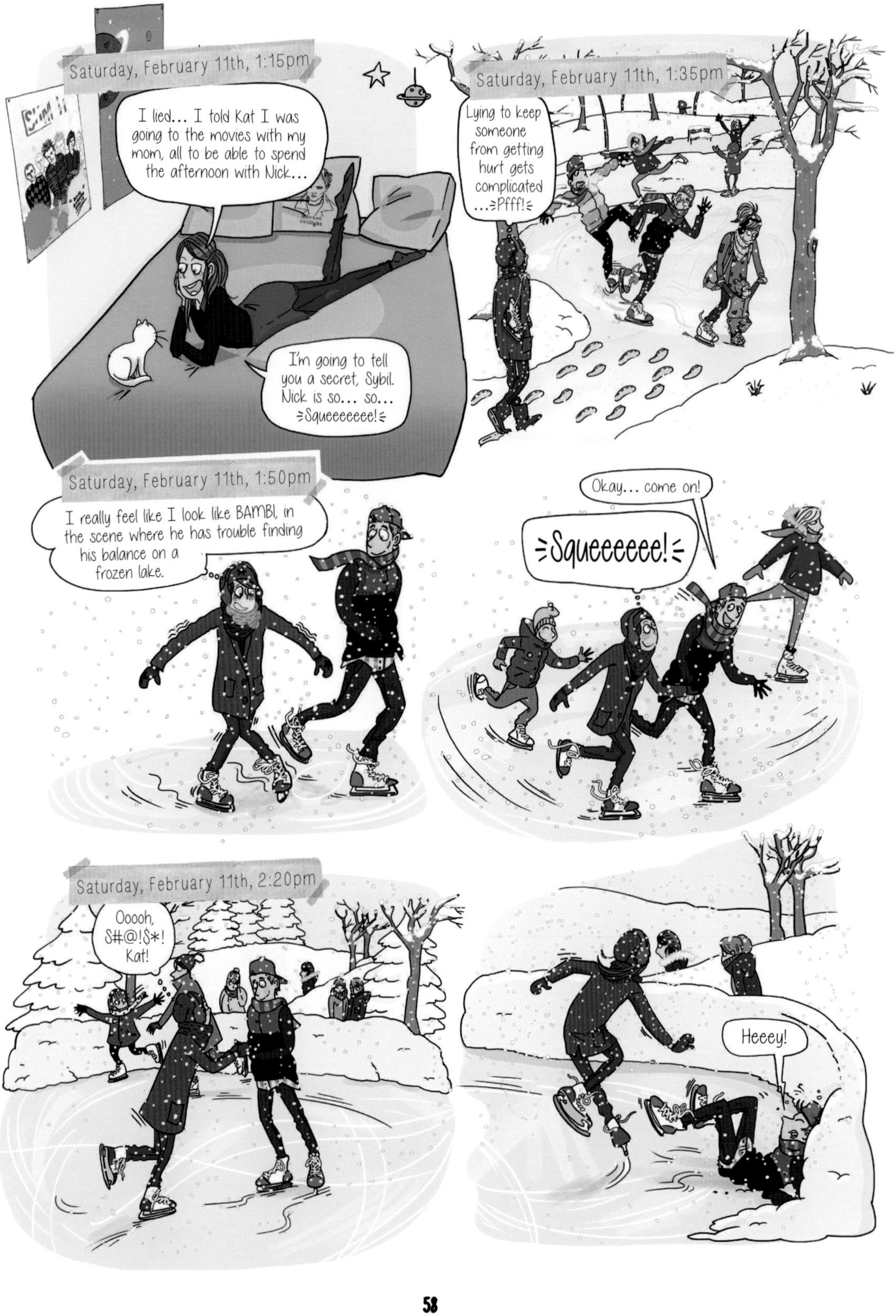
Saturday, February 11th, 1:15pm
I lied... I told Kat I was going to the movies with my mom, all to be able to spend the afternoon with Nick...
I'm going to tell you a secret, Sybil. Nick is so... so... Squeeeeeee!
Saturday, February 11th, 1:35pm
Lying to keep someone from getting hurt gets complicated ...Pfff!
Saturday, February 11th, 1:50pm
I really feel like I look like BAMBI, in the scene where he has trouble finding his balance on a frozen lake.
Okay... come on!
Squeeeeee!
Saturday, February 11th, 2:20pm
Ooooh, S#@!$*! Kat!
Heeey!

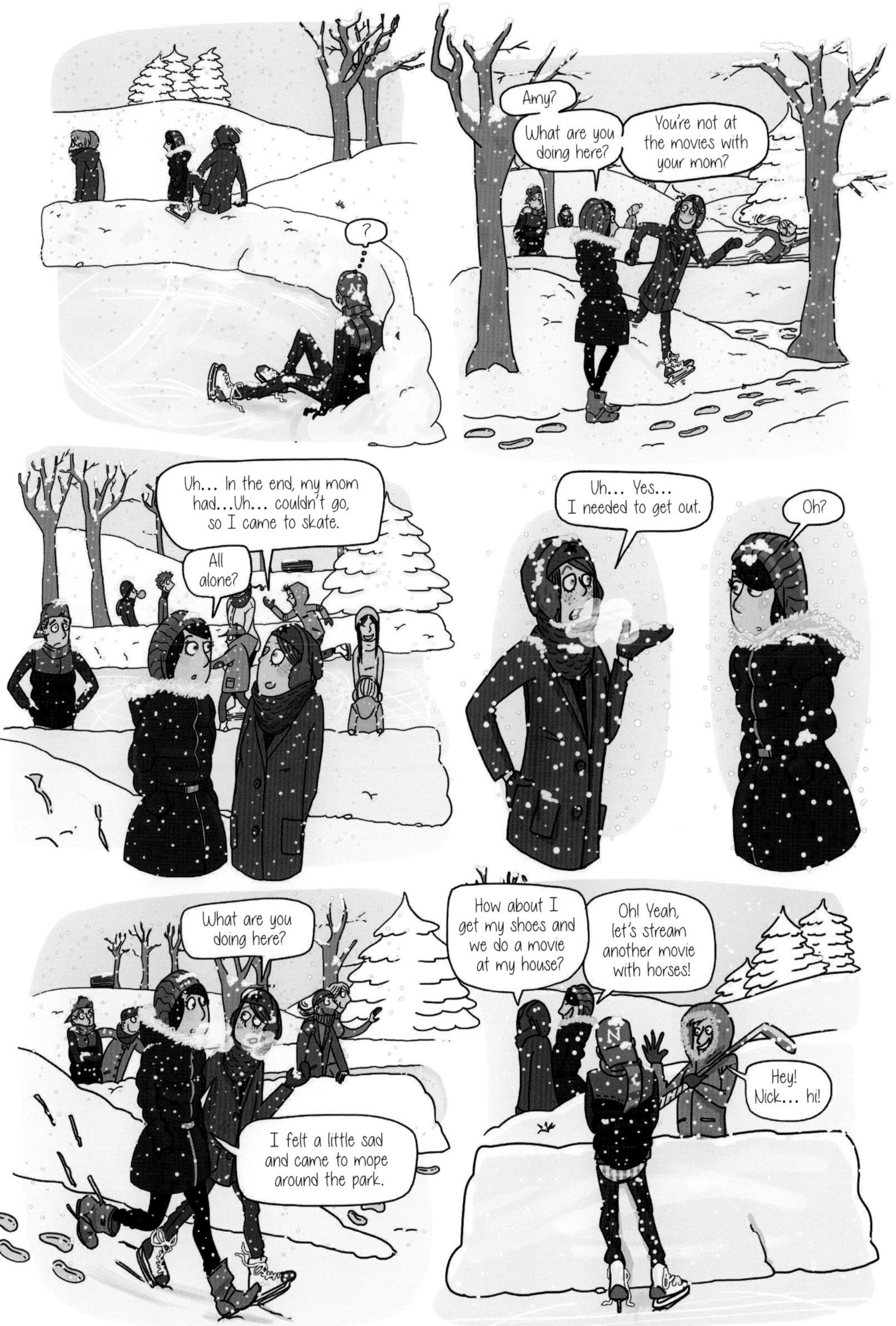
?
Amy?
What are you doing here?
You're not at the movies with your mom?
Uh... In the end, my mom had...Uh... couldn't go, so I came to skate.
All alone?
Uh... Yes... I needed to get out.
Oh?
What are you doing here?
I felt a little sad and came to mope around the park.
How about I get my shoes and we do a movie at my house?
Oh! Yeah, let's stream another movie with horses!
Hey! Nick... hi!

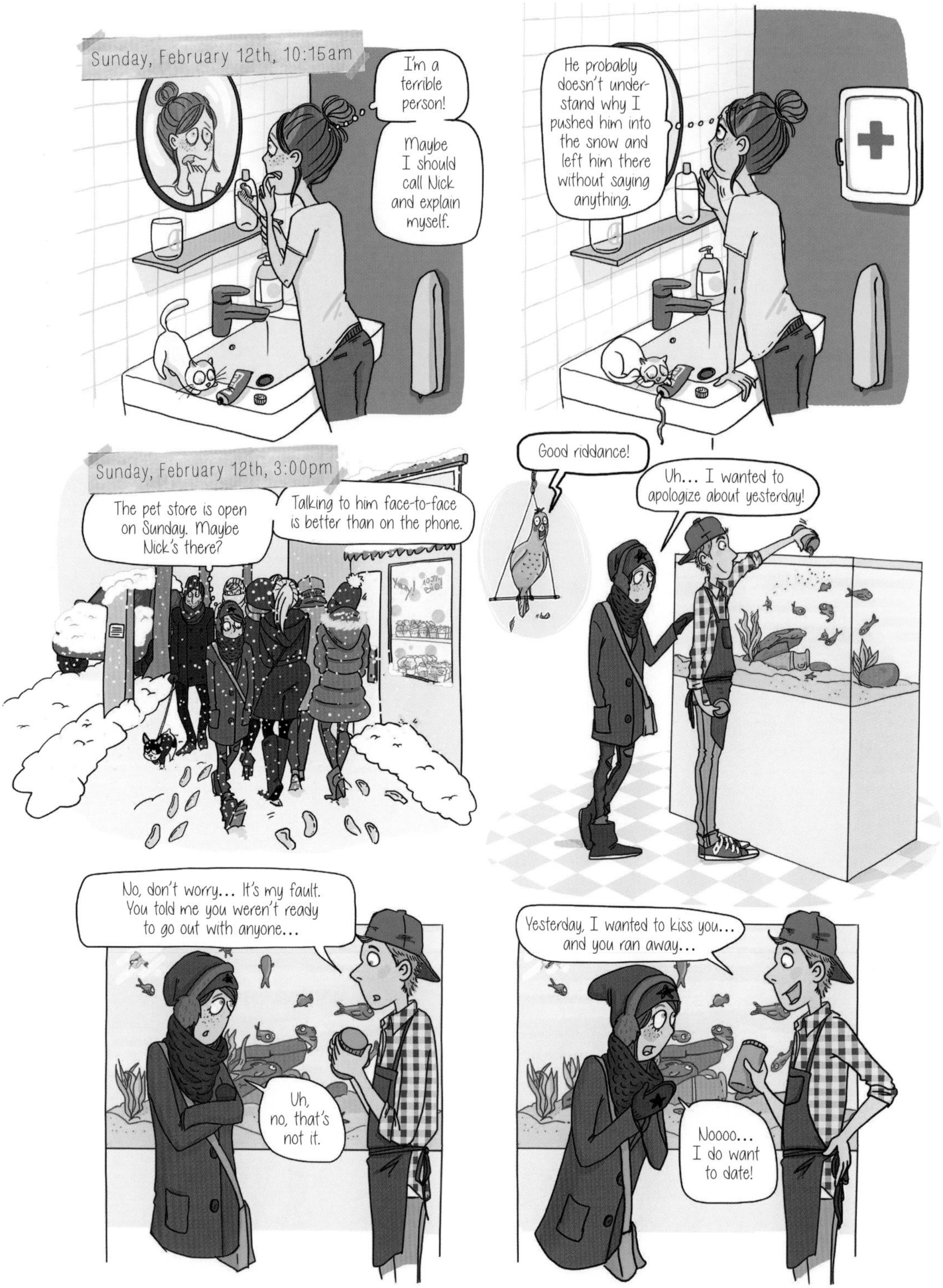
Sunday, February 12th, 10:15am
I'm a terrible person!
Maybe I should call Nick and explain myself.
He probably doesn't understand why I pushed him into the snow and left him there without saying anything.
Sunday, February 12th, 3:00pm
The pet store is open on Sunday. Maybe Nick's there?
Talking to him face-to-face is better than on the phone.
Good riddance!
Uh... I wanted to apologize about yesterday!
No, don't worry... It's my fault. You told me you weren't ready to go out with anyone...
Uh, no, that's not it.
Yesterday, I wanted to kiss you... and you ran away...
Noooo... I do want to date!

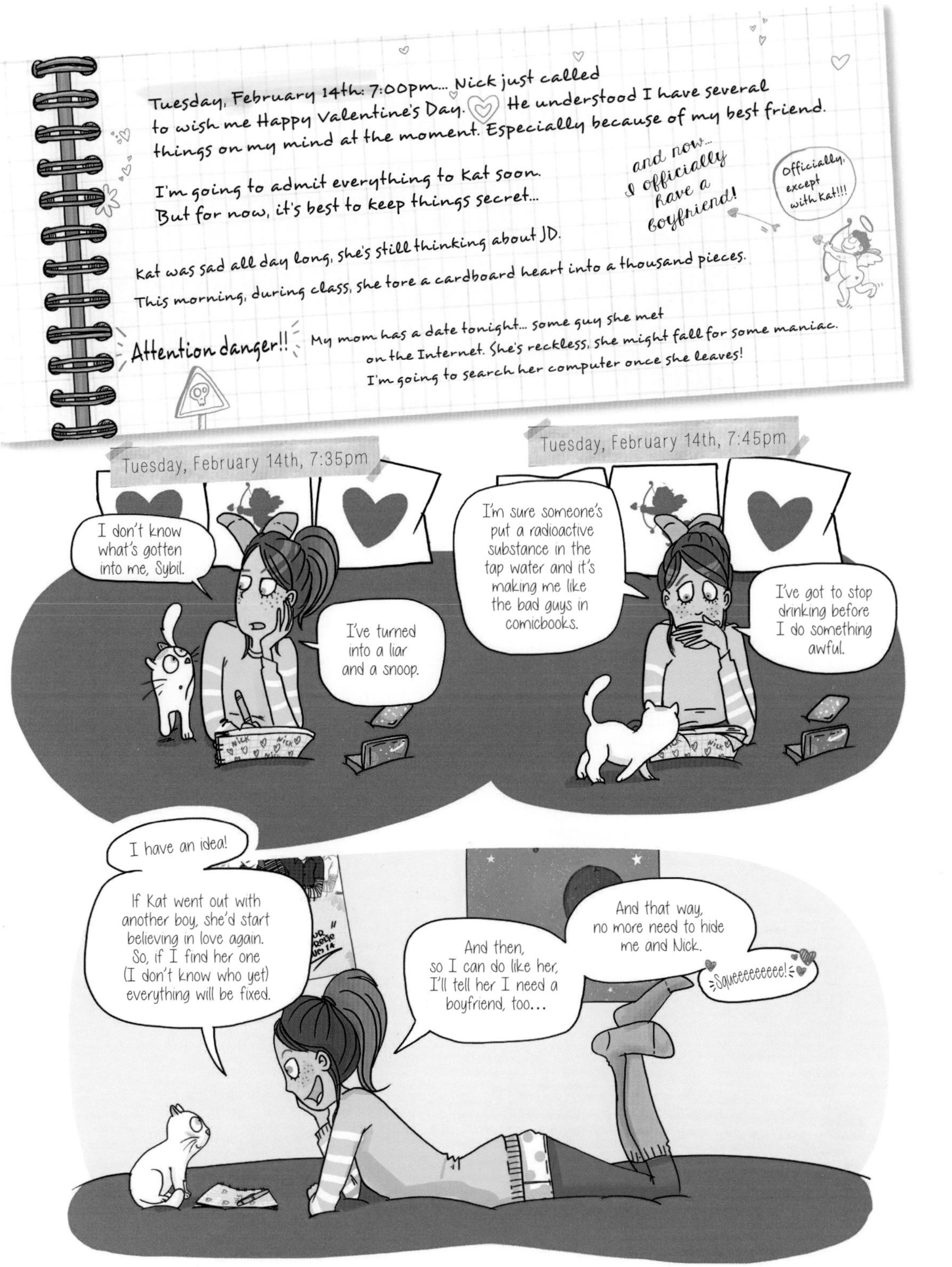
Tuesday, February 14th: 7:00pm... Nick just called to wish me Happy Valentine's Day. He understood I have several things on my mind at the moment. Especially because of my best friend.
I'm going to admit everything to Kat soon. But for now, it's best to keep things secret...
and now... I officially have a boyfriend!
Officially, except with Kat!!!
Kat was sad all day long, she's still thinking about JD.
This morning, during class, she tore a cardboard heart into a thousand pieces.
Attention danger!!
My mom has a date tonight... some guy she met on the Internet. She's reckless, she might fall for some maniac.
I'm going to search her computer once she leaves!
Tuesday, February 14th, 7:35pm
I don't know what's gotten into me, Sybil.
I've turned into a liar and a snoop.
Tuesday, February 14th, 7:45pm
I'm sure someone's put a radioactive substance in the tap water and it's making me like the bad guys in comicbooks.
I've got to stop drinking before I do something awful.
I have an idea!
If Kat went out with another boy, she'd start believing in love again. So, if I find her one (I don't know who yet) everything will be fixed.
And then, so I can do like her, I'll tell her I need a boyfriend, too...
And that way, no more need to hide me and Nick.
Squeeeeeeeee!

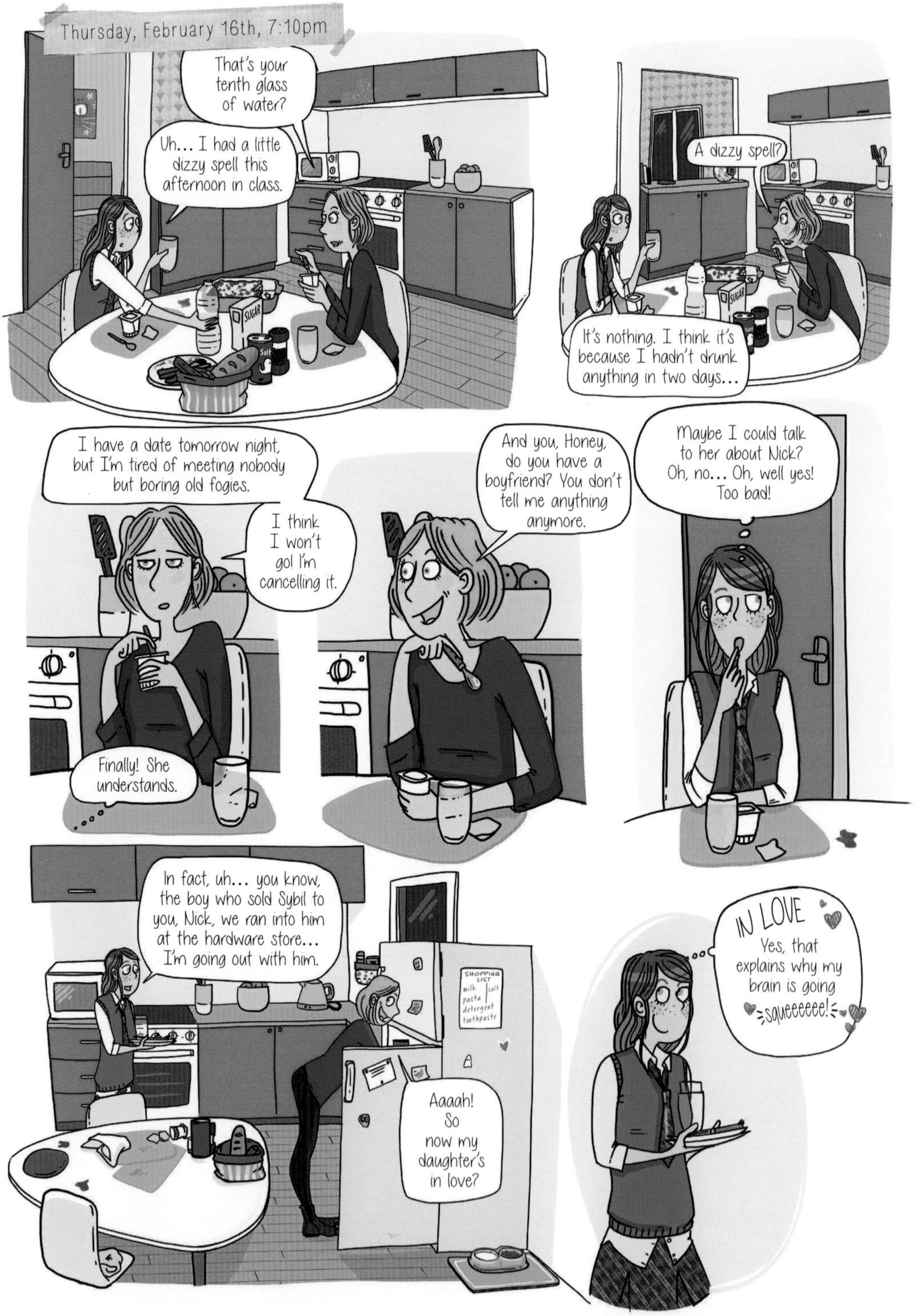
Thursday, February 16th, 7:10pm
That's your tenth glass of water?
Uh... I had a little dizzy spell this afternoon in class.
A dizzy spell?
It's nothing. I think it's because I hadn't drunk anything in two days...
I have a date tomorrow night, but I'm tired of meeting nobody but boring old fogies.
I think I won't go! I'm cancelling it.
Finally! She understands.
And you, Honey, do you have a boyfriend? You don't tell me anything anymore.
Maybe I could talk to her about Nick? Oh, no... Oh, well yes! Too bad!
In fact, uh... you know, the boy who sold Sybil to you, Nick, we ran into him at the hardware store... I'm going out with him.
SHOPPING LIST
milk
salt
pasta
detergent
toothpaste
Aaaah! So now my daughter's in love?
IN LOVE
Yes, that explains why my brain is going squeeeeee!

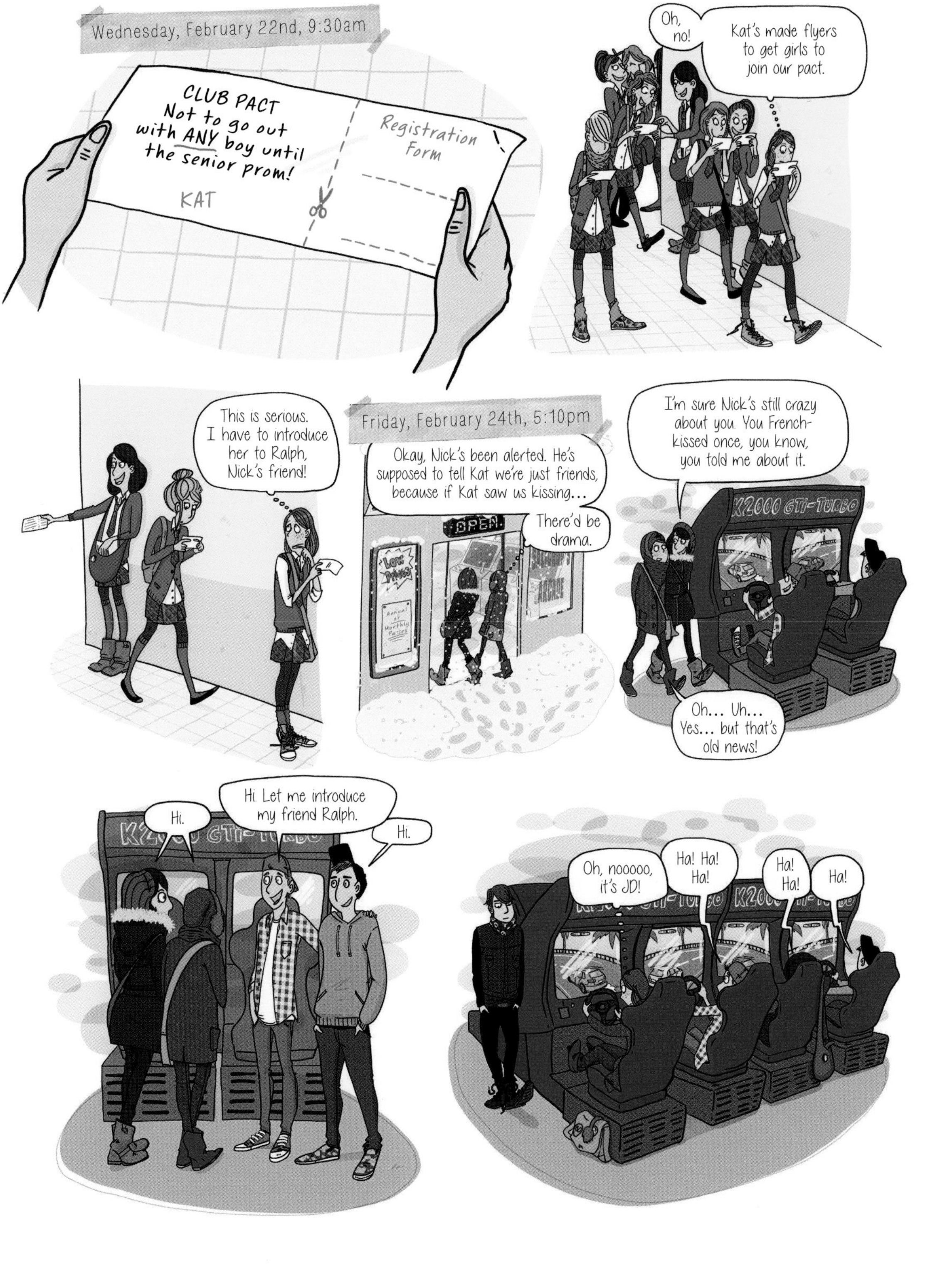

Wednesday, February 22nd, 9:30am
CLUB PACT
Not to go out with ANY boy until the senior prom!
KAT
Registration Form
Oh, no!
Kat's made flyers to get girls to join our pact.
This is serious. I have to introduce her to Ralph, Nick's friend!
Friday, February 24th, 5:10pm
Okay, Nick's been alerted. He's supposed to tell Kat we're just friends, because if Kat saw us kissing...
There'd be drama.
OPEN
I'm sure Nick's still crazy about you. You French-kissed once, you know, you told me about it.
K2000 GTI-TURBO
Oh... Uh... Yes... but that's old news!
Hi.
Hi. Let me introduce my friend Ralph.
Hi.
Oh, nooooo, it's JD!
Ha! Ha! Ha!
Ha! Ha!
Ha!

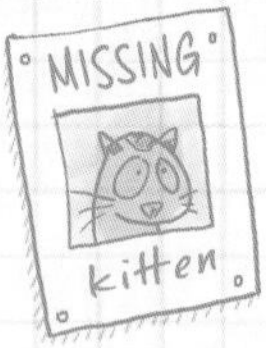
MISSING
kitten

March

Blowing a fuse

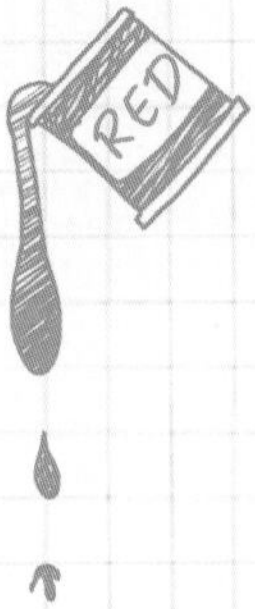
RED

A lot's happened since February 24th.
Okay, first of all at the arcade:

It wasn't love at first sight between Kat and Ralph. Must say he has a special kind of humor. Kat told him she loved horses. He answered: "I can tell, your breath is like theirs... Ha Ha! Gotcha!"

No comment!

Afterwards, Kat and I ran into JD. I told him to his face he was pretentious, and that if he didn't know what that meant, he could just open a dictionary. "You know, that's a book that's almost as fat as your head!"
And I added, "You know, that's worse than being pretentious... Your feet stink!"
And Kat added: "And worse than being pretentious... Your feet stink!"
And we ran away together. Laughing.

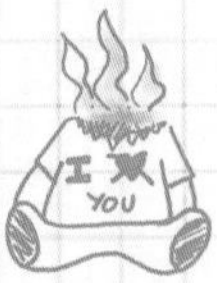
YOU

Okay, it's Saturday, February 25th when everything goes bad:

Nick and I were walking together in the park, I was wanting to tell him I loved him. And before speaking to him, we kissed.... But... But... Julianne came along with two friends. DISASTER! Julianne brought up the pact, she told me I'd just betrayed her sister. Nick asked me if I was ashamed of him... In short, I wanted to turn into a snowman.

Julianne gave me two weeks to tell Kat I was going out with Nick.
(It's thanks to the hamster thing that I got this reprieve.)

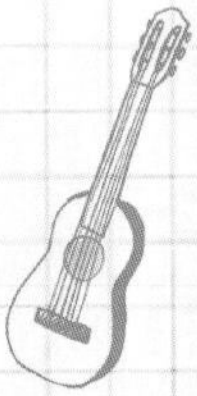

~~TOMMY~~ NICK

I explained everything to Nick... the lie to Kat, the pact... Afterwards, (my teeth chattering because of the cold), I told him: "I (clack clack clack) love (clack clack clack) you (clack clack clack)."
And he said he did too...

Squeeeeeeeeeeeeee!

MUSIC PLUS

Friday, March 3rd: It's Spring Break starting tomorrow!

YEAAAAAAAAAH!

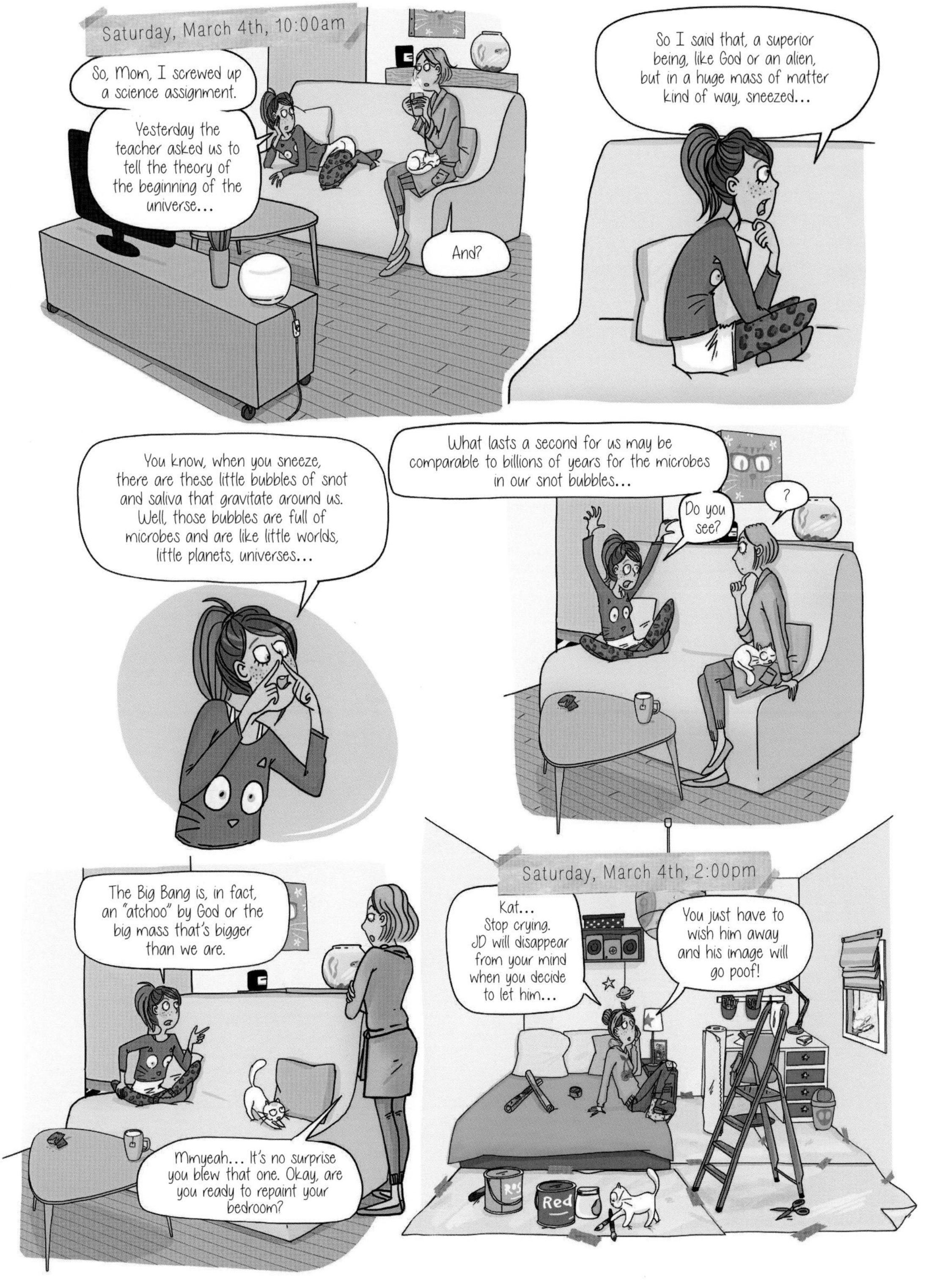

Saturday, March 4th, 10:00am
So, Mom, I screwed up a science assignment.
Yesterday the teacher asked us to tell the theory of the beginning of the universe...
And?
So I said that, a superior being, like God or an alien, but in a huge mass of matter kind of way, sneezed...
You know, when you sneeze, there are these little bubbles of snot and saliva that gravitate around us. Well, those bubbles are full of microbes and are like little worlds, little planets, universes...
What lasts a second for us may be comparable to billions of years for the microbes in our snot bubbles...
Do you see?
?
The Big Bang is, in fact, an "atchoo" by God or the big mass that's bigger than we are.
Mmyeah... It's no surprise you blew that one. Okay, are you ready to repaint your bedroom?
Saturday, March 4th, 2:00pm
Kat... Stop crying. JD will disappear from your mind when you decide to let him...
You just have to wish him away and his image will go poof!
Red

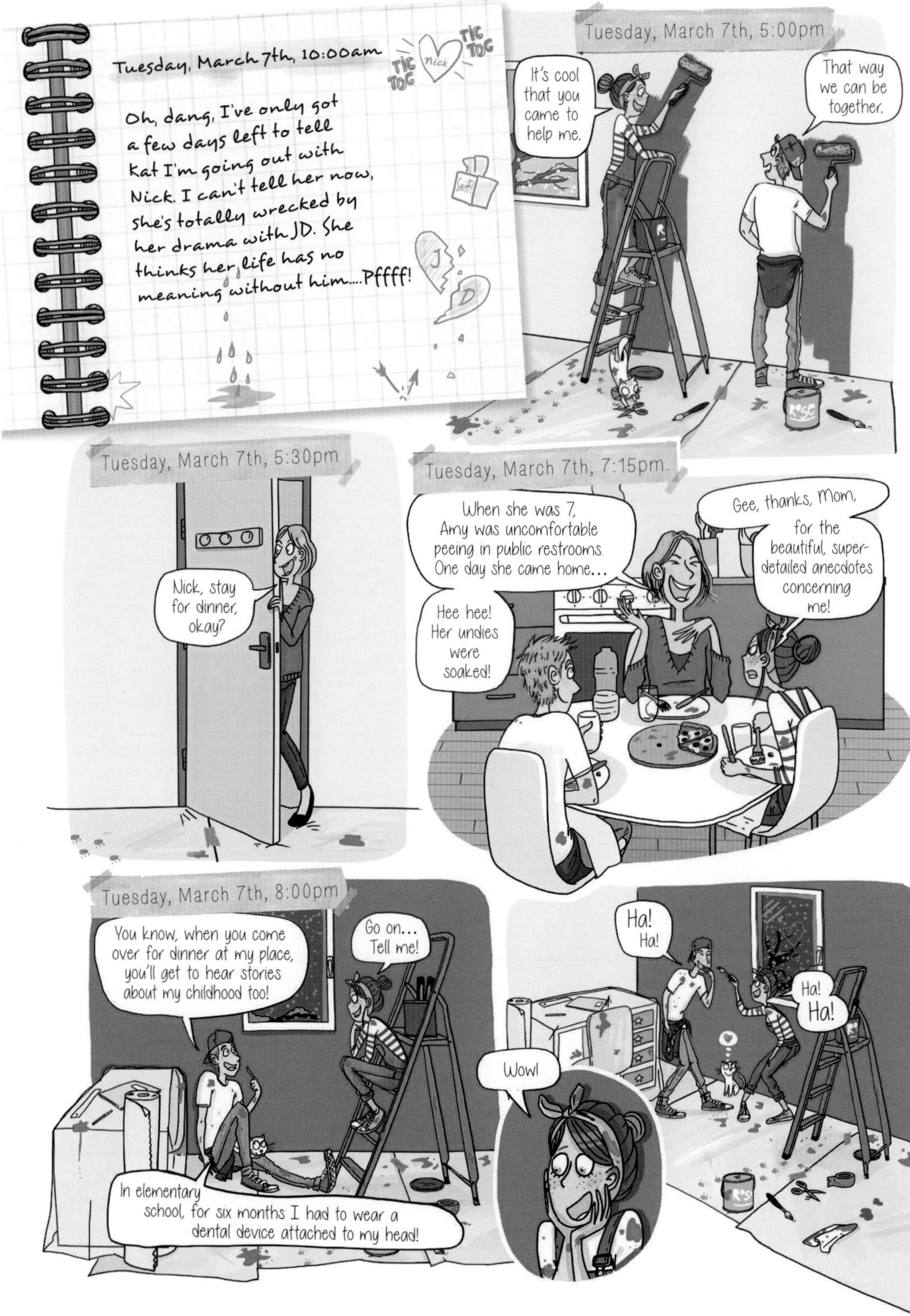

Tuesday, March 7th, 10:00am
Oh, dang, I've only got a few days left to tell Kat I'm going out with Nick. I can't tell her now, she's totally wrecked by her drama with JD. She thinks her life has no meaning without him....Pffff!
TIC TOC
Nick
TIC TOC
Sniff!
J
D
Tuesday, March 7th, 5:00pm
It's cool that you came to help me.
That way we can be together.
Tuesday, March 7th, 5:30pm
Nick, stay for dinner, okay?
Tuesday, March 7th, 7:15pm.
When she was 7, Amy was uncomfortable peeing in public restrooms. One day she came home…
Hee hee! Her undies were soaked!
Gee, thanks, Mom,
for the beautiful, super-detailed anecdotes concerning me!
Tuesday, March 7th, 8:00pm
You know, when you come over for dinner at my place, you'll get to hear stories about my childhood too!
Go on… Tell me!
In elementary school, for six months I had to wear a dental device attached to my head!
Wow!
Ha! Ha!
Ha! Ha!

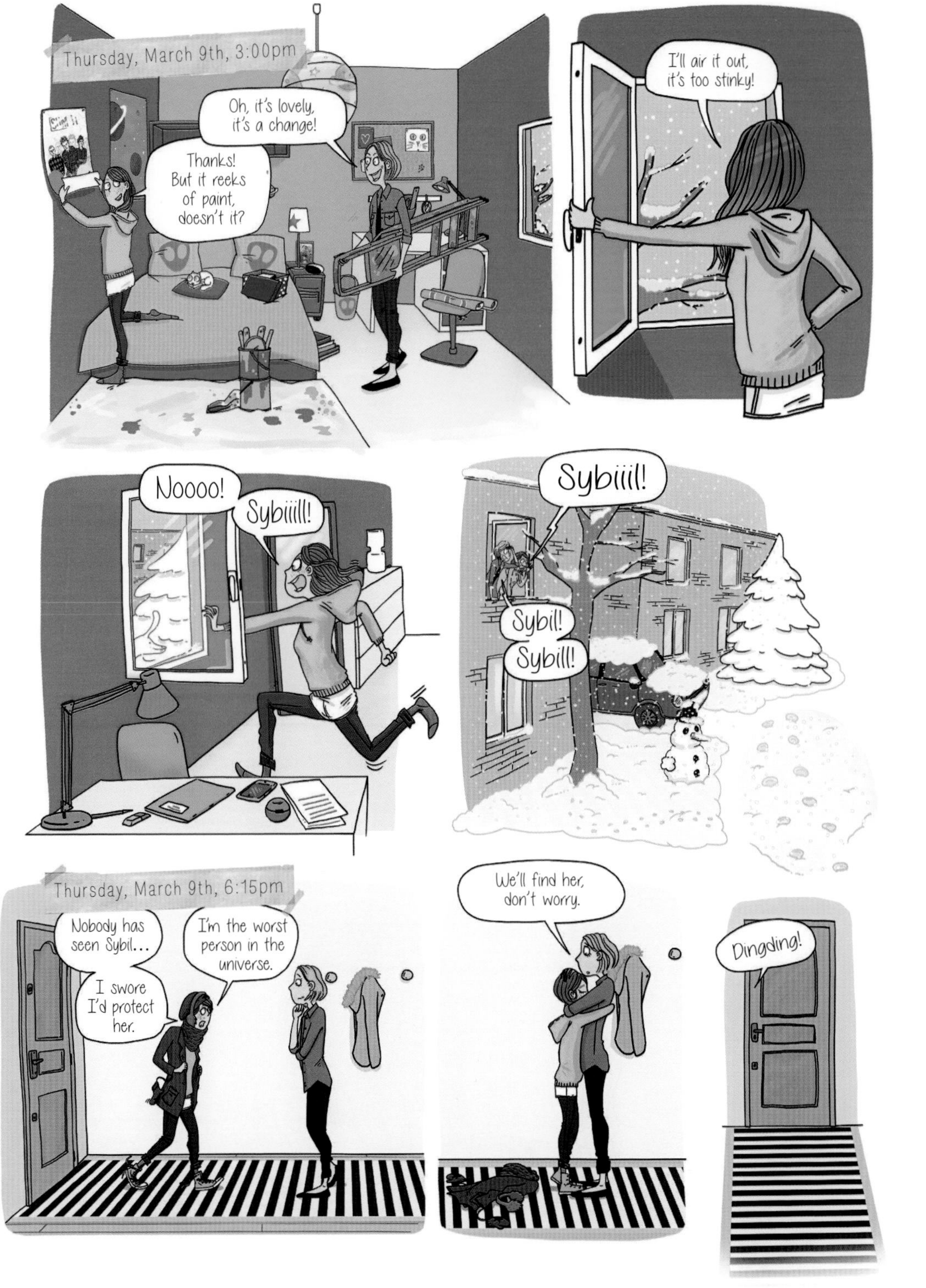

Thursday, March 9th, 3:00pm
Oh, it's lovely, it's a change!
Thanks! But it reeks of paint, doesn't it?
I'll air it out, it's too stinky!
Noooo!
Sybiiill!
Sybiiil!
Sybil!
Sybill!
Thursday, March 9th, 6:15pm
Nobody has seen Sybil...
I swore I'd protect her.
I'm the worst person in the universe.
We'll find her, don't worry.
Dingding!

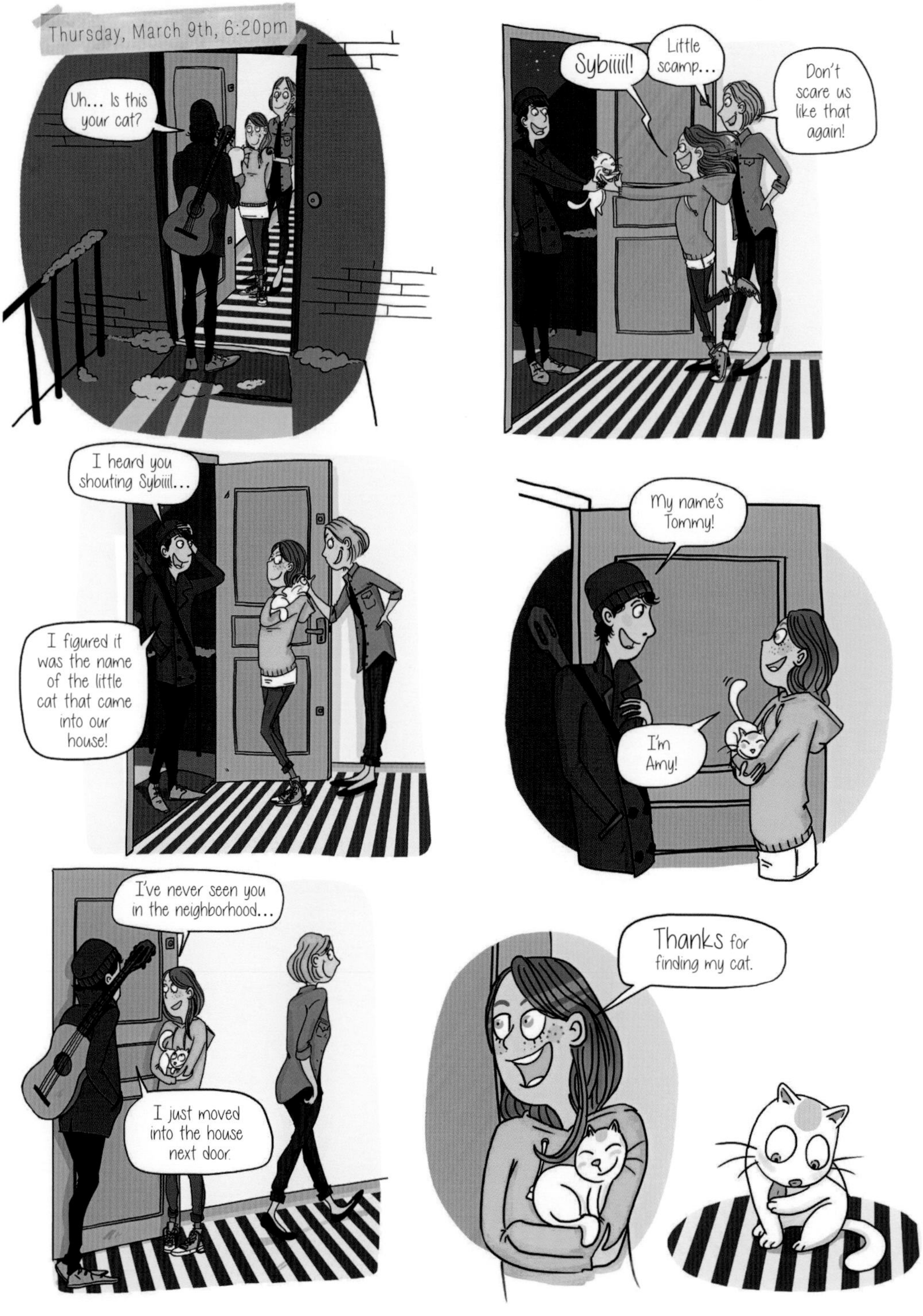
Thursday, March 9th, 6:20pm
Uh... Is this your cat?
Sybiiiil!
Little scamp...
Don't scare us like that again!
I heard you shouting Sybiiil...
I figured it was the name of the little cat that came into our house!
My name's Tommy!
I'm Amy!
I've never seen you in the neighborhood...
I just moved into the house next door.
Thanks for finding my cat.

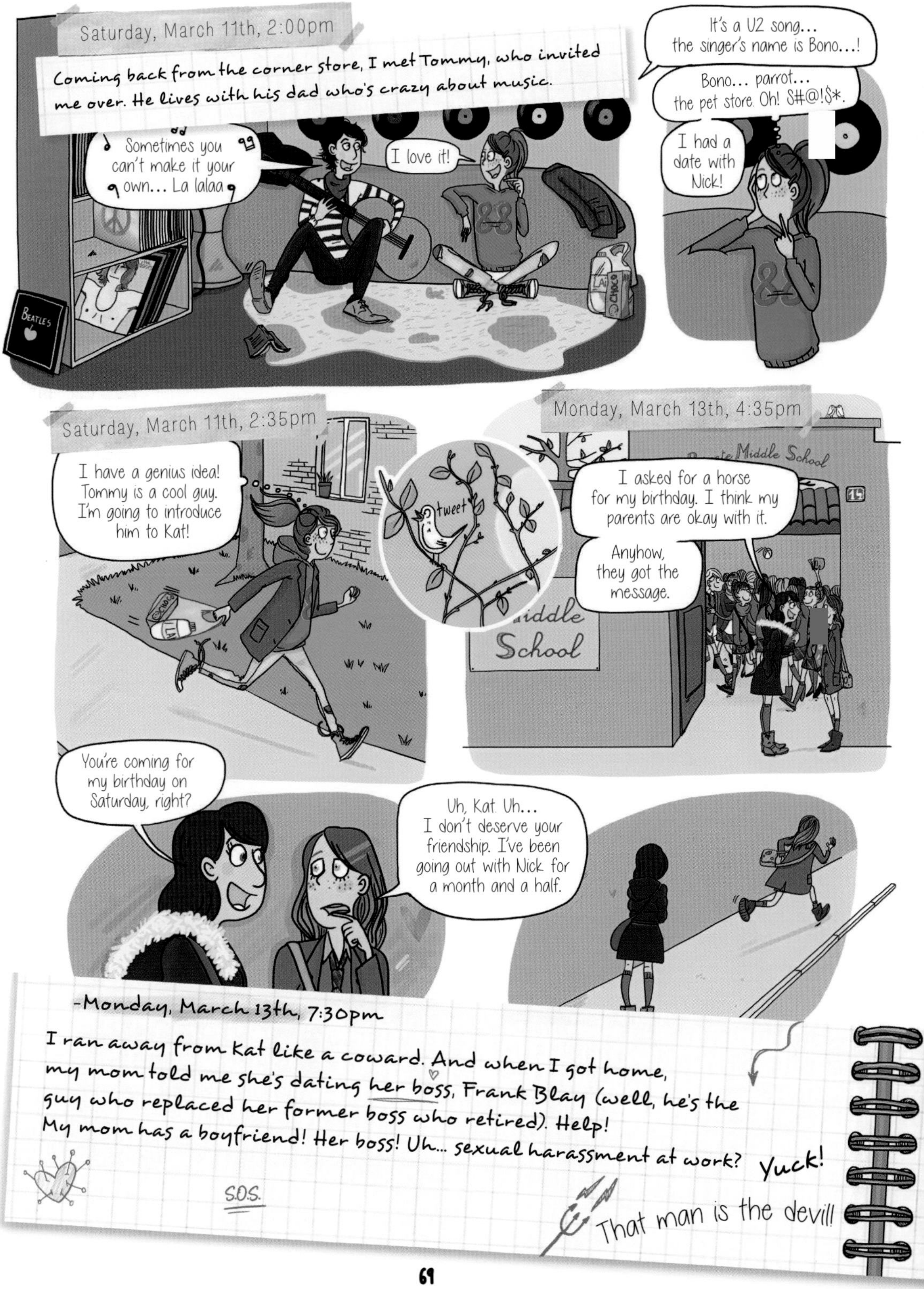
Saturday, March 11th, 2:00pm
Coming back from the corner store, I met Tommy, who invited me over. He lives with his dad who's crazy about music.
Sometimes you can't make it your own... La lalaa
I love it!
BEATLES
It's a U2 song... the singer's name is Bono...!
Bono... parrot... the pet store. Oh! $#@!$*.
I had a date with Nick!
Saturday, March 11th, 2:35pm
I have a genius idea! Tommy is a cool guy. I'm going to introduce him to Kat!
tweet
Monday, March 13th, 4:35pm
Middle School
I asked for a horse for my birthday. I think my parents are okay with it.
Anyhow, they got the message.
Middle School
You're coming for my birthday on Saturday, right?
Uh, Kat. Uh... I don't deserve your friendship. I've been going out with Nick for a month and a half.
-Monday, March 13th, 7:30pm
I ran away from Kat like a coward. And when I got home, my mom told me she's dating her boss, Frank Blay (well, he's the guy who replaced her former boss who retired). Help! My mom has a boyfriend! Her boss! Uh... sexual harassment at work?
Yuck!
S.O.S.
That man is the devil!

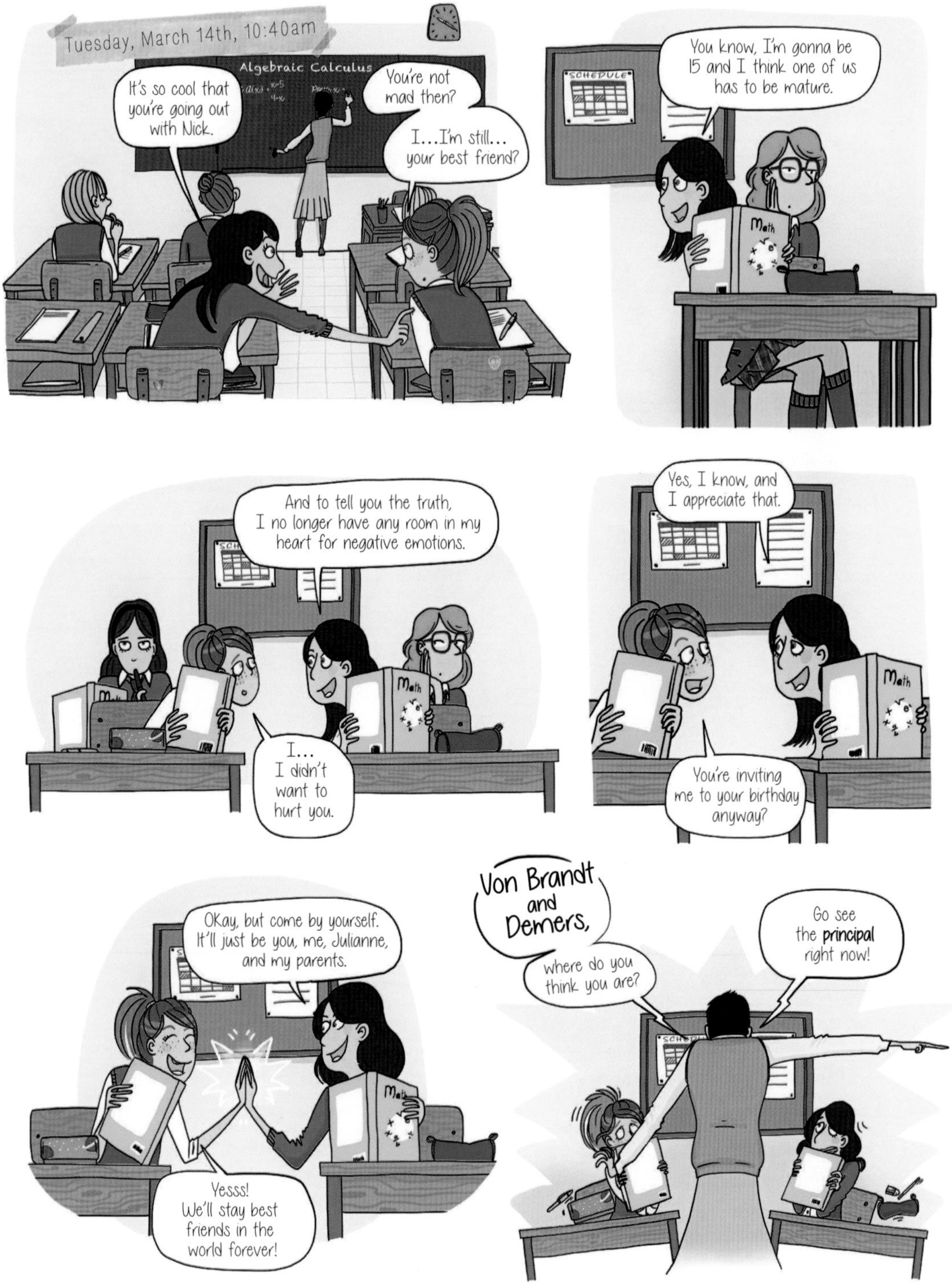

Tuesday, March 14th, 10:40am
Algebraic Calculus
It's so cool that you're going out with Nick.
You're not mad then?
I...I'm still... your best friend?
You know, I'm gonna be 15 and I think one of us has to be mature.
Math
And to tell you the truth, I no longer have any room in my heart for negative emotions.
I... I didn't want to hurt you.
Yes, I know, and I appreciate that.
You're inviting me to your birthday anyway?
OKay, but come by yourself. It'll just be you, me, Julianne, and my parents.
Yesss! We'll stay best friends in the world forever!
Von Brandt and Demers,
where do you think you are?
Go see the **principal** right now!

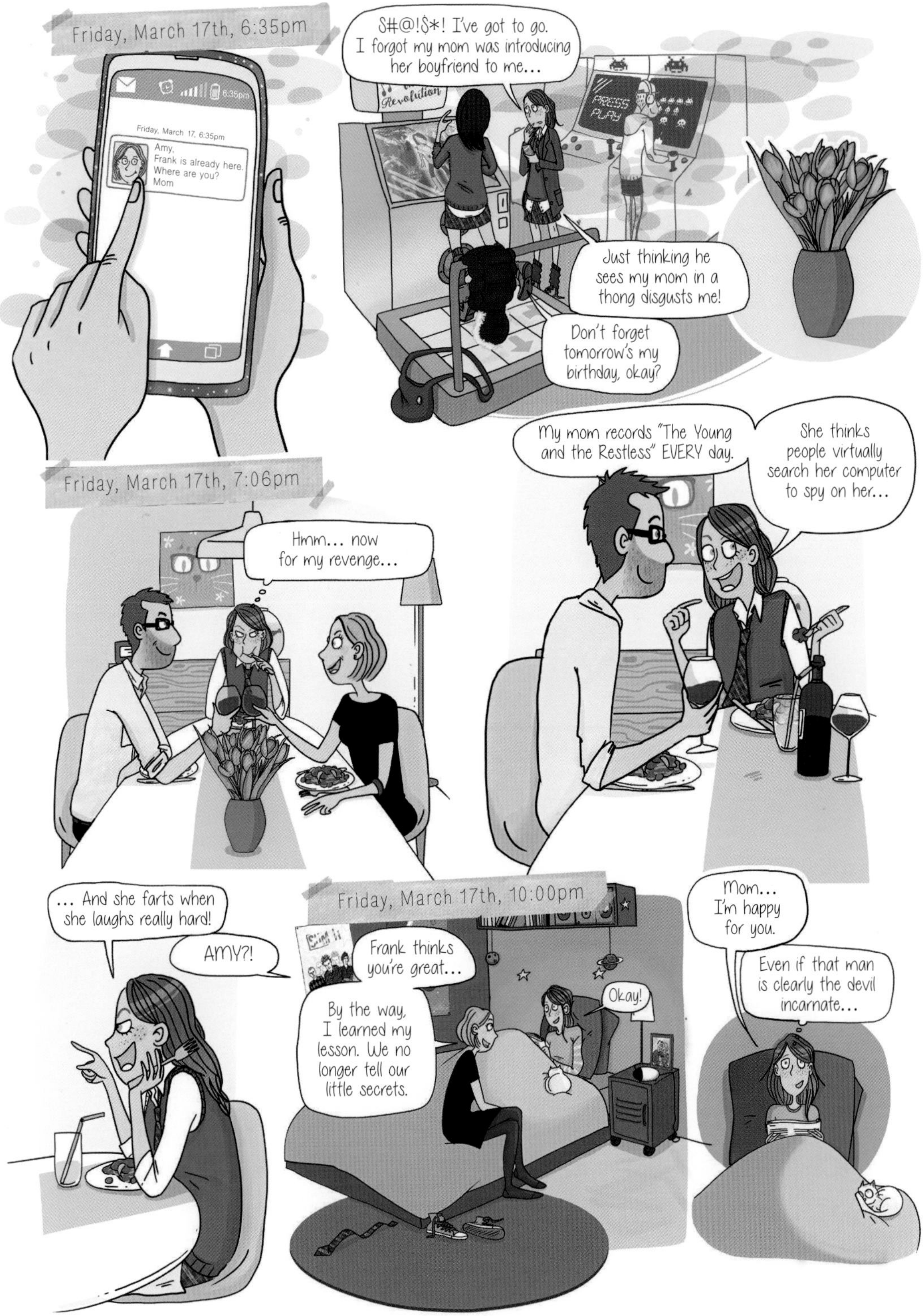

Friday, March 17th, 6:35pm
6:35pm
Friday, March 17, 6:35pm
Amy,
Frank is already here.
Where are you?
Mom
S#@!$*! I've got to go. I forgot my mom was introducing her boyfriend to me...
PRESS PLAY
Just thinking he sees my mom in a thong disgusts me!
Don't forget tomorrow's my birthday, okay?
Friday, March 17th, 7:06pm
Hmm... now for my revenge...
My mom records "The Young and the Restless" EVERY day.
She thinks people virtually search her computer to spy on her...
... And she farts when she laughs really hard!
AMY?!
Friday, March 17th, 10:00pm
Frank thinks you're great...
By the way, I learned my lesson. We no longer tell our little secrets.
Okay!
Mom... I'm happy for you.
Even if that man is clearly the devil incarnate...

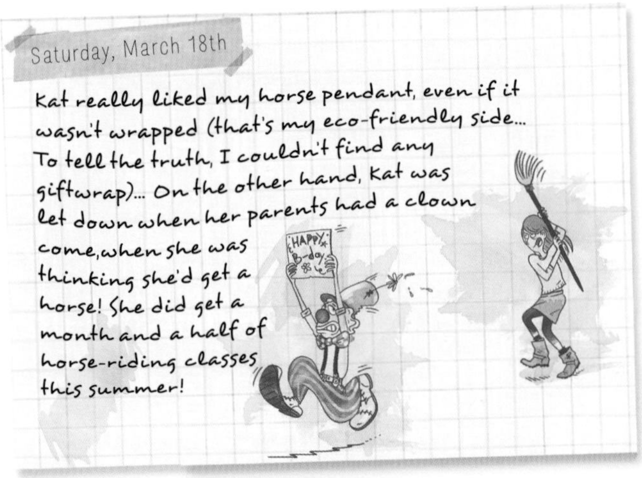
Saturday, March 18th
Kat really liked my horse pendant, even if it wasn't wrapped (that's my eco-friendly side... To tell the truth, I couldn't find any giftwrap)... On the other hand, Kat was let down when her parents had a clown come, when she was thinking she'd get a horse! She did get a month and a half of horse-riding classes this summer!
HAPPY B-day

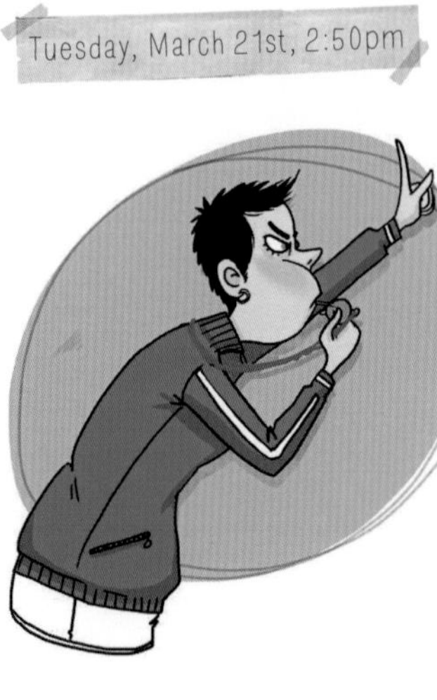
Tuesday, March 21st, 2:50pm

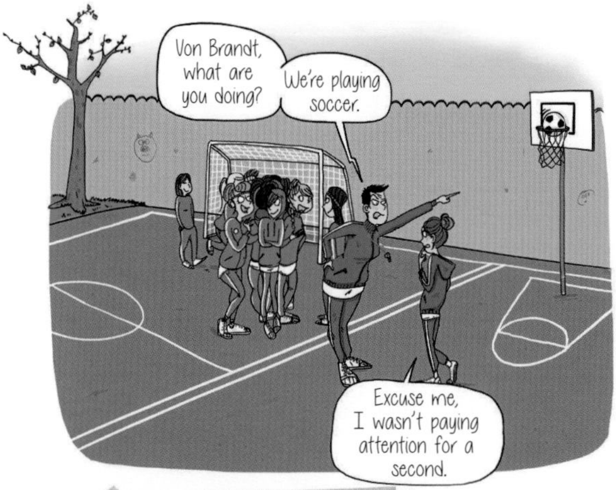
Von Brandt, what are you doing?
We're playing soccer.
Excuse me, I wasn't paying attention for a second.

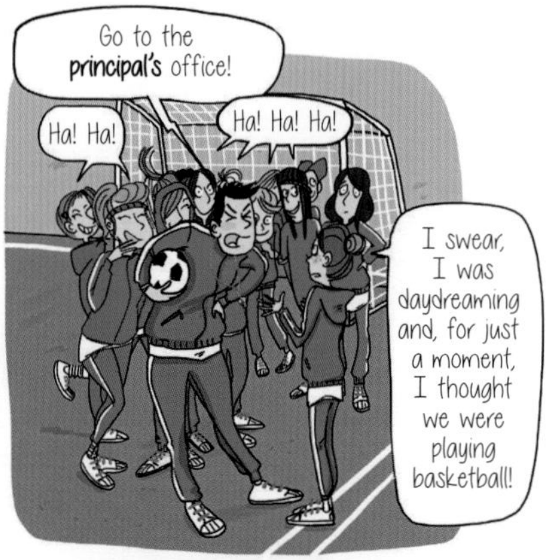
Go to the **principal's** office!
Ha! Ha!
Ha! Ha! Ha!
I swear, I was daydreaming and, for just a moment, I thought we were playing basketball!

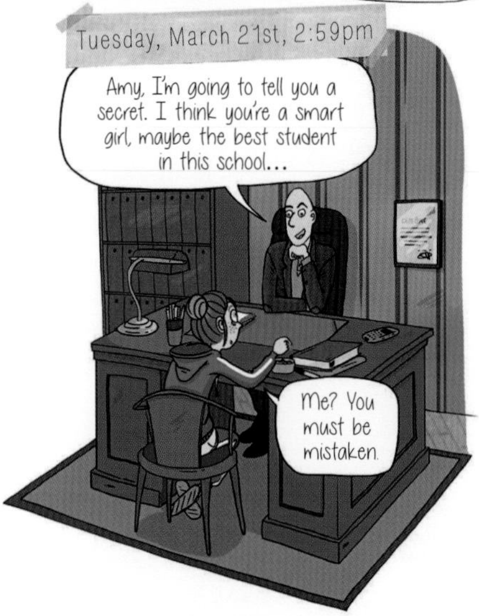
Tuesday, March 21st, 2:59pm
Amy, I'm going to tell you a secret. I think you're a smart girl, maybe the best student in this school...
Me? You must be mistaken.

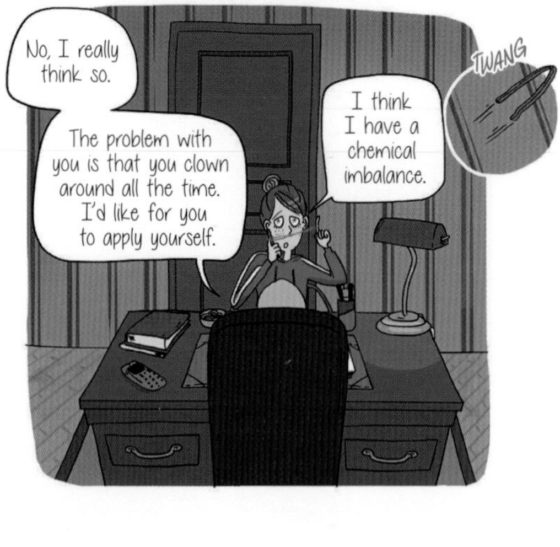
No, I really think so.
The problem with you is that you clown around all the time. I'd like for you to apply yourself.
I think I have a chemical imbalance.
TWANG

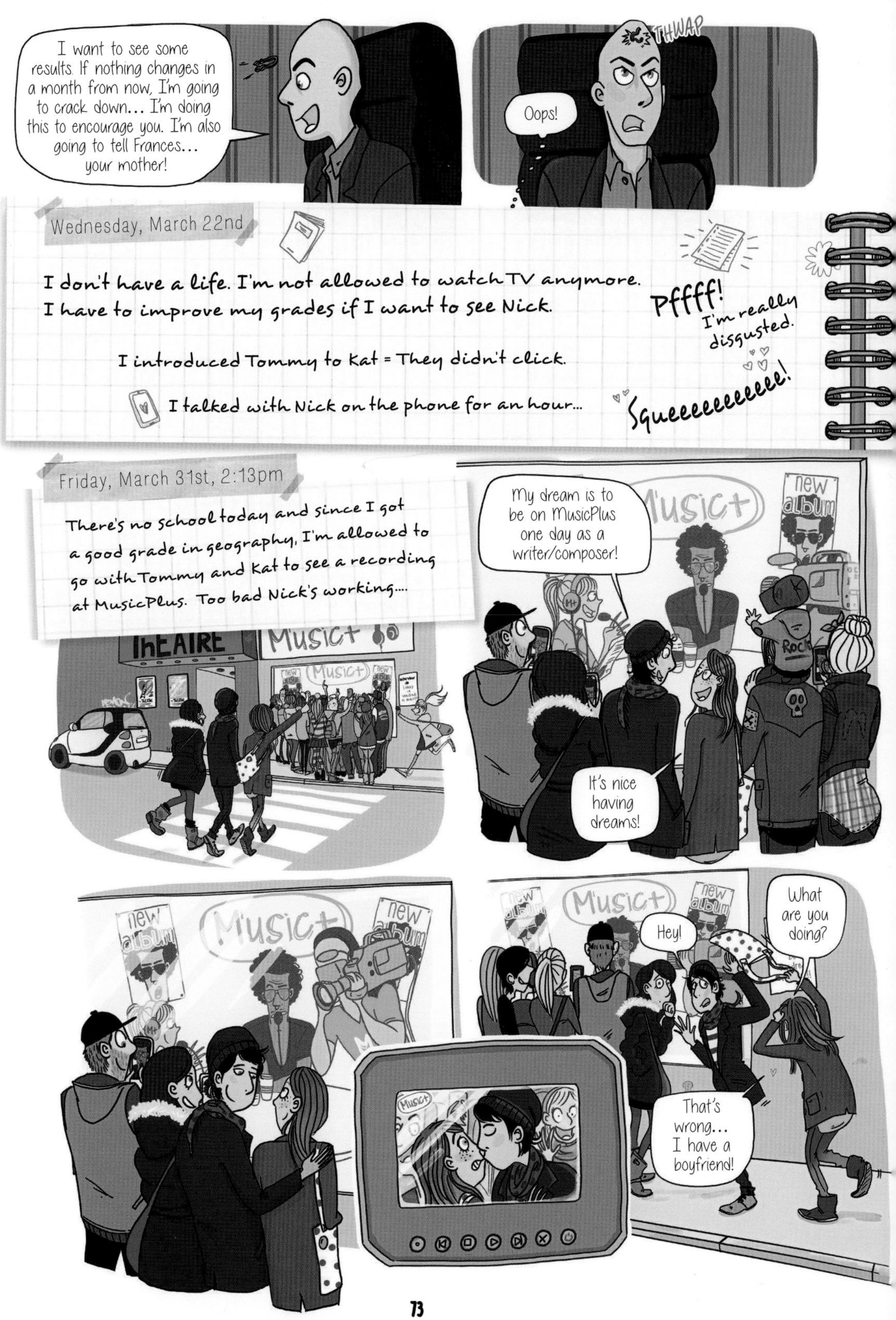
I want to see some results. If nothing changes in a month from now, I'm going to crack down… I'm doing this to encourage you. I'm also going to tell Frances… your mother!
THWAP
Oops!
Wednesday, March 22nd
I don't have a life. I'm not allowed to watch TV anymore. I have to improve my grades if I want to see Nick.
Pffff! I'm really disgusted.
I introduced Tommy to Kat = They didn't click.
I talked with Nick on the phone for an hour...
Squeeeeeeeeee!
Friday, March 31st, 2:13pm
There's no school today and since I got a good grade in geography, I'm allowed to go with Tommy and Kat to see a recording at MusicPlus. Too bad Nick's working....
THEATRE
Music+
new album
My dream is to be on MusicPlus one day as a writer/composer!
It's nice having dreams!
Hey!
What are you doing?
That's wrong… I have a boyfriend!

APRIL
A thousand pieces

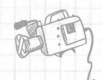

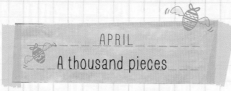

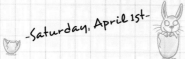

-Saturday, April 1st-

7:00am: With a little luck, the host will have stuttered right at the moment when Tommy kissed me, and MusicPlus won't broadcast that part of the show.

7:15am: Or better yet, the camera operator wasn't filming in our direction anymore.

8:20am: Unless I call MusicPlus to ask them (kindly) not to broadcast that sequence.

(If I explain to them, they'll understand!)

8:25am: If I explain the situation to Nick, he might understand, too... After all, I'm not the one who kissed Tommy.
Anyhow, I clearly rejected him.

He loves
me
a little
a lot
not at all

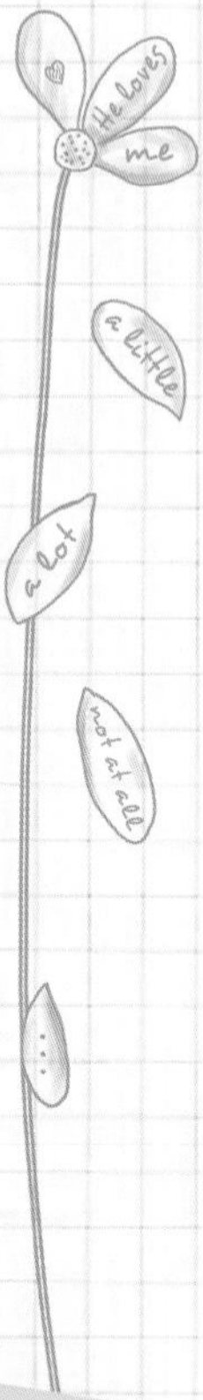

8:30am: Maybe Nick saw the broadcast live yesterday?

No...he was working... **whew!**

8:31am: What if he finds out when the reruns come on?

8:40am: I'll invite Nick to the movies and tell him everything.

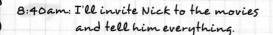

SUMMER
VACATION
It'll soon be
My
Birthday
15 years old
Yipee!

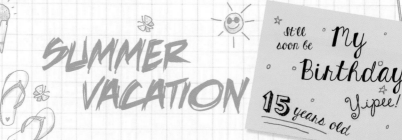

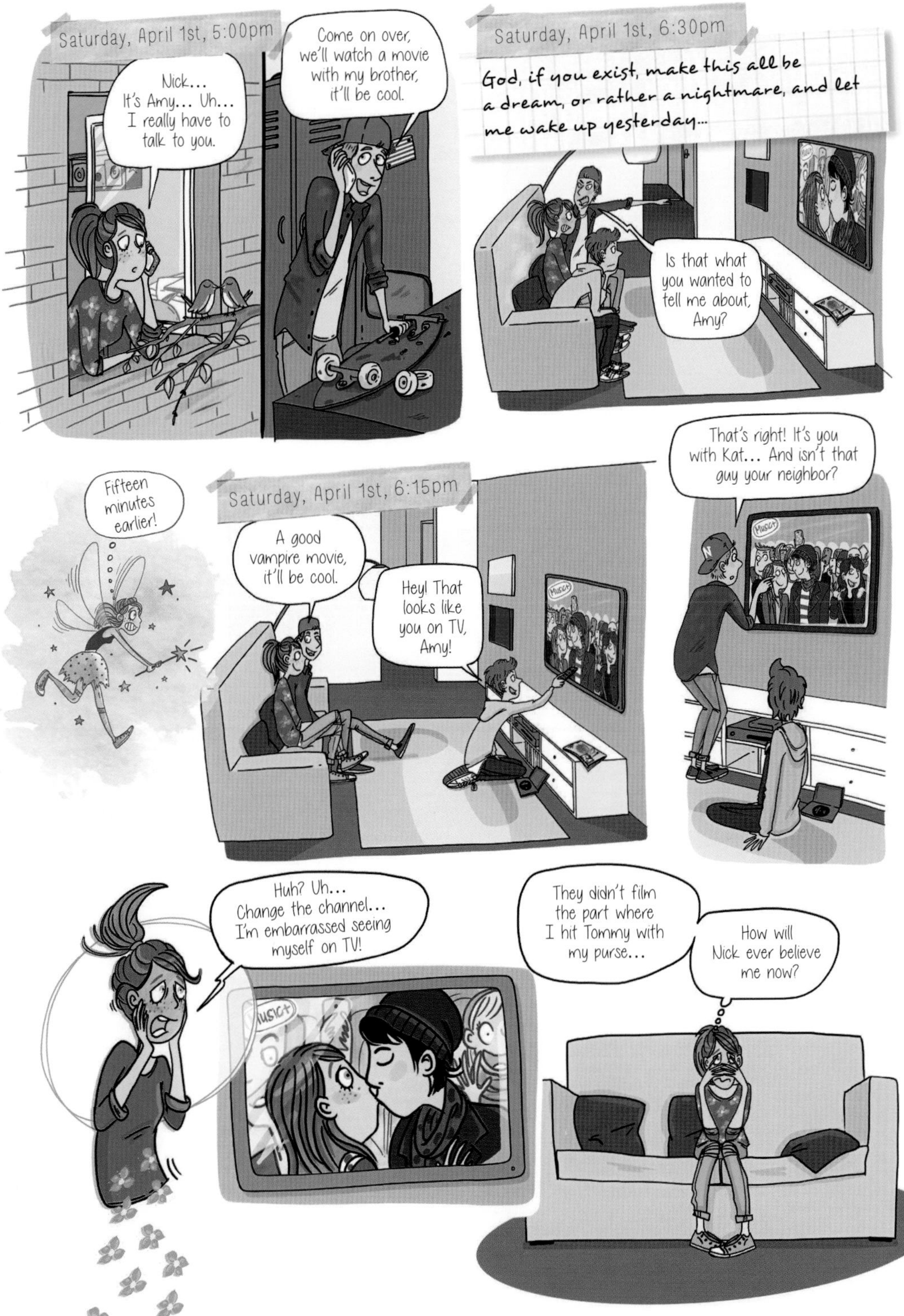
Saturday, April 1st, 5:00pm
Nick... It's Amy... Uh... I really have to talk to you.
Come on over, we'll watch a movie with my brother, it'll be cool.
Saturday, April 1st, 6:30pm
God, if you exist, make this all be a dream, or rather a nightmare, and let me wake up yesterday...
Is that what you wanted to tell me about, Amy?
Fifteen minutes earlier!
Saturday, April 1st, 6:15pm
A good vampire movie, it'll be cool.
Hey! That looks like you on TV, Amy!
Music+
That's right! It's you with Kat... And isn't that guy your neighbor?
Huh? Uh... Change the channel... I'm embarrassed seeing myself on TV!
They didn't film the part where I hit Tommy with my purse...
How will Nick ever believe me now?

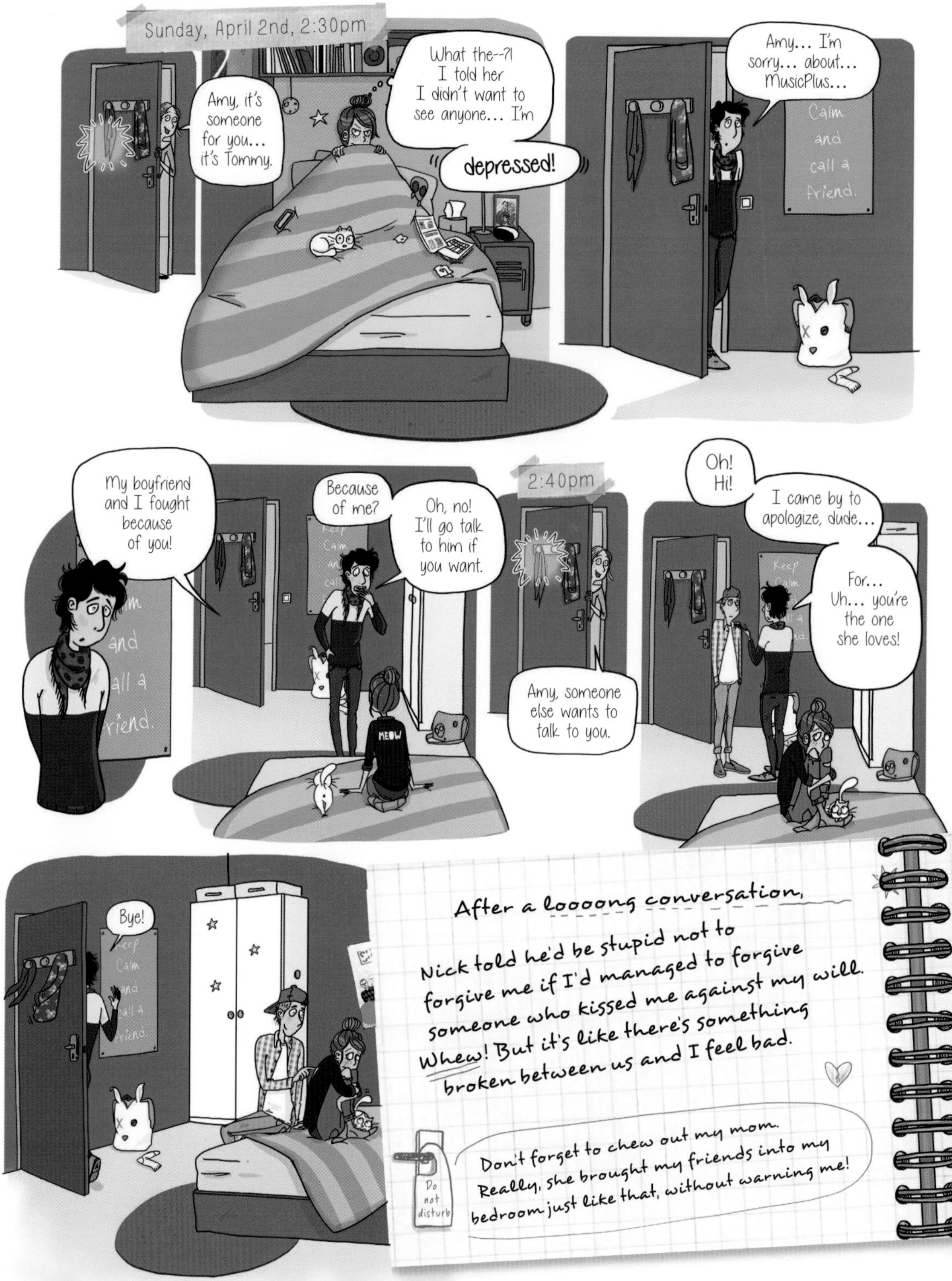

Sunday, April 2nd, 2:30pm
Amy, it's someone for you... it's Tommy.
What the--?! I told her I didn't want to see anyone... I'm
depressed!
Amy... I'm sorry... about... MusicPlus...
Calm and call a friend.
My boyfriend and I fought because of you!
Because of me?
Oh, no! I'll go talk to him if you want.
MEOW
2:40pm
Amy, someone else wants to talk to you.
Oh! Hi!
I came by to apologize, dude...
For... Uh... you're the one she loves!
Bye!
After a loooong conversation,
Nick told he'd be stupid not to forgive me if I'd managed to forgive someone who kissed me against my will.
Whew! But it's like there's something broken between us and I feel bad.
Do not disturb
Don't forget to chew out my mom. Really, she brought my friends into my bedroom just like that, without warning me!

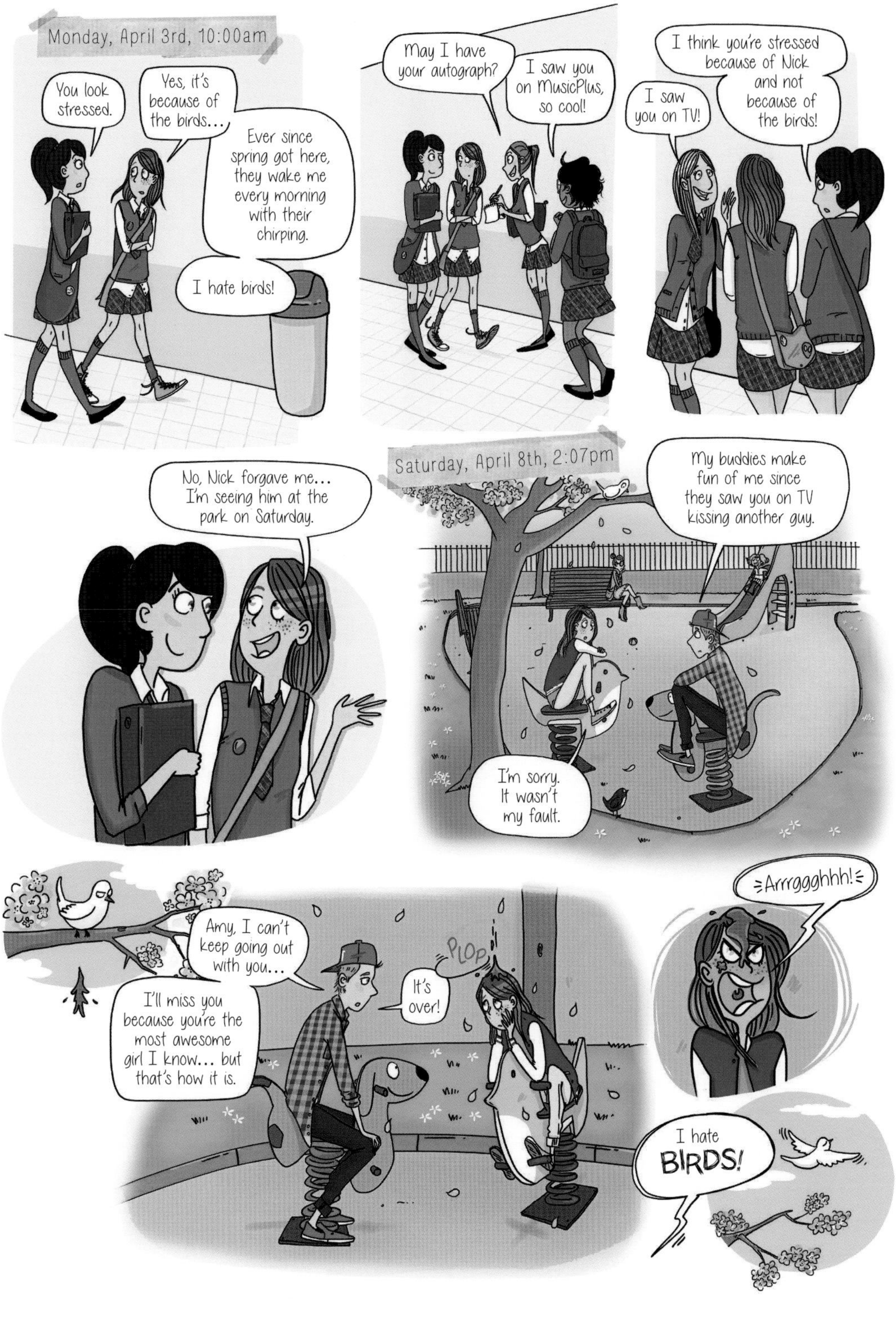
Monday, April 3rd, 10:00am
You look stressed.
Yes, it's because of the birds…
Ever since spring got here, they wake me every morning with their chirping.
I hate birds!
May I have your autograph?
I saw you on MusicPlus, so cool!
I saw you on TV!
I think you're stressed because of Nick and not because of the birds!
No, Nick forgave me… I'm seeing him at the park on Saturday.
Saturday, April 8th, 2:07pm
My buddies make fun of me since they saw you on TV kissing another guy.
I'm sorry. It wasn't my fault.
Amy, I can't keep going out with you…
I'll miss you because you're the most awesome girl I know… but that's how it is.
PLOP
It's over!
Arrrggghhh!
I hate BIRDS!

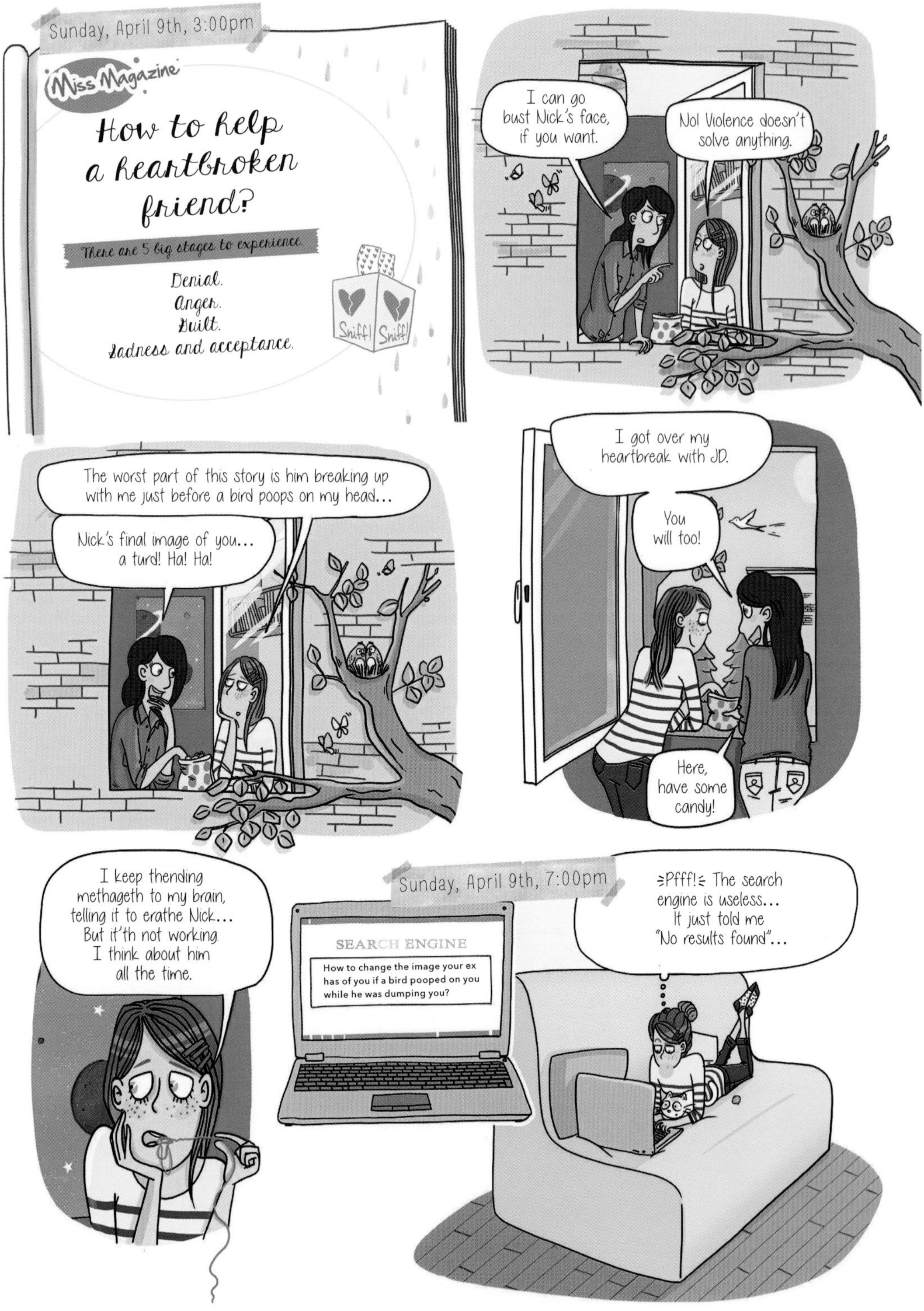

Sunday, April 9th, 3:00pm
Miss Magazine
How to help a heartbroken friend?
There are 5 big stages to experience.
Denial.
Anger.
Guilt.
Sadness and acceptance.
Sniff! Sniff!
I can go bust Nick's face, if you want.
No! Violence doesn't solve anything.
The worst part of this story is him breaking up with me just before a bird poops on my head...
Nick's final image of you... a turd! Ha! Ha!
I got over my heartbreak with JD.
You will too!
Here, have some candy!
I keep thending methageth to my brain, telling it to erathe Nick... But it'th not working. I think about him all the time.
Sunday, April 9th, 7:00pm
SEARCH ENGINE
How to change the image your ex has of you if a bird pooped on you while he was dumping you?
≥Pfff!≤ The search engine is useless... It just told me "No results found"...

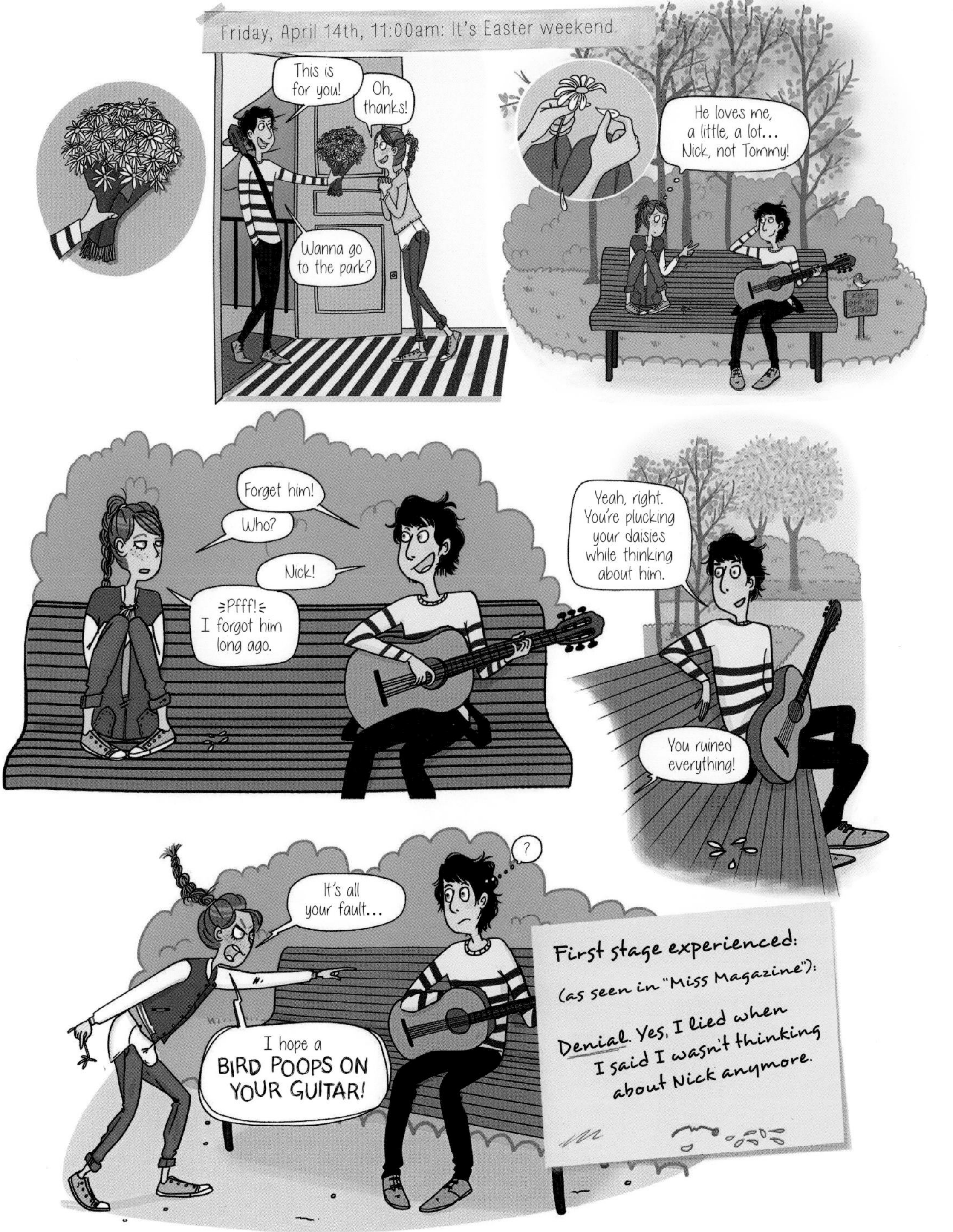
Friday, April 14th, 11:00am: It's Easter weekend.
This is for you!
Oh, thanks!
Wanna go to the park?
He loves me, a little, a lot... Nick, not Tommy!
KEEP OFF THE GRASS
Forget him!
Who?
Nick!
Pfff! I forgot him long ago.
Yeah, right. You're plucking your daisies while thinking about him.
You ruined everything!
?
It's all your fault...
I hope a BIRD POOPS ON YOUR GUITAR!
First stage experienced:
(as seen in "Miss Magazine"):
Denial. Yes, I lied when I said I wasn't thinking about Nick anymore.

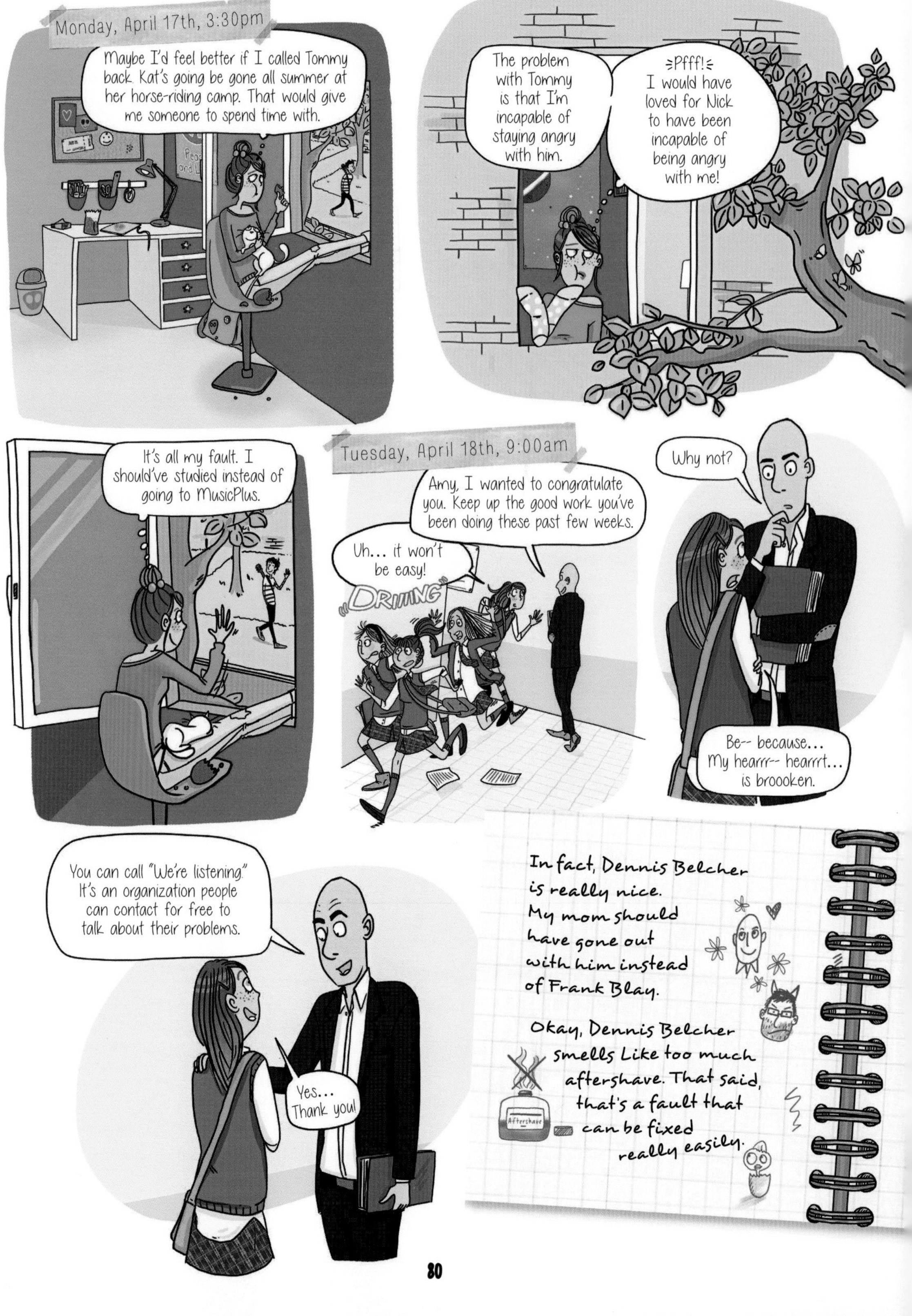
Monday, April 17th, 3:30pm
Maybe I'd feel better if I called Tommy back. Kat's going be gone all summer at her horse-riding camp. That would give me someone to spend time with.
The problem with Tommy is that I'm incapable of staying angry with him.
Pfff! I would have loved for Nick to have been incapable of being angry with me!
It's all my fault. I should've studied instead of going to MusicPlus.
Tuesday, April 18th, 9:00am
Amy, I wanted to congratulate you. Keep up the good work you've been doing these past few weeks.
Uh... it won't be easy!
DRIIIING
Why not?
Be-- because... My hearrr-- hearrrt... is broooken.
You can call "We're listening." It's an organization people can contact for free to talk about their problems.
Yes... Thank you!
In fact, Dennis Belcher is really nice. My mom should have gone out with him instead of Frank Blay.
Okay, Dennis Belcher smells like too much aftershave. That said, that's a fault that can be fixed really easily.
Aftershave

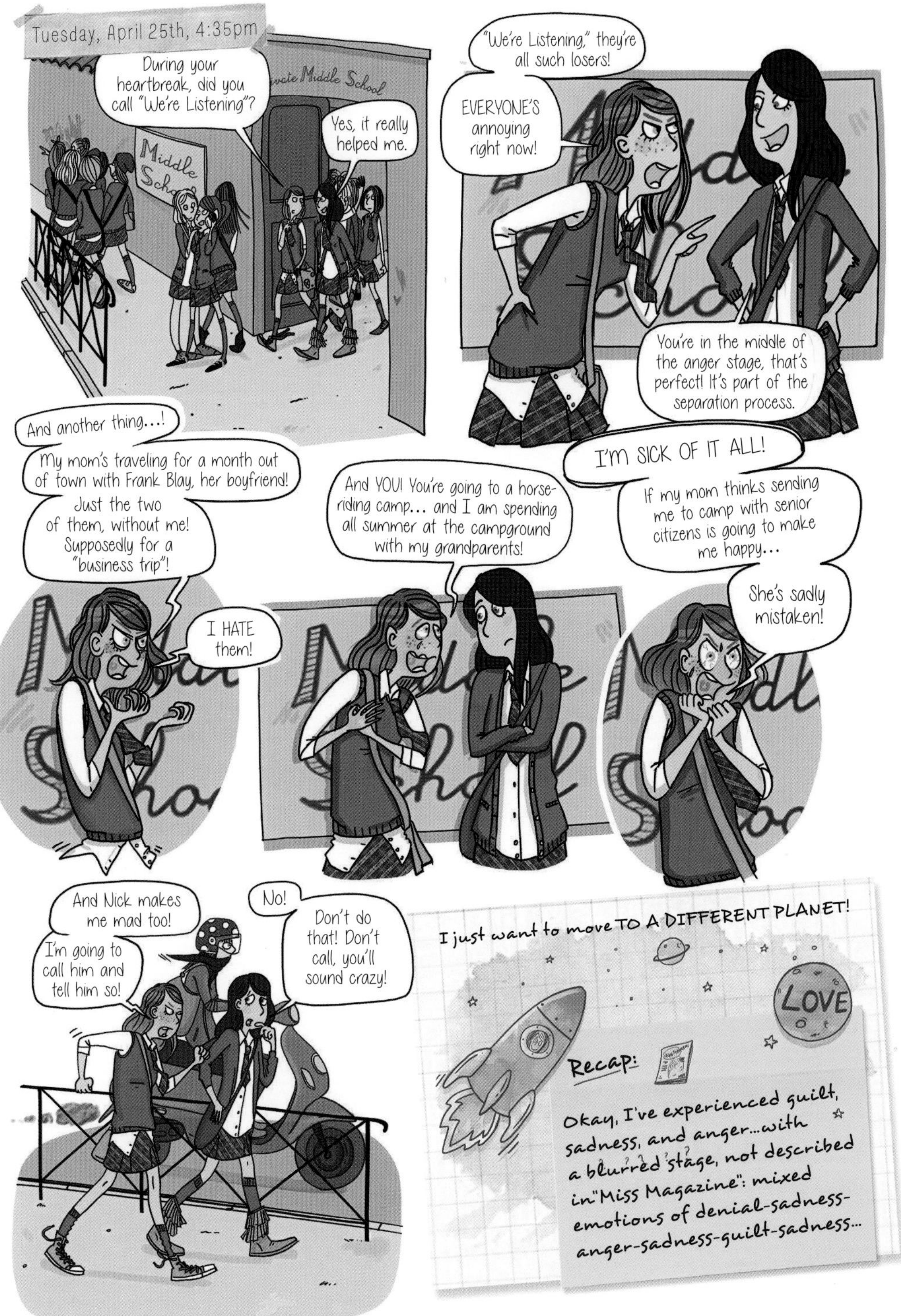

Tuesday, April 25th, 4:35pm
Private Middle School
Middle School
During your heartbreak, did you call "We're Listening"?
Yes, it really helped me.
"We're Listening," they're all such losers!
EVERYONE'S annoying right now!
You're in the middle of the anger stage, that's perfect! It's part of the separation process.
And another thing...!
My mom's traveling for a month out of town with Frank Blay, her boyfriend!
Just the two of them, without me! Supposedly for a "business trip"!
I HATE them!
And YOU! You're going to a horse-riding camp... and I am spending all summer at the campground with my grandparents!
I'M SICK OF IT ALL!
If my mom thinks sending me to camp with senior citizens is going to make me happy...
She's sadly mistaken!
And Nick makes me mad too!
I'm going to call him and tell him so!
No!
Don't do that! Don't call, you'll sound crazy!
I just want to move TO A DIFFERENT PLANET!
LOVE
Recap:
Okay, I've experienced guilt, sadness, and anger...with a blurred stage, not described in "Miss Magazine": mixed emotions of denial-sadness-anger-sadness-guilt-sadness...

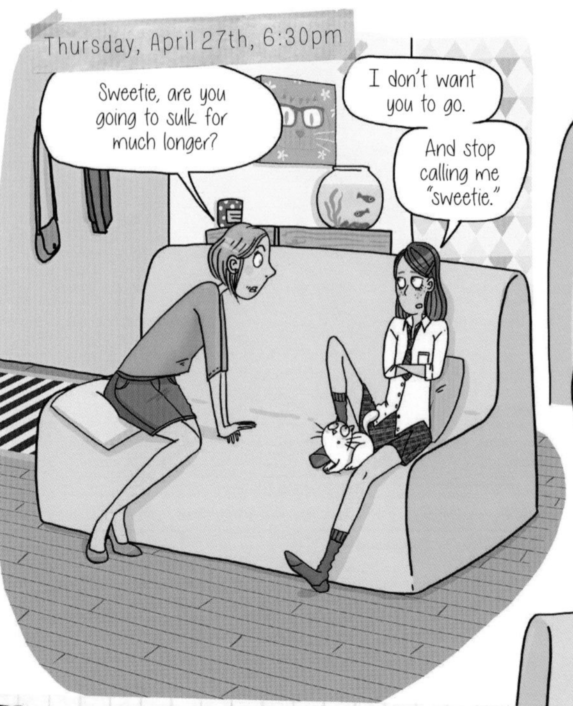
Thursday, April 27th, 6:30pm
Sweetie, are you going to sulk for much longer?
I don't want you to go.
And stop calling me "sweetie."

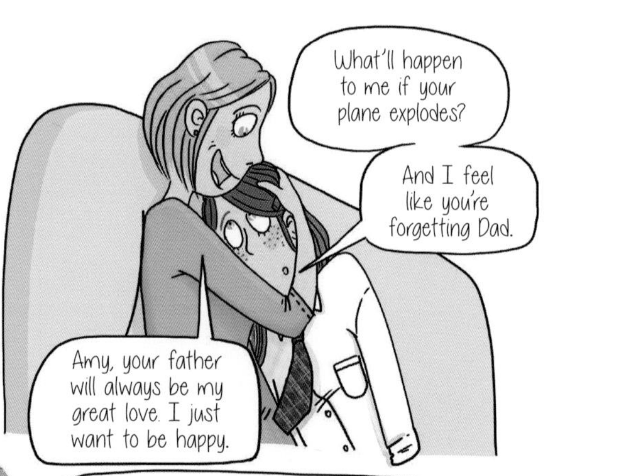
What'll happen to me if your plane explodes?
And I feel like you're forgetting Dad.
Amy, your father will always be my great love. I just want to be happy.

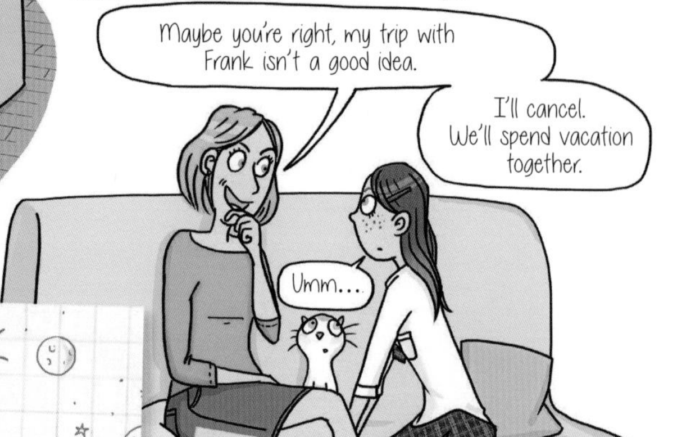
Maybe you're right, my trip with Frank isn't a good idea.
I'll cancel. We'll spend vacation together.
Umm...

-Friday, April 28th, 10:00pm

This afternoon, I did something without thinking. I walked out of school to go see my mom at her job. I ran, ran, and ran. While running, all the events of the last months tumbled through my mind: My 1st love, my lies to Kat, my mom's first boyfriend since my dad's death, Tommy, my annoying neighbor becoming my friend, my bad grades at school... When I saw my mother, I told her not to cancel her trip with her boyfriend. I want her to be happy.

I'm going to be 15 this summer, and it's time for me to grow up!

Kat told me hurting is part of life. Sometimes you experience difficult things, but you have to get over them and keep on dreaming...

Final stages: sadness and acceptance. Hmmmm... as for those, I think it'll take a little bit longer, because if I do manage to stop hurting a little less, I'll never forget Nick.

And that's okay!

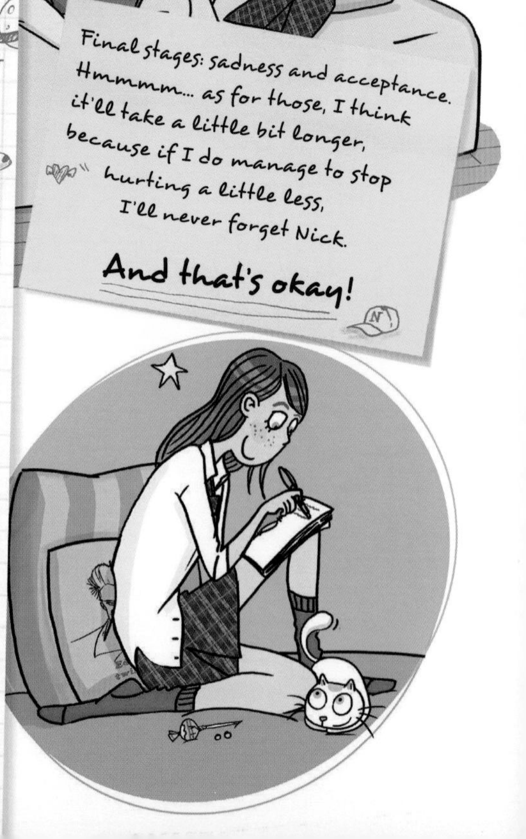

Charmz chat™

Hey! Don't you know you're not supposed to look at other people's diaries?! Well, maybe we can make an exception for AMY'S DIARY…? Welcome to AMY'S DIARY #1 "Space Alien… Almost?," based on the novels by India Desjardins, adapted by Véronique Grisseaux, writer, and Laëtitia Aynié, artist. We hope you enjoyed getting to really know Amy Von Brandt and her friends and family in this graphic novel. Maybe it's because we've enjoyed taking this peek into her diary, but it's easy to imagine Amy, Kat, and all the rest as our own real "friends," even though they are fictitious characters. The same is true regarding the friendliness of the stars of other Charmz titles:

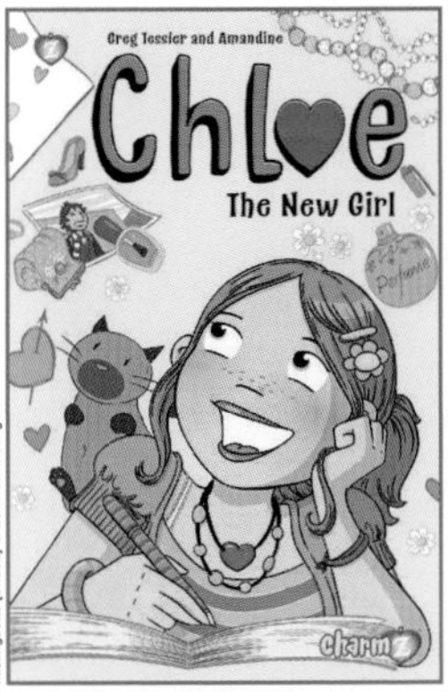

Greg Tessier and Amandine
Chloe
The New Girl
charmz

Chloe, a middle-schooler falling in and out of love, is the star of CHLOE. And we like her almost as much as her besties Mark and Fatou do.

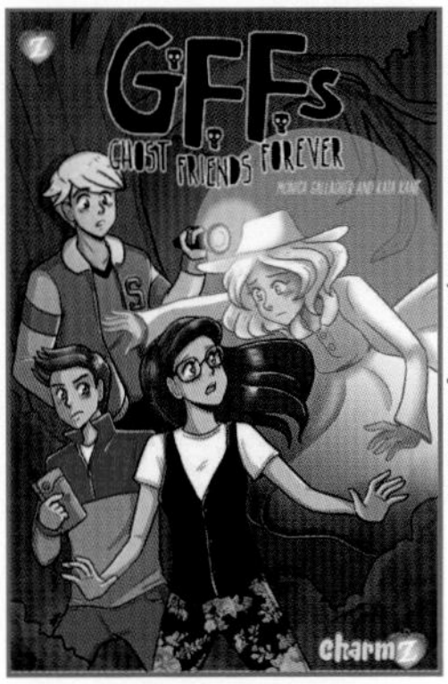

GFFs
Ghost Friends Forever
charmz

G.F.F.s GHOST FRIENDS FOREVER involves a love triangle between paranormal investigator Sophia Greene-Campos, her ex-boyfriend Jake, and Whitney, an actual ghost. How cool would it be to have a friend who's a ghost-hunter or an actual ghost?

Or imagine living in another time, and having a friend who is almost like a super-hero? In SCARLET ROSE, swashbuckling vigilante Maud must search for her father's killer while also figuring out where things stand with her masked crime-fighting partner, The Fox.

In SWEETIES, we meet and befriend an entire "blended" family, that is the result of when Cherry Costello's dad, Paddy, marries Charlotte, the mother of Skye, Coco, Honey, and Summer Tanberry. While they're trying to figure out the best way to get along with each other, we get to know each sister very well. (SWEETIES, like AMY'S DIARY is based on a series of novels. SWEETIES is based on the "The Chocolate Box Girls" by Cathy Cassidy, and also adapted into comics by Véronique Grisseaux.)

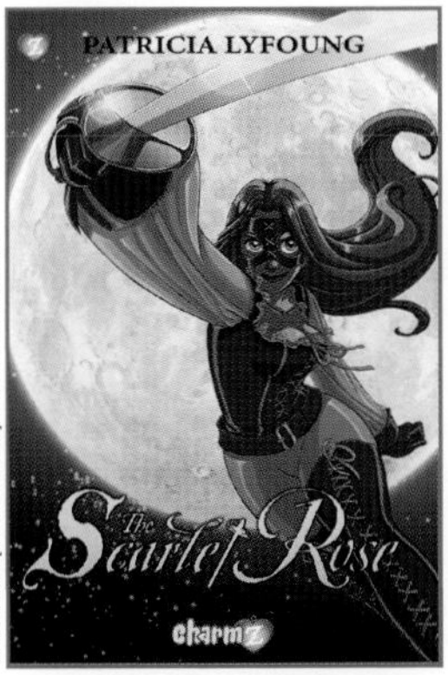

PATRICIA LYFOUNG
The Scarlet Rose
charmz

Or if you really want to get weird, check this Charmz series out: STITCHED is about Crimson Volania Mulch, a patchwork girl, who wakes up in a cemetery, soon to discover it's actually a lively place full of potential new relationships and friendships.

Coming soon to Charmz is someone we're sure you'll like: Meet MONICA! She's had the same friends most of her life, but now their relationships are changing just as they're becoming teenagers. When Monica was little she was the leader of her group of friends, and if any of them got out of line, she'd let 'em have it and wallop them with her plush bunny rabbit. Monica's main rival to lead her gang was Jimmy Five, who now prefers to be called "J-Five." He's matured to the point where being leader of the gang is no longer a priority, now he's focused on trying to make the planet a better place. Smudge is the one into sports, the more radical, the better. Maggy, is a caring friend that loves cats, and is into taking better care of her body. She's focused on proper nutrition, exercise, and sports. Look for all of these new friends and more in MONICA ADVENTURES #1 "Who Can Afford the Price of Friendship Today?" and #2 "We Fought Each Other as Kids… Now We're in Love?!"

While the major theme tying all the Charmz graphic novels together is romance, friendship is a big factor in each title as well. Each Charmz graphic novel is almost like visiting friends and catching up with their lives. Whether their lives are close to ours (Amy, Chloe, Monica) or from another time (Maud) or even somewhat supernatural (Sophia and Crimson), what comes through in each series is that they all have the special qualities that we seek in choosing our friends. And that's why we all love spending time with them. And on the following pages, you'll get to spend a little time with special previews of MONICA ADVENTURES #1 (in black and white, in a style resembling Manga) and SCARLET ROSE #1 (in full-color, in the traditional European graphic novel style).

Speaking of which, don't miss AMY'S DIARY #2 "The World's Upside Down" coming soon, where things don't go exactly as Amy has hoped in regards to her love life. We suspect Amy could use a friend in her next graphic novel, so we hope you'll be there!

Thanks,

Jim

Editor-in-Chief

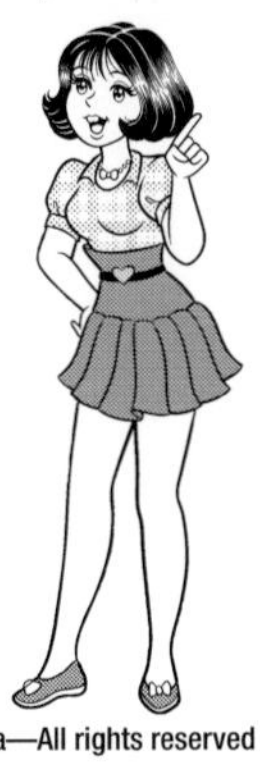

STAY IN TOUCH!
(That's what friends do!)

EMAIL:	salicrup@papercutz.com
WEB:	Papercutz.com
TWITTER:	@papercutzgn
INSTAGRAM:	@papercutzgn
FACEBOOK:	PAPERCUTZGRAPHICNOVELS
FANMAIL:	Charmz, 160 Broadway, Suite 700, East Wing, New York, NY 10038

Bonus! Here's a preview of THE SCARLET ROSE #1
"I Knew I'd Meet You"...

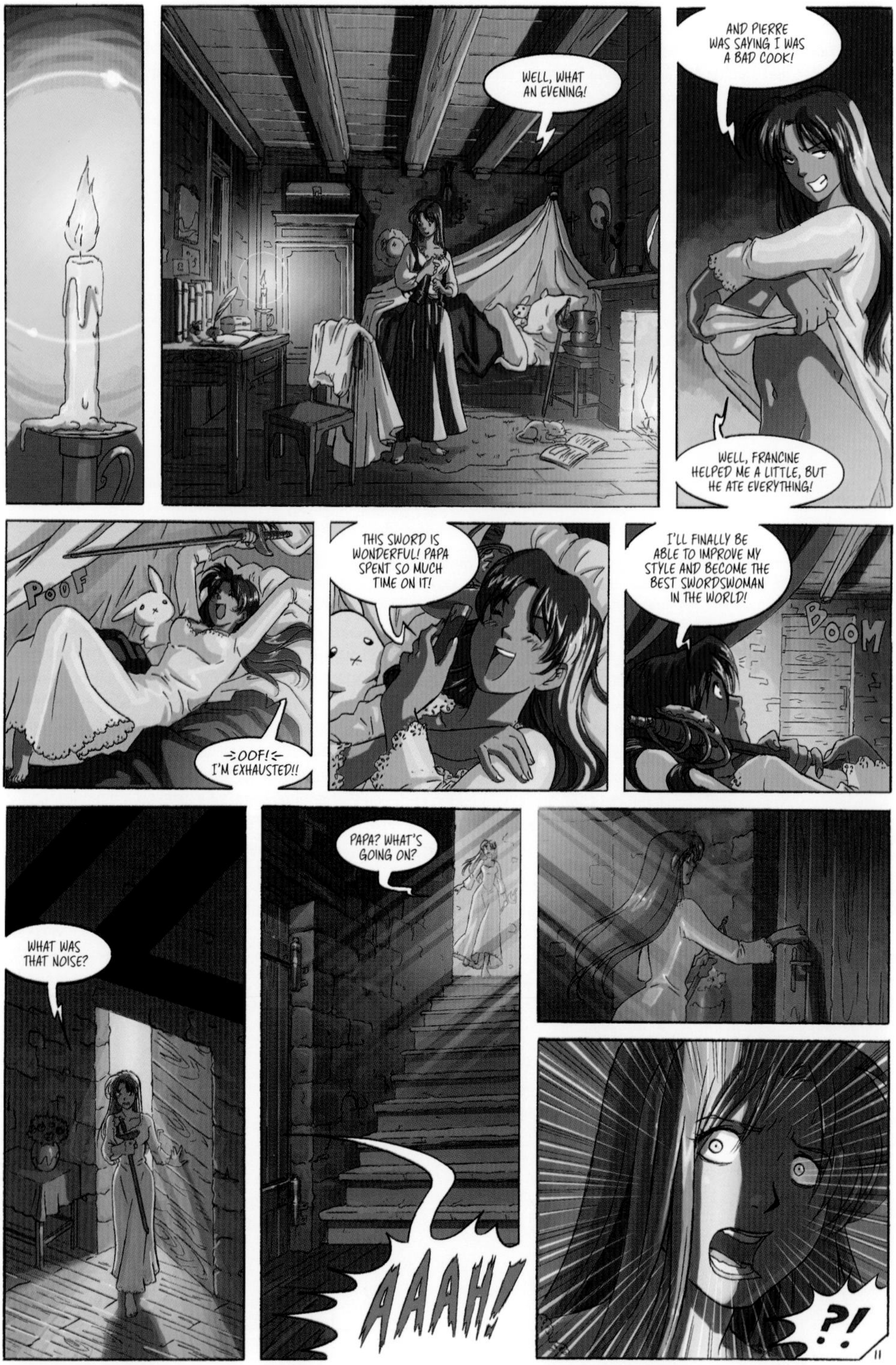
WELL, WHAT AN EVENING!
AND PIERRE WAS SAYING I WAS A BAD COOK!
WELL, FRANCINE HELPED ME A LITTLE, BUT HE ATE EVERYTHING!
POOF
OOF! I'M EXHAUSTED!!
THIS SWORD IS WONDERFUL! PAPA SPENT SO MUCH TIME ON IT!
I'LL FINALLY BE ABLE TO IMPROVE MY STYLE AND BECOME THE BEST SWORDSWOMAN IN THE WORLD!
BOOM
WHAT WAS THAT NOISE?
PAPA? WHAT'S GOING ON?
AAAH!
?!
11

THE SCARLET ROSE by Patricia Lyfoung. La Rose écarlate © Éditions Delcourt – 2005.

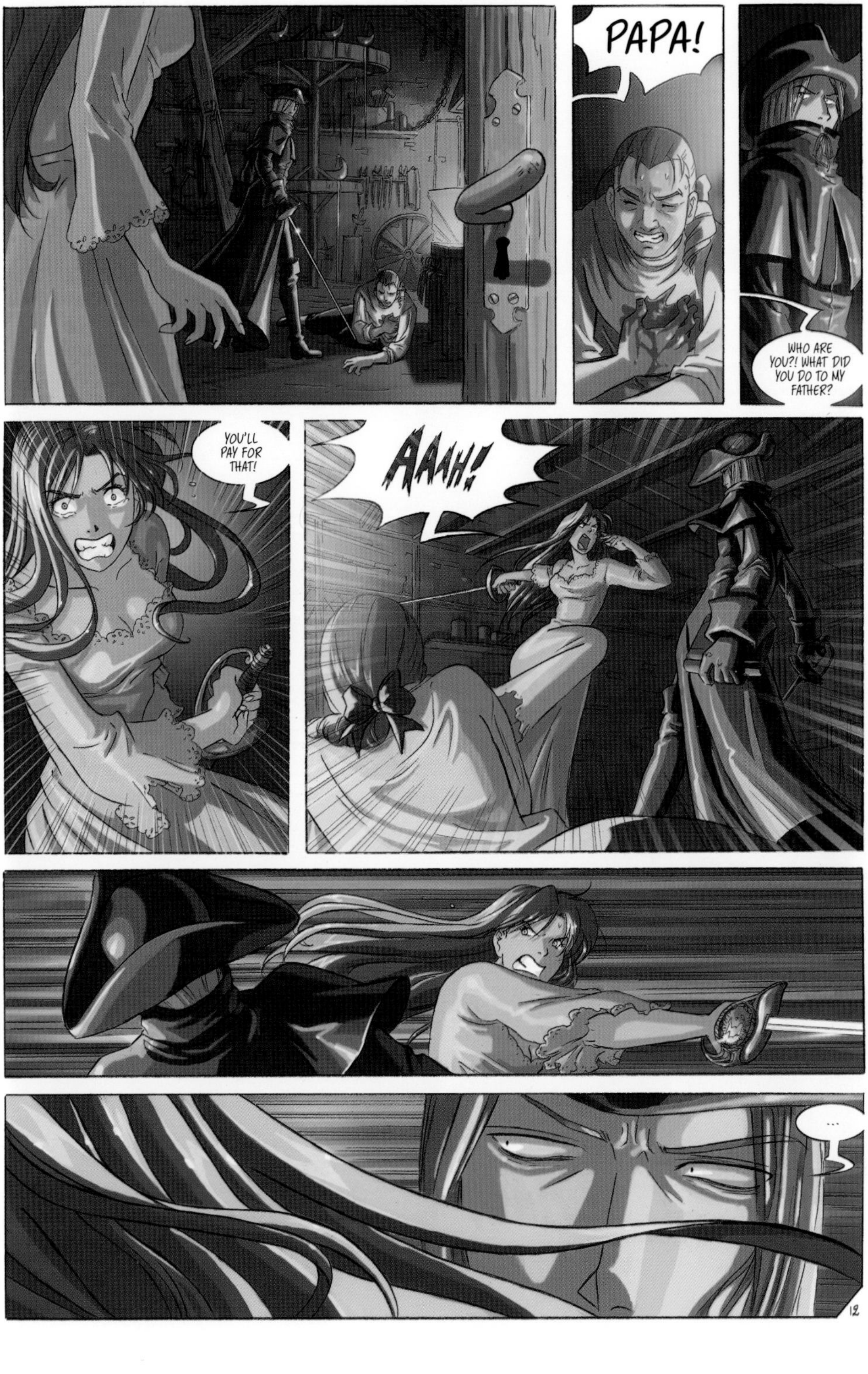
PAPA!
WHO ARE YOU?! WHAT DID YOU DO TO MY FATHER?
YOU'LL PAY FOR THAT!
AAAH!
...

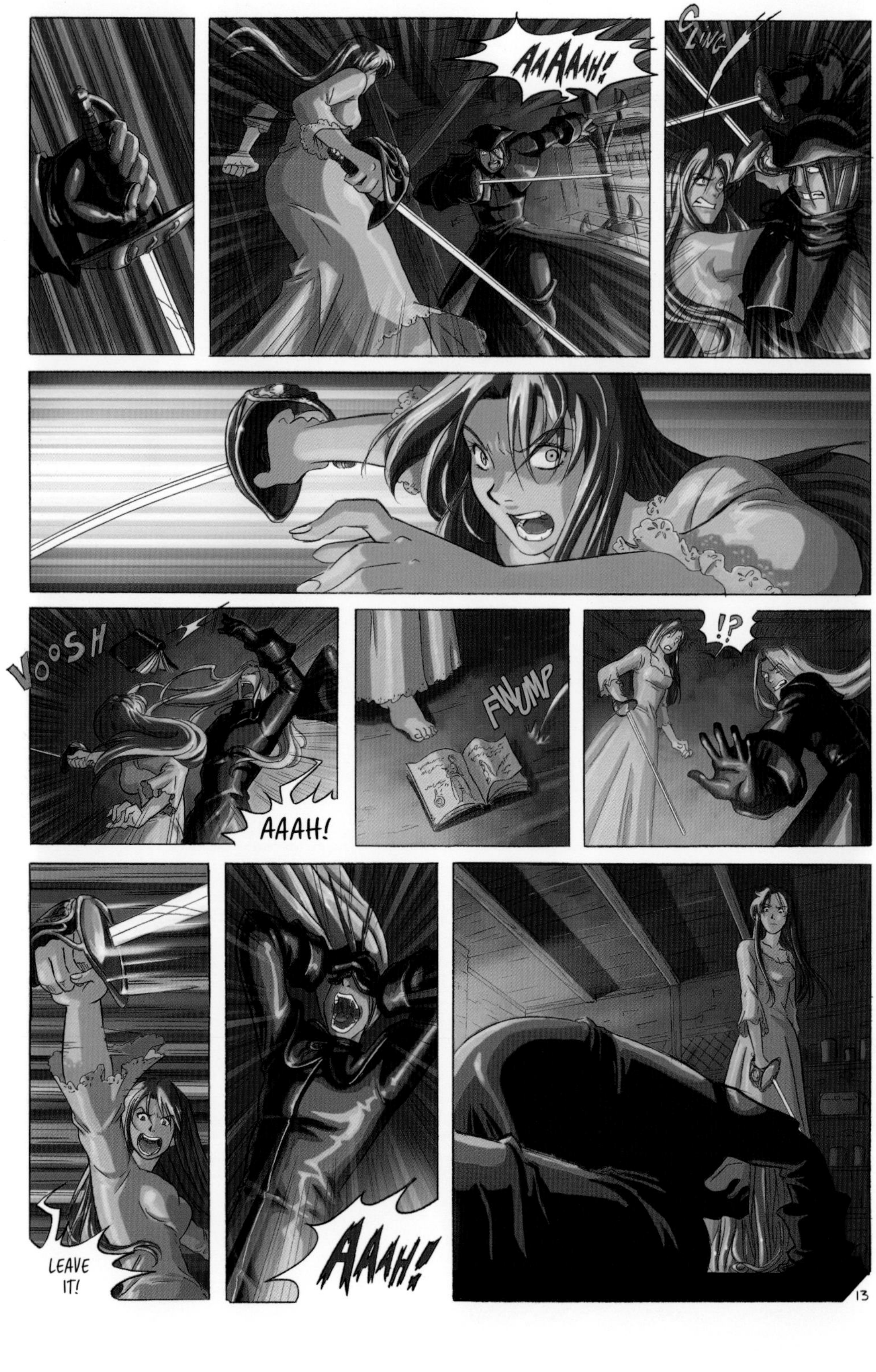
AAAAAH!
CLING
VOOSH
AAAH!
FWUMP
!?
LEAVE IT!
AAAH!

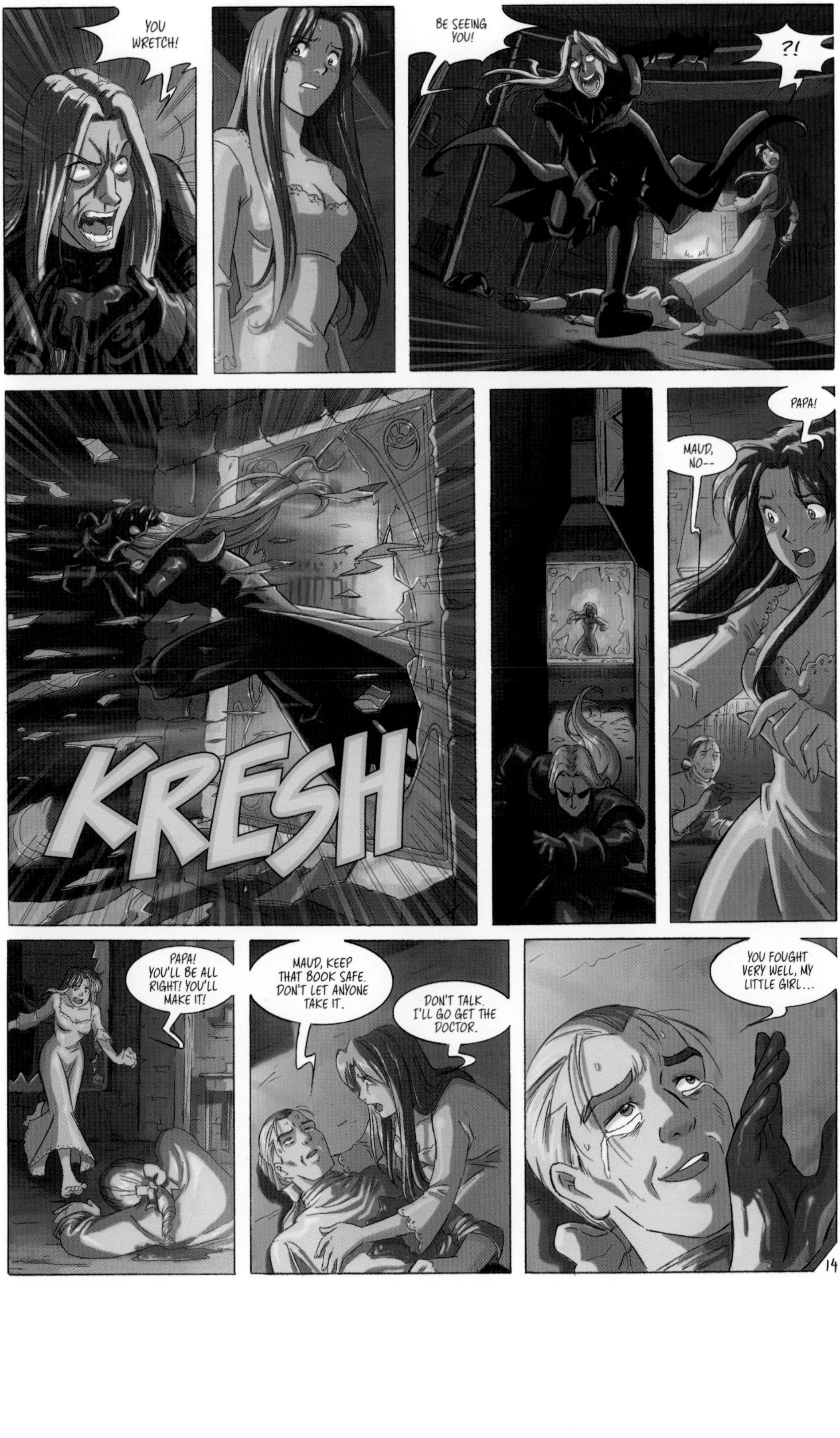
YOU WRETCH!
BE SEEING YOU!
?!
KRESH
PAPA!
MAUD, NO--
PAPA! YOU'LL BE ALL RIGHT! YOU'LL MAKE IT!
MAUD, KEEP THAT BOOK SAFE. DON'T LET ANYONE TAKE IT.
DON'T TALK. I'LL GO GET THE DOCTOR.
YOU FOUGHT VERY WELL, MY LITTLE GIRL...

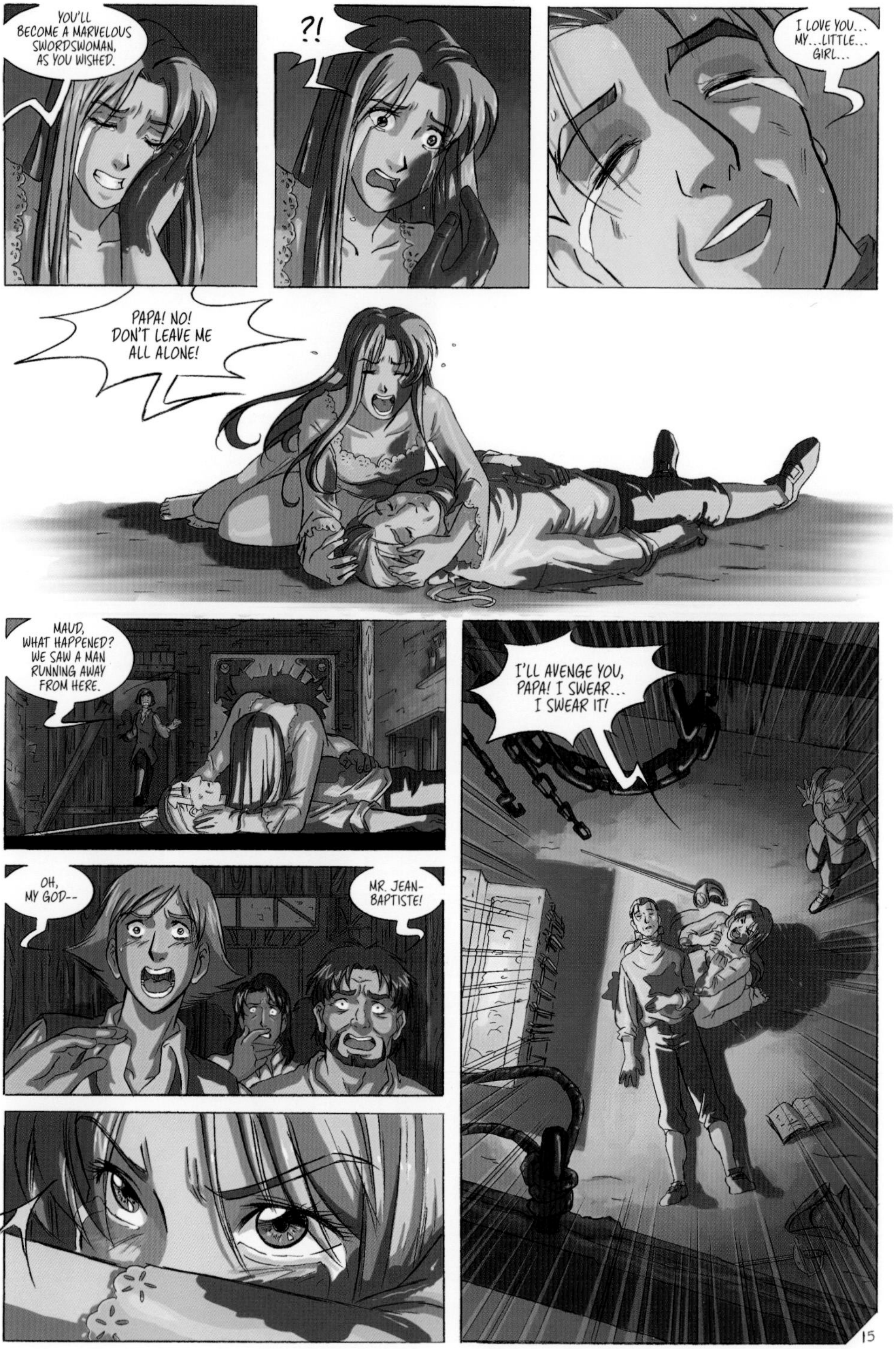
YOU'LL BECOME A MARVELOUS SWORDSWOMAN, AS YOU WISHED.
?!
I LOVE YOU... MY...LITTLE... GIRL...
PAPA! NO! DON'T LEAVE ME ALL ALONE!
MAUD, WHAT HAPPENED? WE SAW A MAN RUNNING AWAY FROM HERE.
OH, MY GOD--
MR. JEAN-BAPTISTE!
I'LL AVENGE YOU, PAPA! I SWEAR... I SWEAR IT!
15

Don't miss THE SCARLET ROSE #1, available now at booksellers everywhere.

Here's a special preview of MONICA'S ADVENTURES #1
"Who Can Afford the Price of Friendship Today?"...

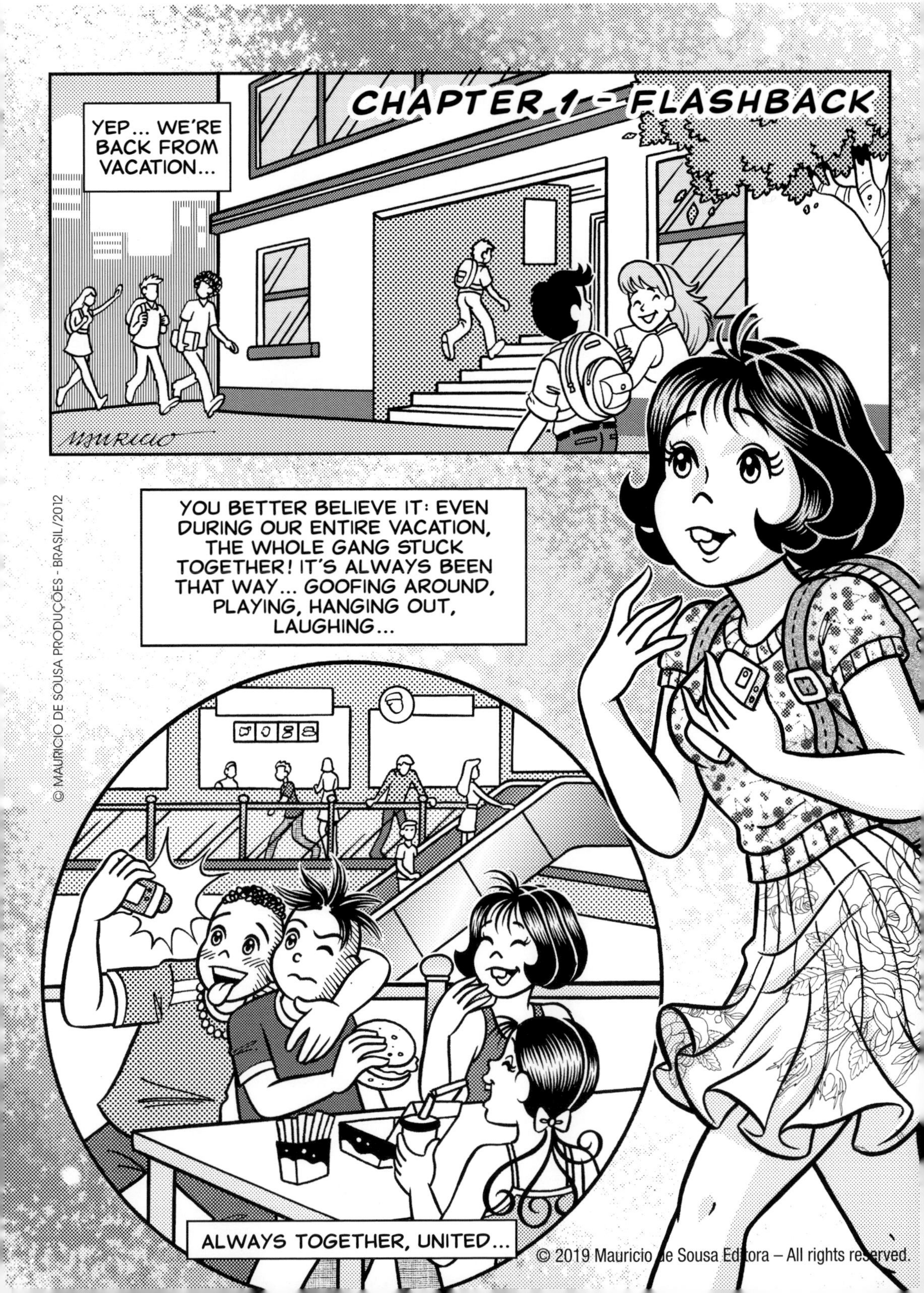
CHAPTER 1 – FLASHBACK
YEP... WE'RE BACK FROM VACATION...
YOU BETTER BELIEVE IT: EVEN DURING OUR ENTIRE VACATION, THE WHOLE GANG STUCK TOGETHER! IT'S ALWAYS BEEN THAT WAY... GOOFING AROUND, PLAYING, HANGING OUT, LAUGHING...
ALWAYS TOGETHER, UNITED...

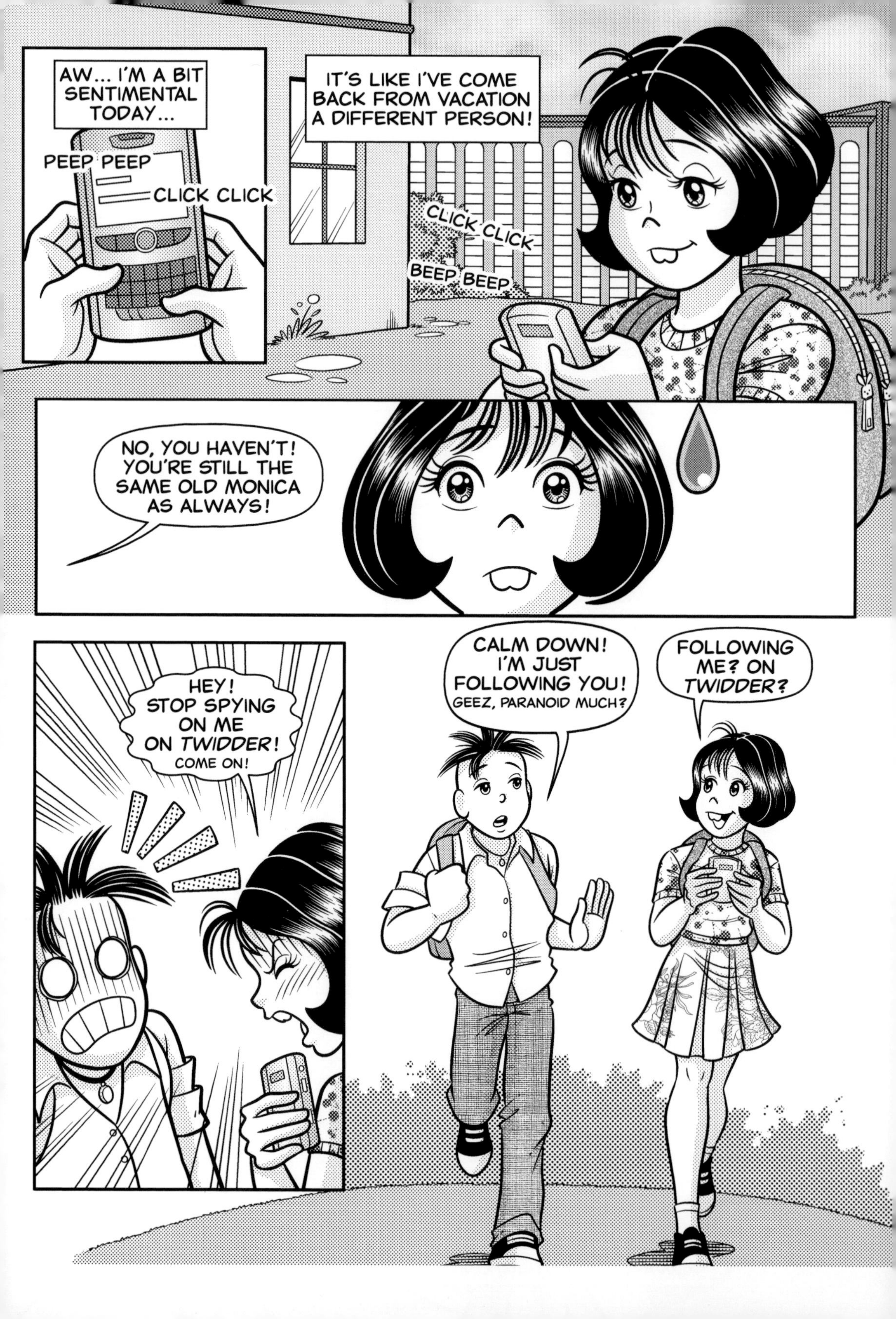
AW... I'M A BIT SENTIMENTAL TODAY...
PEEP PEEP
CLICK CLICK
IT'S LIKE I'VE COME BACK FROM VACATION A DIFFERENT PERSON!
CLICK CLICK
BEEP BEEP
NO, YOU HAVEN'T! YOU'RE STILL THE SAME OLD MONICA AS ALWAYS!
HEY! STOP SPYING ON ME ON *TWIDDER*! COME ON!
CALM DOWN! I'M JUST FOLLOWING YOU! GEEZ, PARANOID MUCH?
FOLLOWING ME? ON *TWIDDER*?

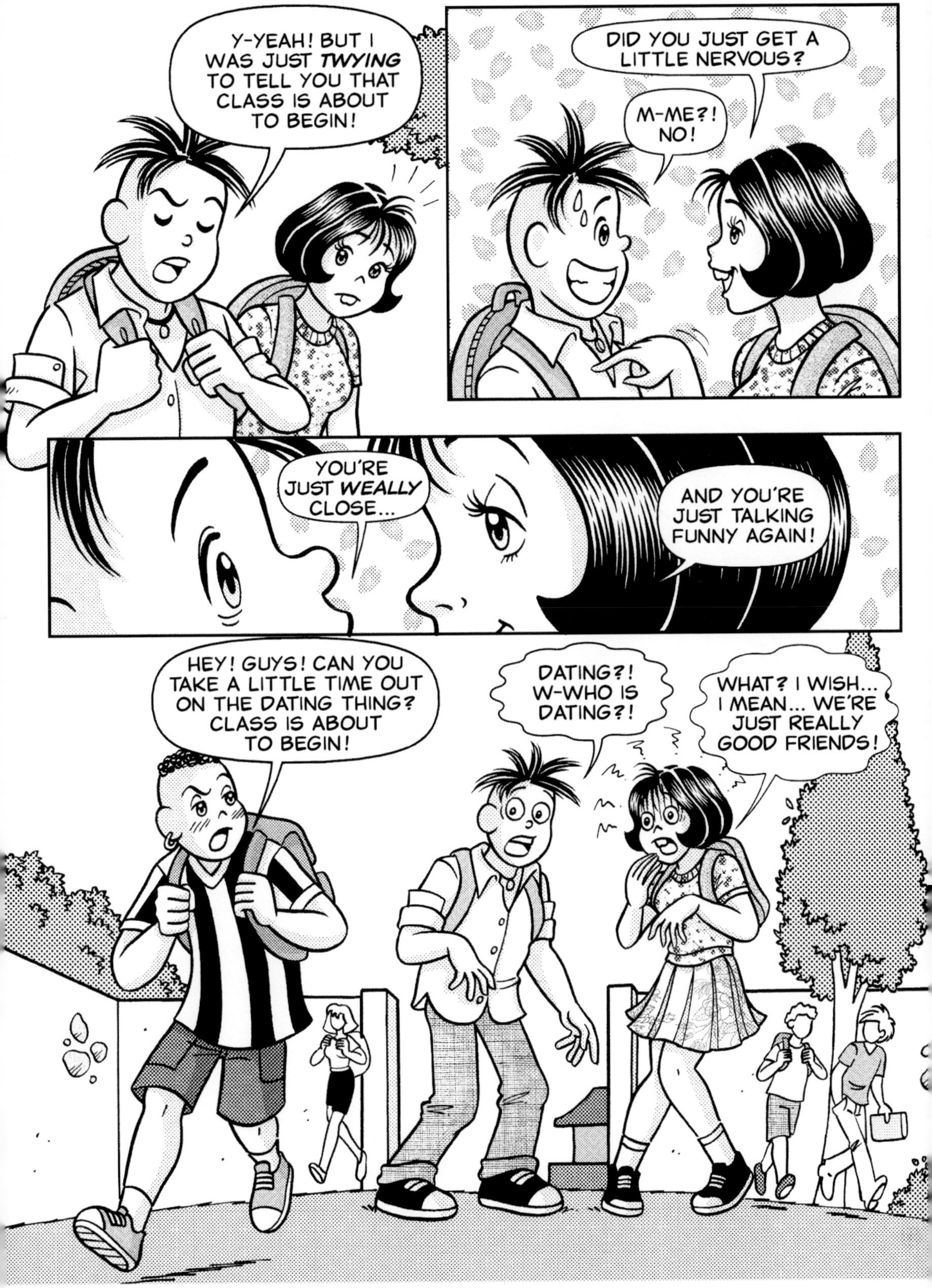
Y-YEAH! BUT I WAS JUST *TWYING* TO TELL YOU THAT CLASS IS ABOUT TO BEGIN!
DID YOU JUST GET A LITTLE NERVOUS?
M-ME?! NO!
YOU'RE JUST *WEALLY* CLOSE...
AND YOU'RE JUST TALKING FUNNY AGAIN!
HEY! GUYS! CAN YOU TAKE A LITTLE TIME OUT ON THE DATING THING? CLASS IS ABOUT TO BEGIN!
DATING?! W-WHO IS DATING?!
WHAT? I WISH... I MEAN... WE'RE JUST REALLY GOOD FRIENDS!

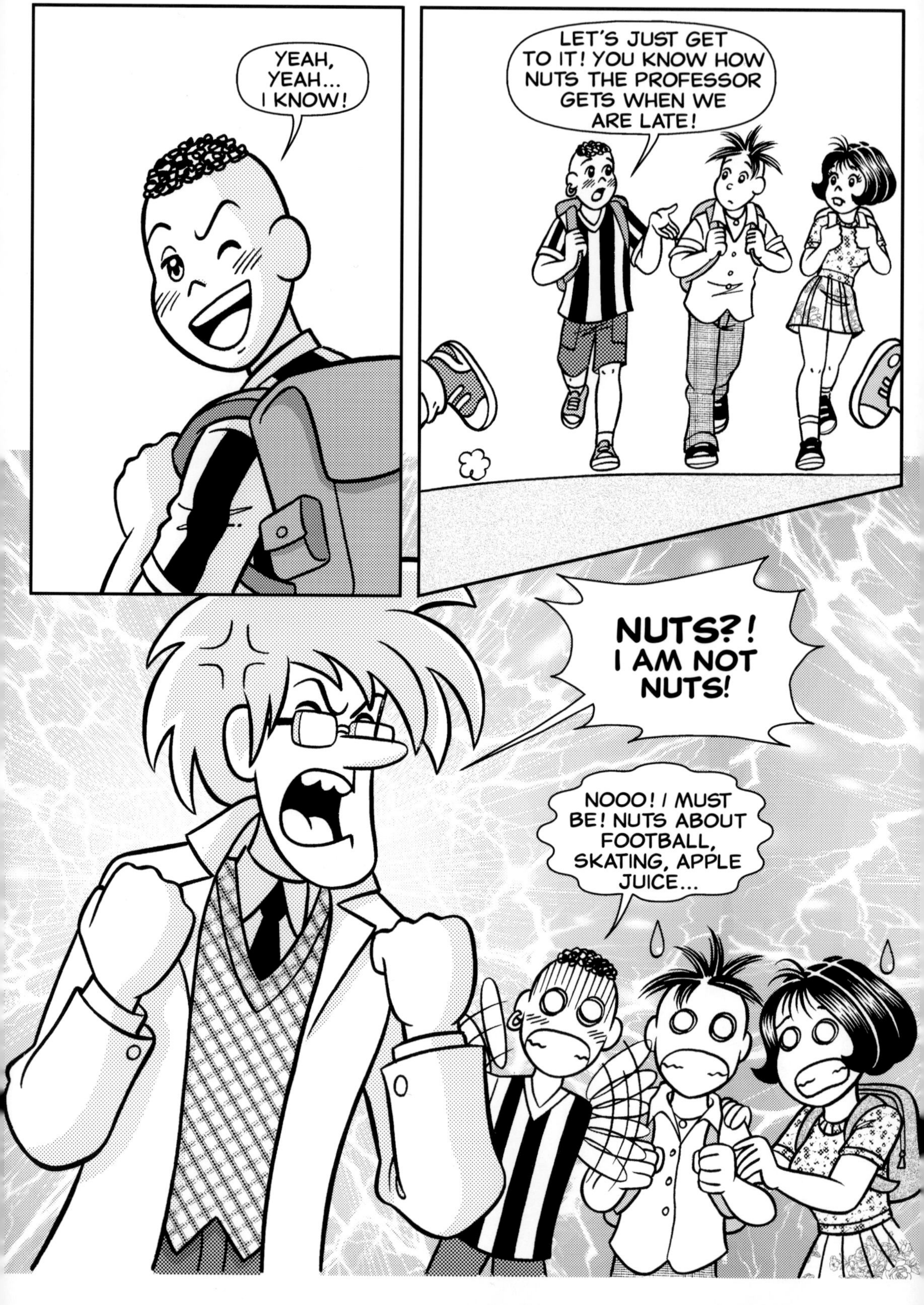
YEAH, YEAH... I KNOW!
LET'S JUST GET TO IT! YOU KNOW HOW NUTS THE PROFESSOR GETS WHEN WE ARE LATE!
NUTS?! I AM NOT NUTS!
NOOO! I MUST BE! NUTS ABOUT FOOTBALL, SKATING, APPLE JUICE...

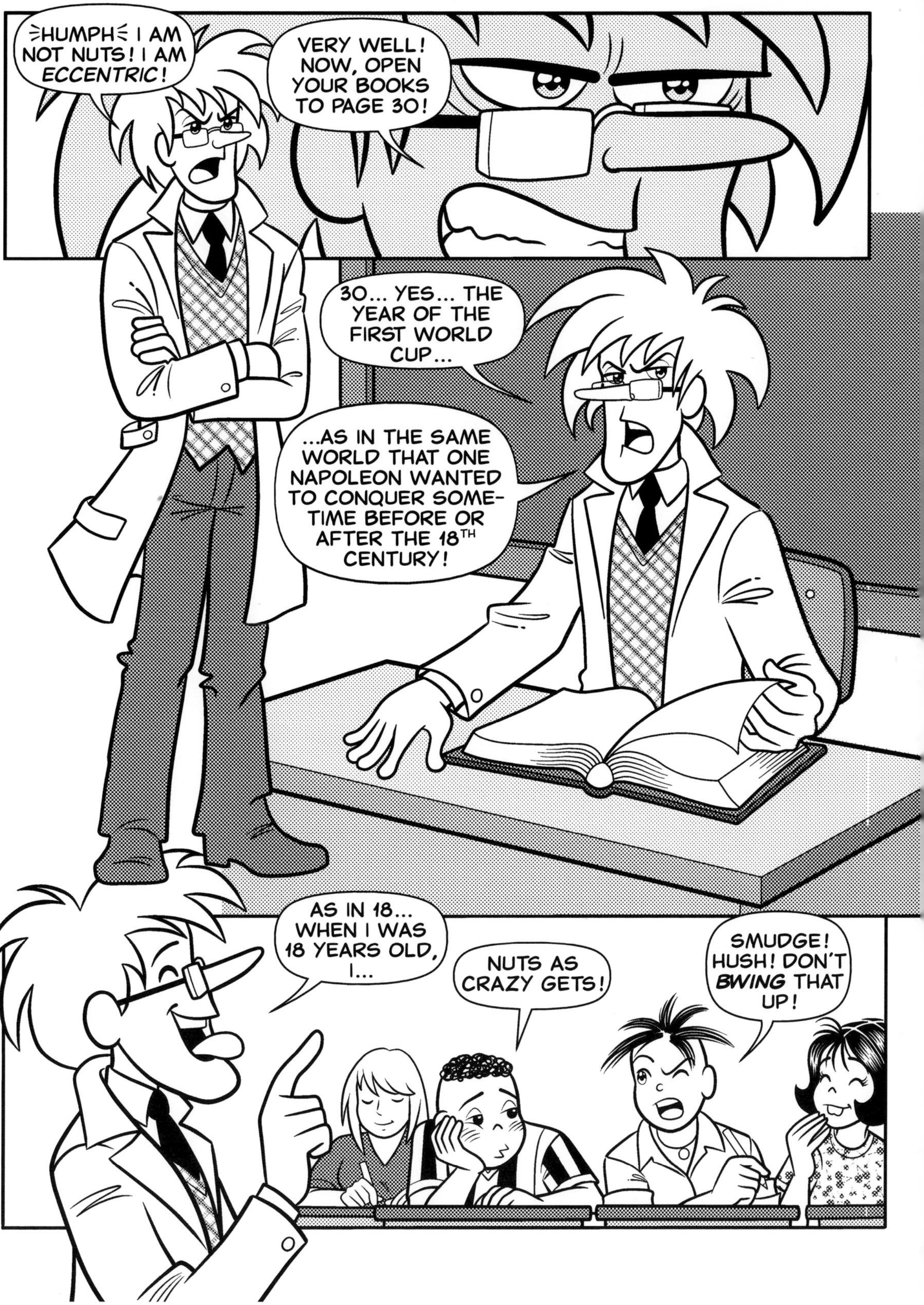
HUMPH I AM NOT NUTS! I AM *ECCENTRIC*!
VERY WELL! NOW, OPEN YOUR BOOKS TO PAGE 30!
30... YES... THE YEAR OF THE FIRST WORLD CUP...
...AS IN THE SAME WORLD THAT ONE NAPOLEON WANTED TO CONQUER SOME-TIME BEFORE OR AFTER THE 18TH CENTURY!
AS IN 18... WHEN I WAS 18 YEARS OLD, I...
NUTS AS CRAZY GETS!
SMUDGE! HUSH! DON'T *BWING* THAT UP!

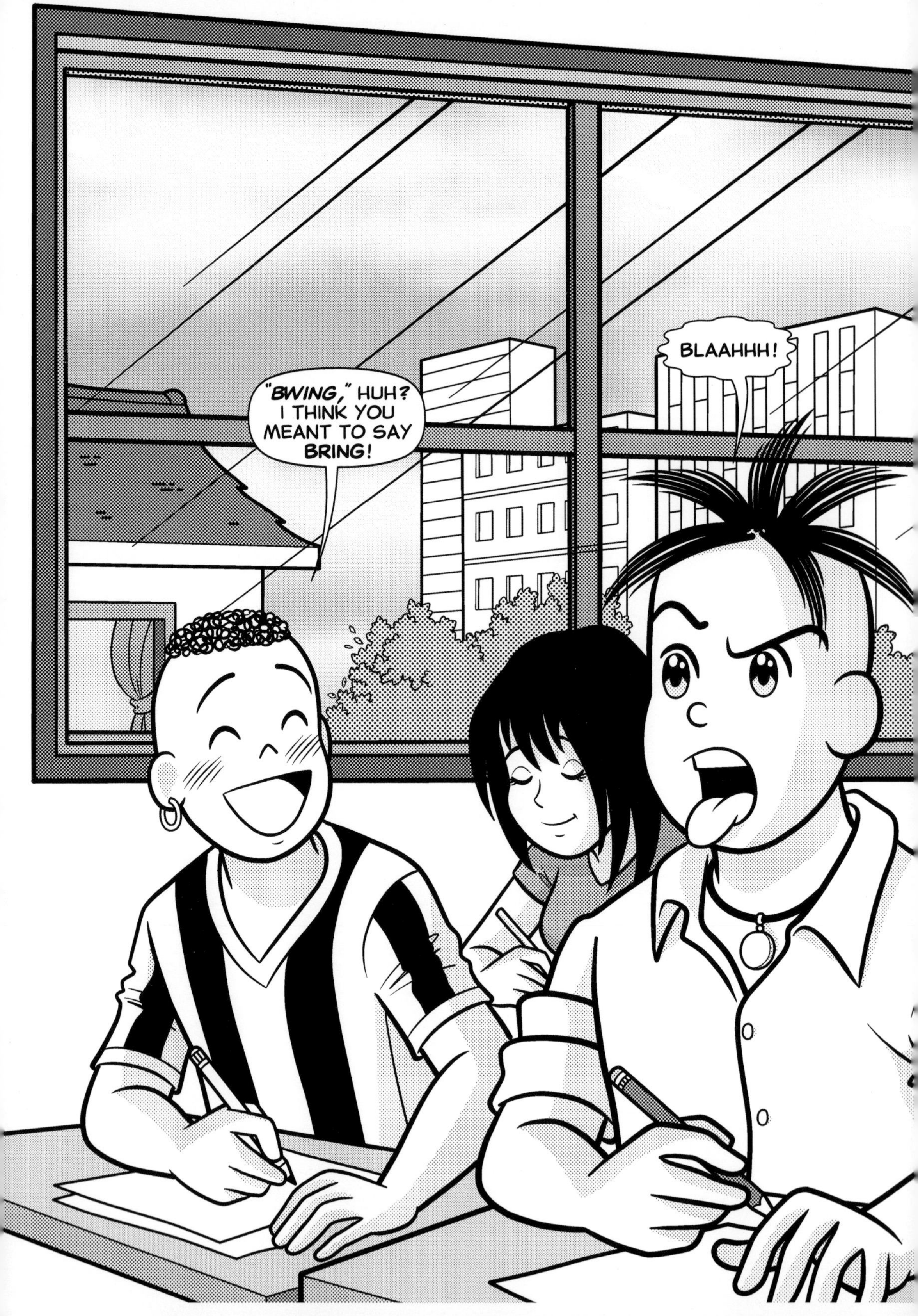
"*BWING,*" HUH? I THINK YOU MEANT TO SAY **BRING**!
BLAAHHH!

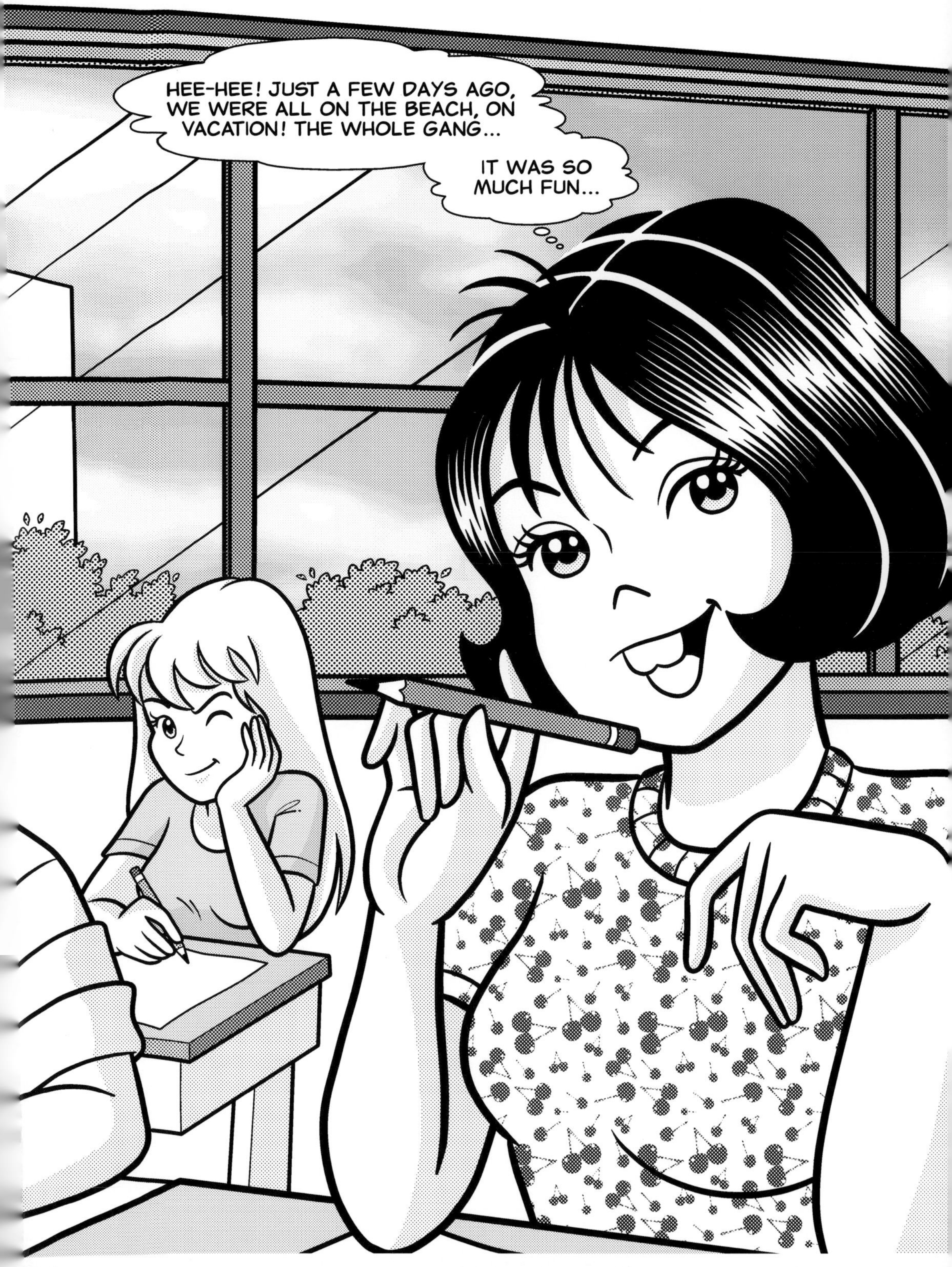
HEE-HEE! JUST A FEW DAYS AGO, WE WERE ALL ON THE BEACH, ON VACATION! THE WHOLE GANG...
IT WAS SO MUCH FUN...

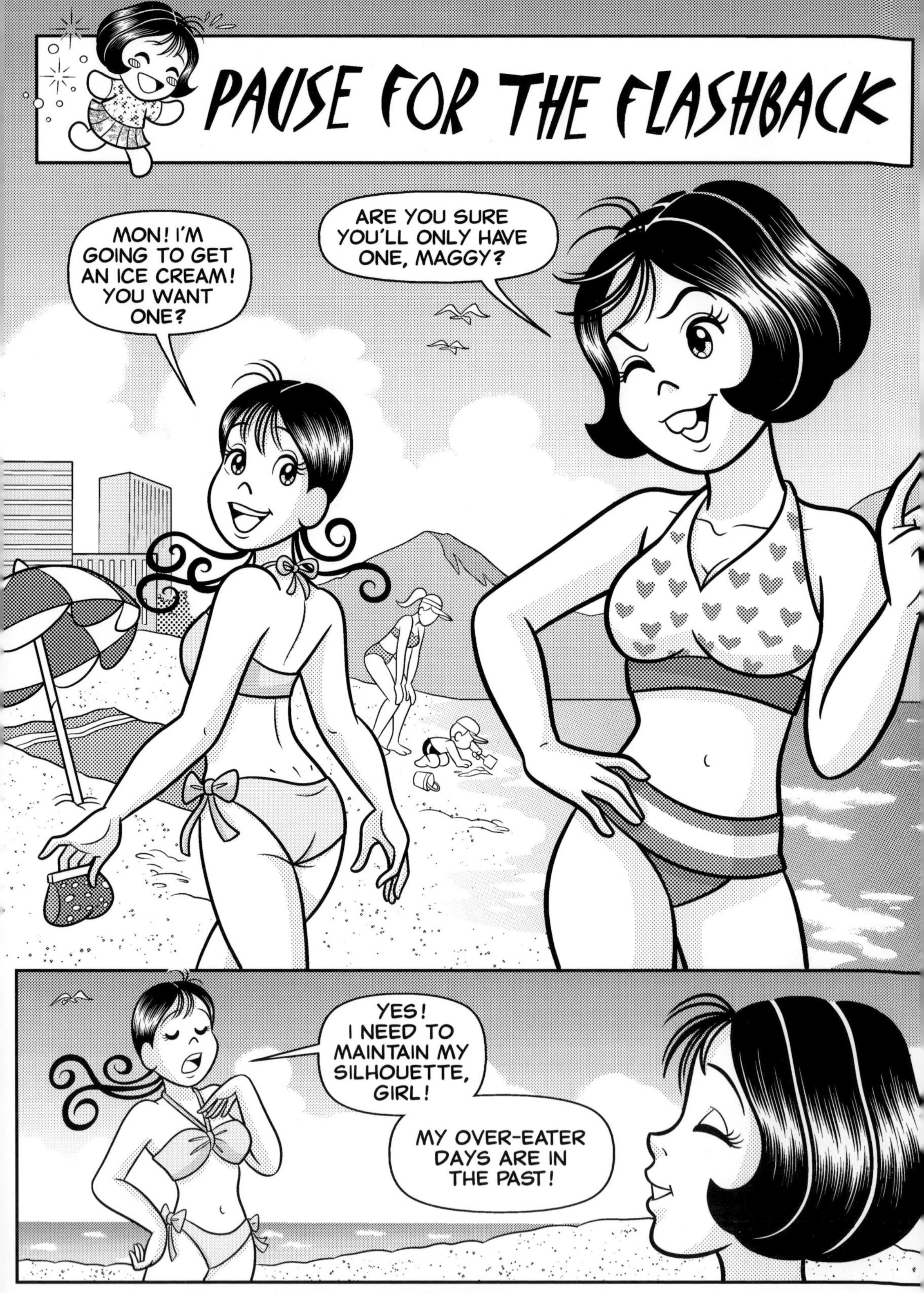
PAUSE FOR THE FLASHBACK
MON! I'M GOING TO GET AN ICE CREAM! YOU WANT ONE?
ARE YOU SURE YOU'LL ONLY HAVE ONE, MAGGY?
YES! I NEED TO MAINTAIN MY SILHOUETTE, GIRL!
MY OVER-EATER DAYS ARE IN THE PAST!